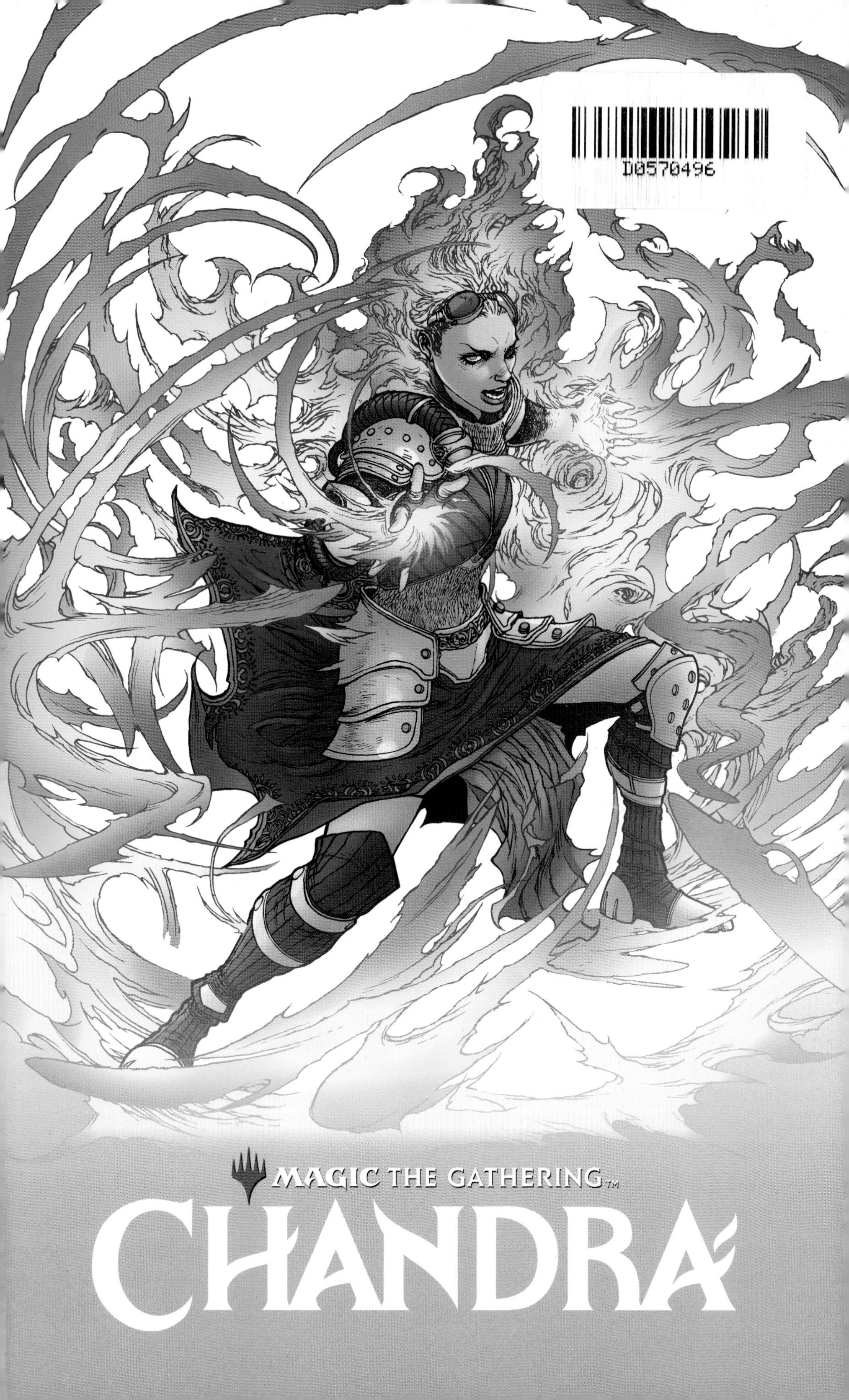



MAGIC THE GATHERING™

# CHANDRA

Facebook: **facebook.com/idwpublishing**
Twitter: **@idwpublishing**
YouTube: **youtube.com/idwpublishing**
Tumblr: **tumblr.idwpublishing.com**
Instagram: **instagram.com/idwpublishing**

ISBN: 978-1-68405-427-5     22 21 20 19     1 2 3 4

**COVER ARTIST**
KEN LASHLEY

**COVER COLORIST**
MATT HERMS

**COLLECTION EDITORS**
JUSTIN EISINGER
and ALONZO SIMON

**COLLECTION DESIGNER**
CLYDE GRAPA

Originally published as MAGIC: THE GATHERING: CHANDRA
issues #1–4.

Chris Ryall, President, Publisher, & CCO
John Barber, Editor-In-Chief
Cara Morrison, Chief Financial Officer
Matt Ruzicka, Chief Accounting Officer
David Hedgecock, Associate Publisher
Jerry Bennington, VP of New Product Development
Lorelei Bunjes, VP of Digital Services
Justin Eisinger, Editorial Director, Graphic Novels & Collections
Eric Moss, Senior Director, Licensing and Business Development

Ted Adams and Robbie Robbins, IDW Founders

Special thanks to Daniel Ketchum, Elizabeth Artale, Megan Ruggiero, Brad
Thompson, Jeremy Jarvis, Nic Kelman, Wizards of the Coast, and Hasbro for
their invaluable assistance.

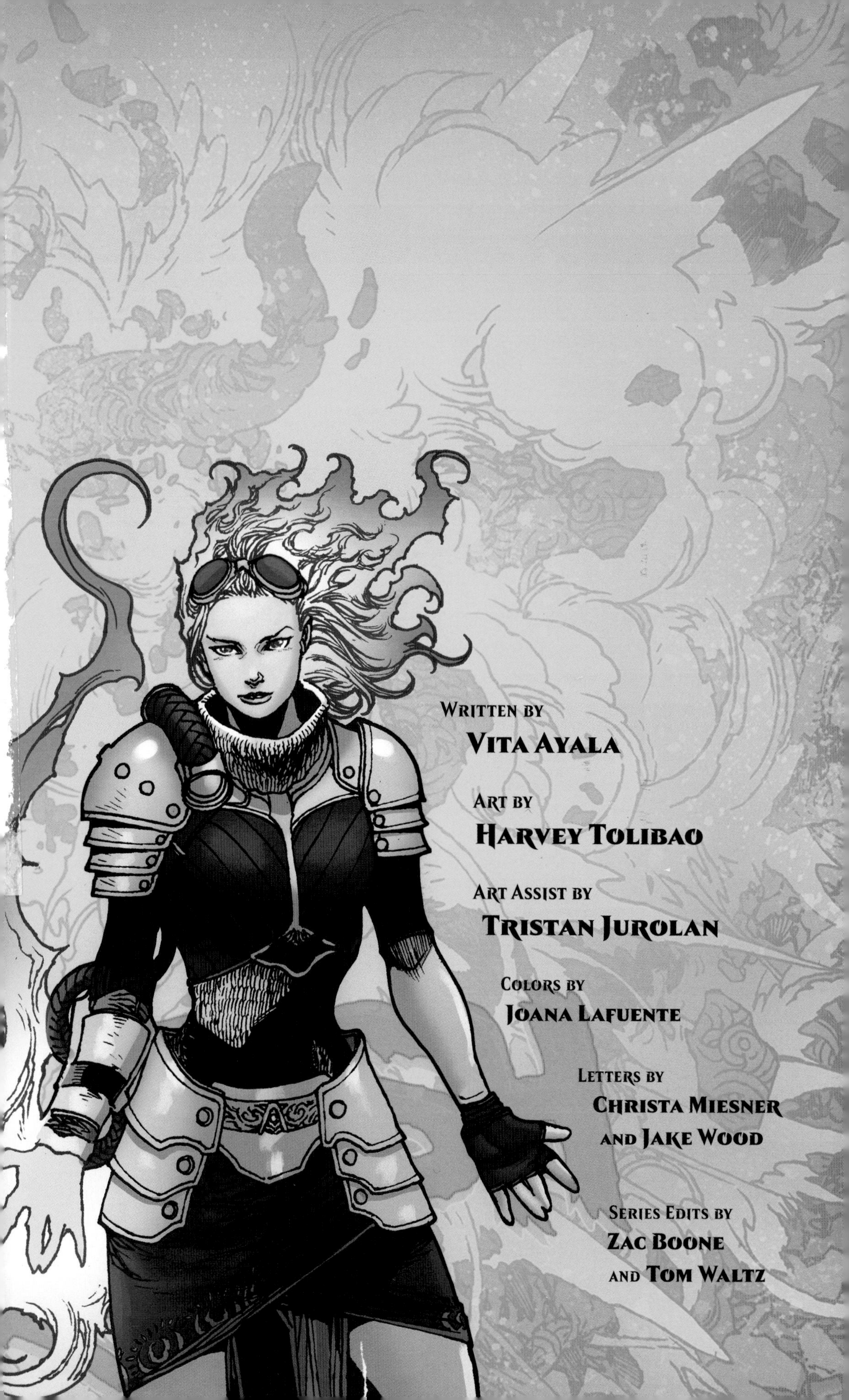

Written by
**Vita Ayala**

Art by
**Harvey Tolibao**

Art Assist by
**Tristan Jurolan**

Colors by
**Joana Lafuente**

Letters by
**Christa Miesner and Jake Wood**

Series Edits by
**Zac Boone and Tom Waltz**

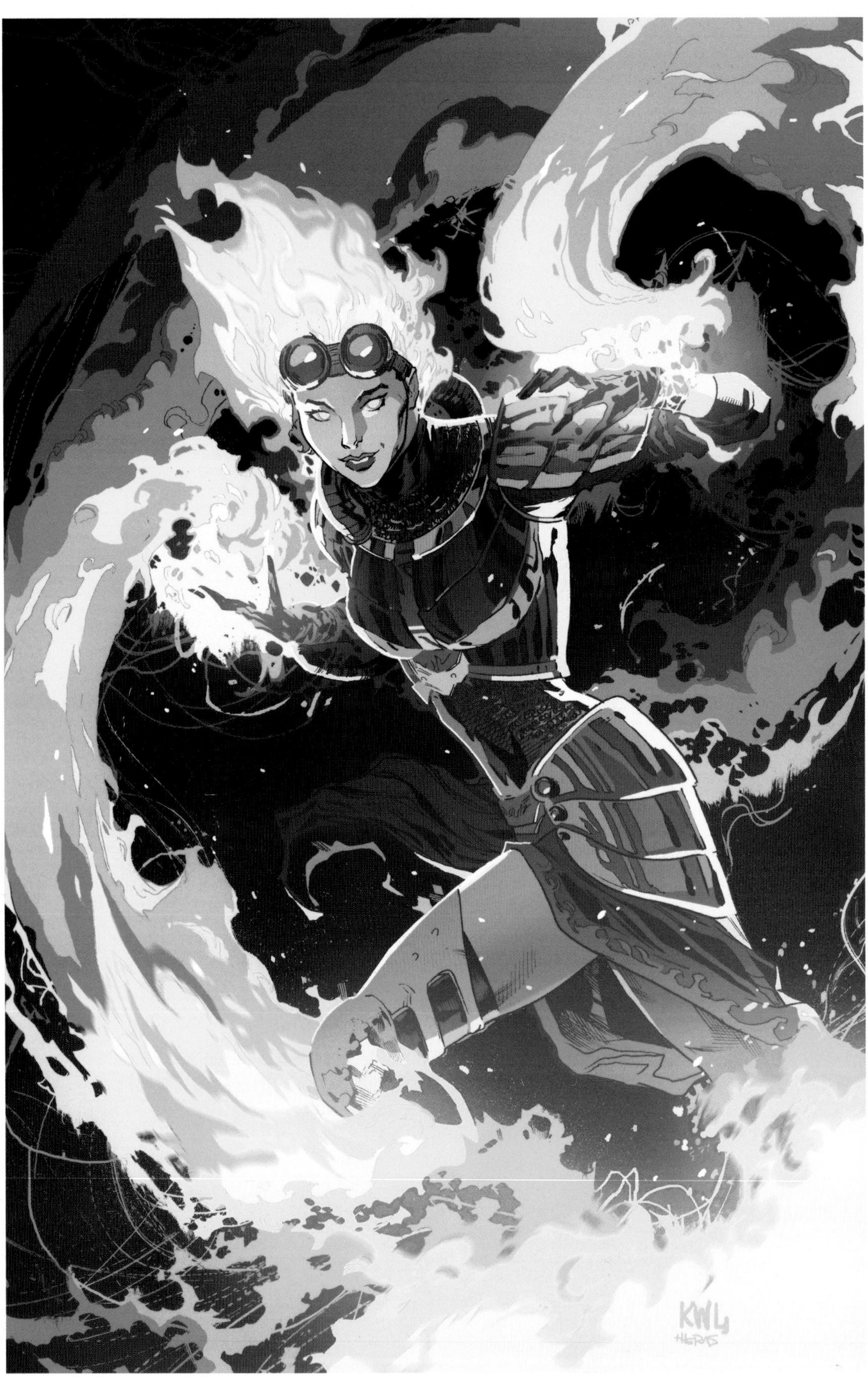

Art by Ken Lashley • Colors by Matt Herms

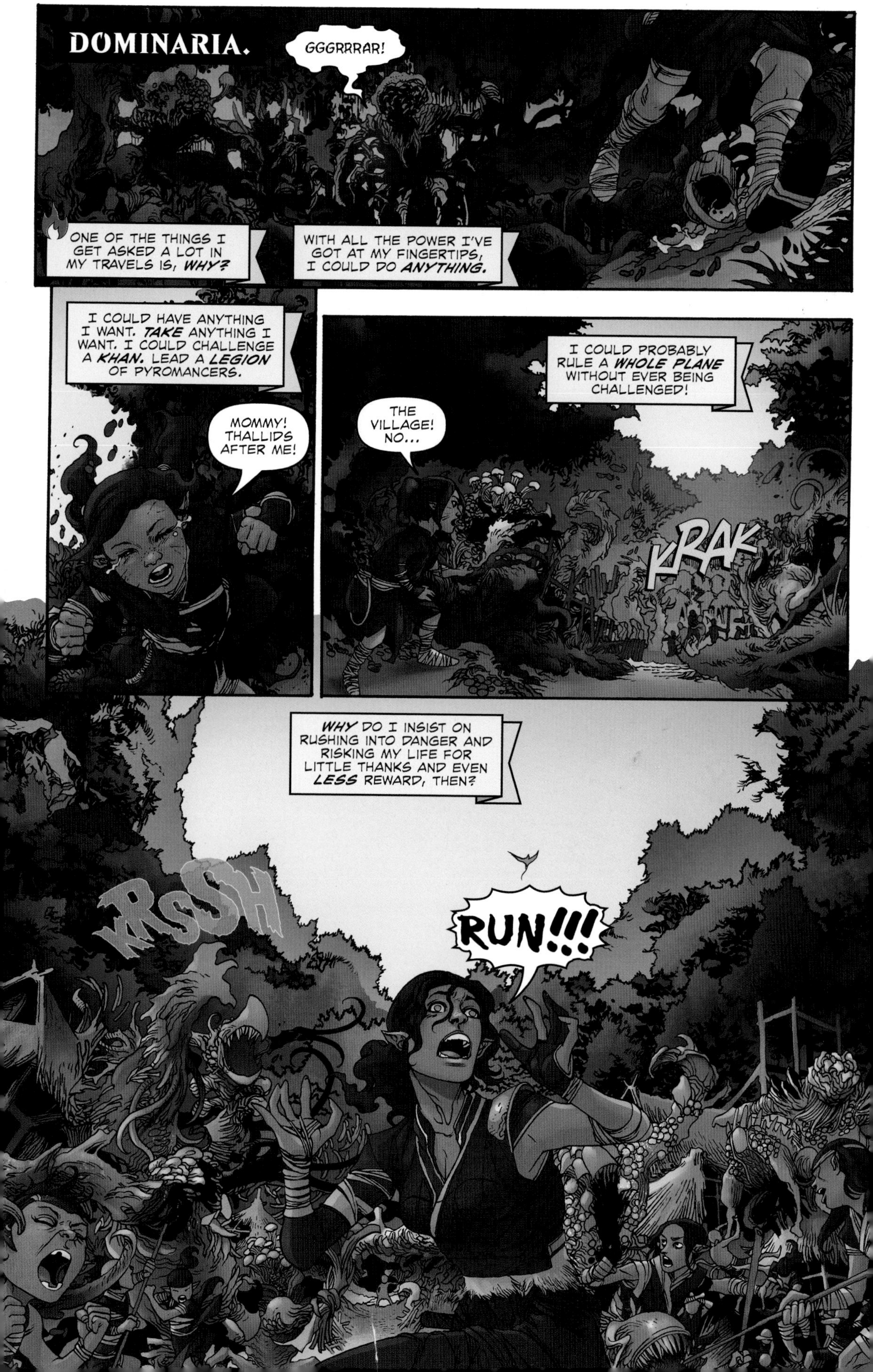
DOMINARIA.
GGGRRRAR!
ONE OF THE THINGS I GET ASKED A LOT IN MY TRAVELS IS, WHY?
WITH ALL THE POWER I'VE GOT AT MY FINGERTIPS, I COULD DO ANYTHING.
I COULD HAVE ANYTHING I WANT. TAKE ANYTHING I WANT. I COULD CHALLENGE A KHAN. LEAD A LEGION OF PYROMANCERS.
MOMMY! THALLIDS AFTER ME!
I COULD PROBABLY RULE A WHOLE PLANE WITHOUT EVER BEING CHALLENGED!
THE VILLAGE! NO...
KRAK
WHY DO I INSIST ON RUSHING INTO DANGER AND RISKING MY LIFE FOR LITTLE THANKS AND EVEN LESS REWARD, THEN?
KRSSH
RUN!!!

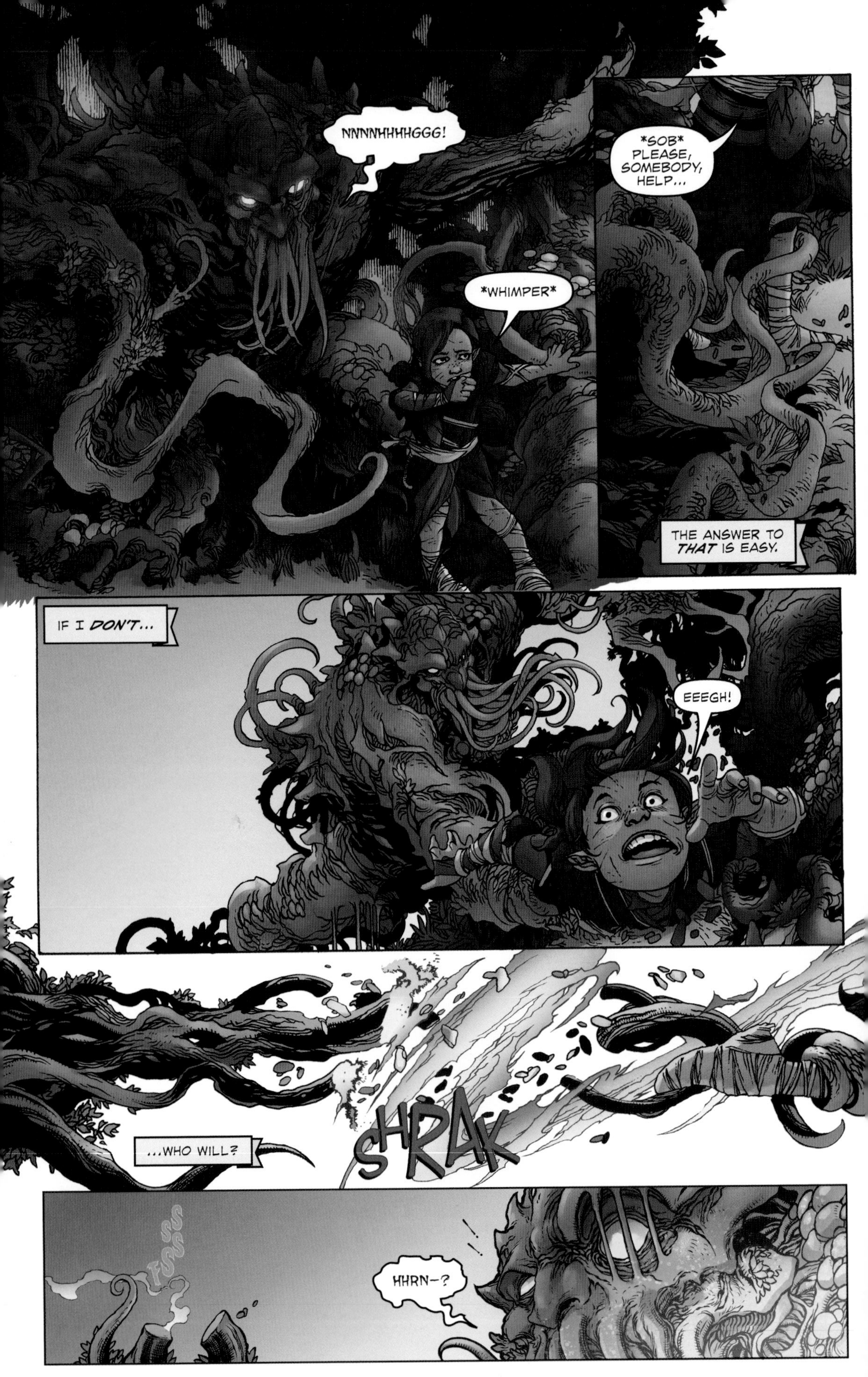
NNNNHHHHGGG!
*WHIMPER*
*SOB* PLEASE, SOMEBODY, HELP...
THE ANSWER TO THAT IS EASY.
IF I DON'T...
EEEGH!
...WHO WILL?
SHRAK
FSSSS
HHRN-?

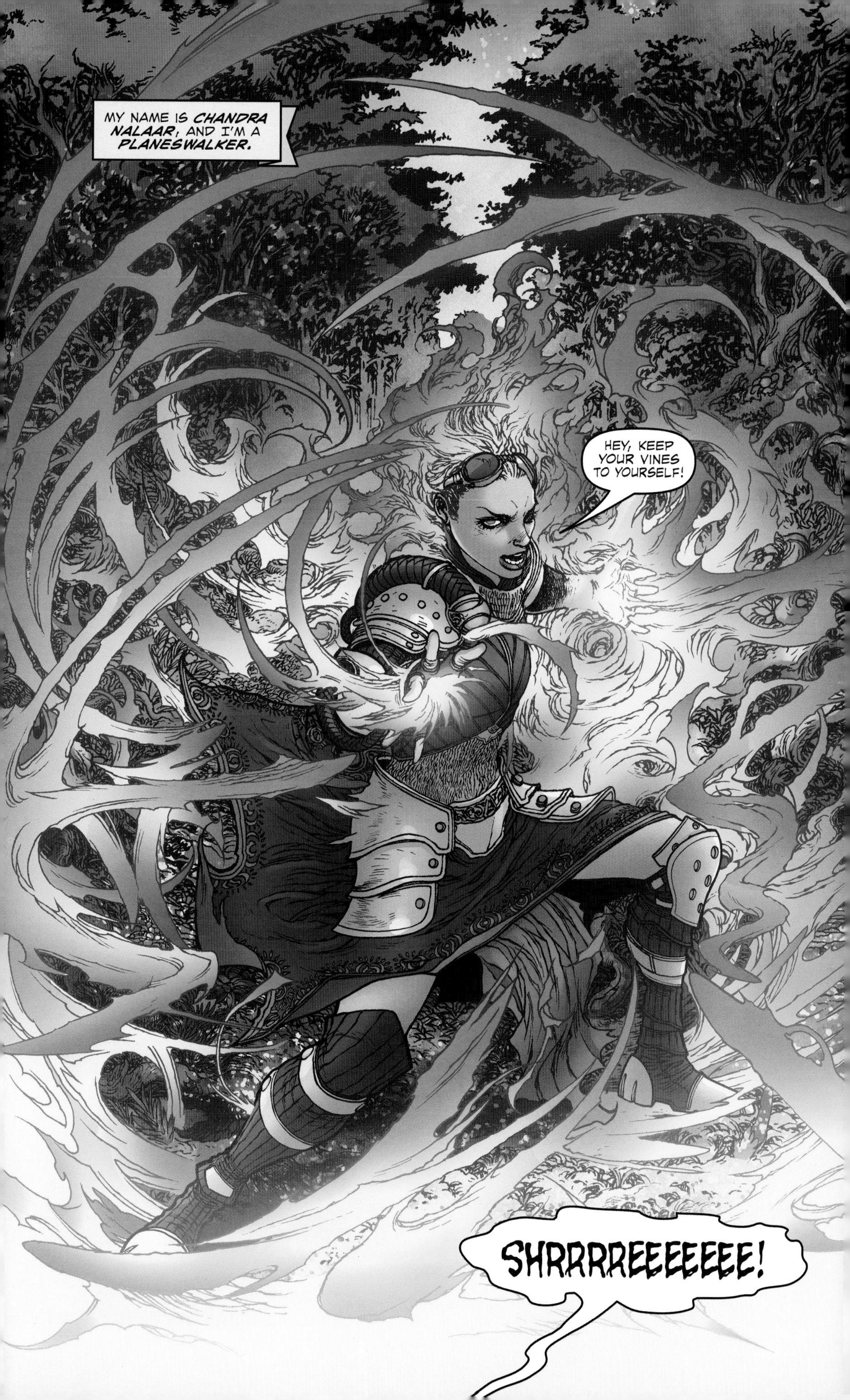
MY NAME IS CHANDRA NALAAR, AND I'M A PLANESWALKER.
HEY, KEEP YOUR VINES TO YOURSELF!
SHRRRREEEEEEE!

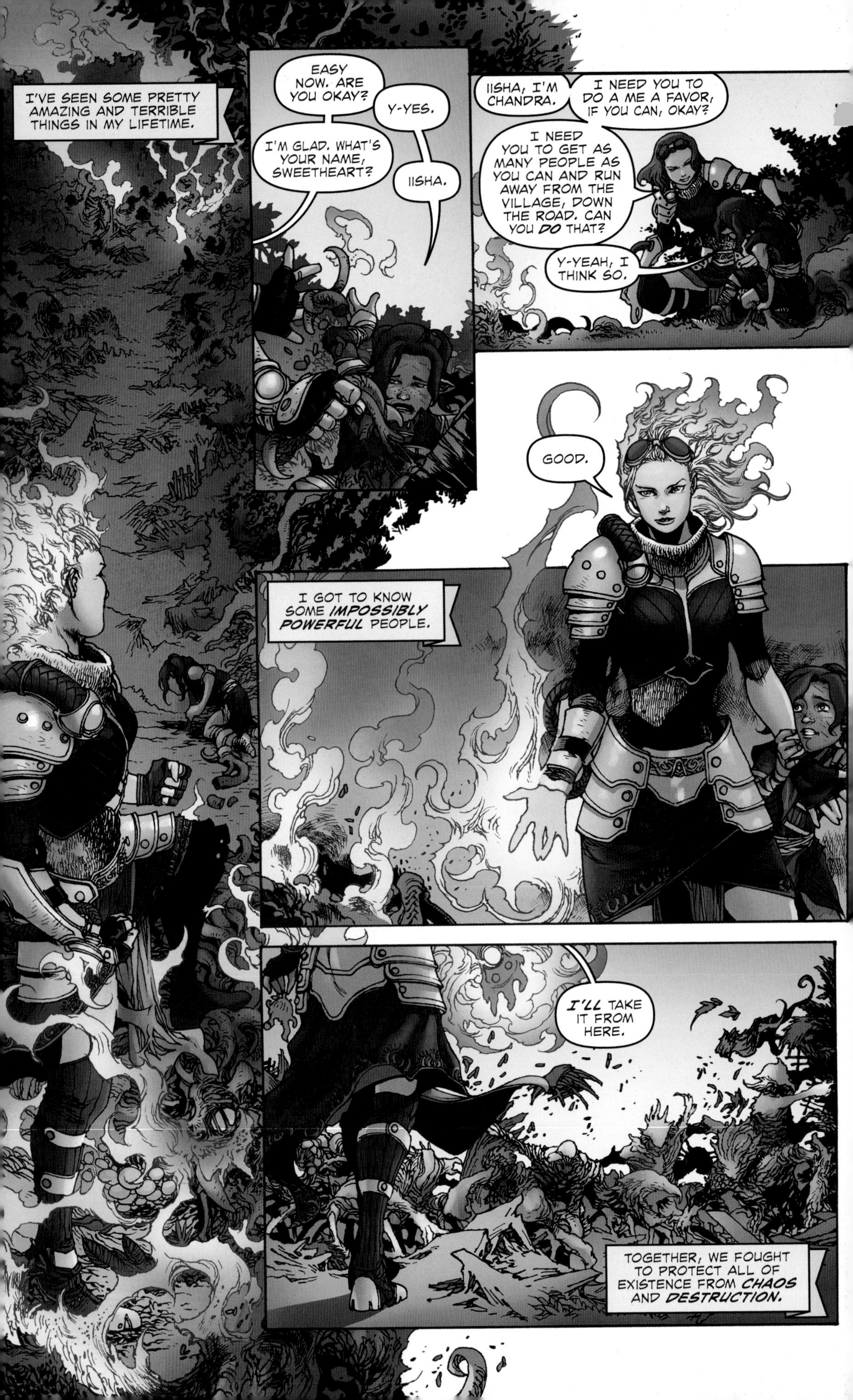

I'VE SEEN SOME PRETTY AMAZING AND TERRIBLE THINGS IN MY LIFETIME.
EASY NOW. ARE YOU OKAY?
Y-YES.
I'M GLAD. WHAT'S YOUR NAME, SWEETHEART?
IISHA.
IISHA, I'M CHANDRA.
I NEED YOU TO DO A ME A FAVOR, IF YOU CAN, OKAY?
I NEED YOU TO GET AS MANY PEOPLE AS YOU CAN AND RUN AWAY FROM THE VILLAGE, DOWN THE ROAD. CAN YOU DO THAT?
Y-YEAH, I THINK SO.
GOOD.
I GOT TO KNOW SOME IMPOSSIBLY POWERFUL PEOPLE.
I'LL TAKE IT FROM HERE.
TOGETHER, WE FOUGHT TO PROTECT ALL OF EXISTENCE FROM CHAOS AND DESTRUCTION.

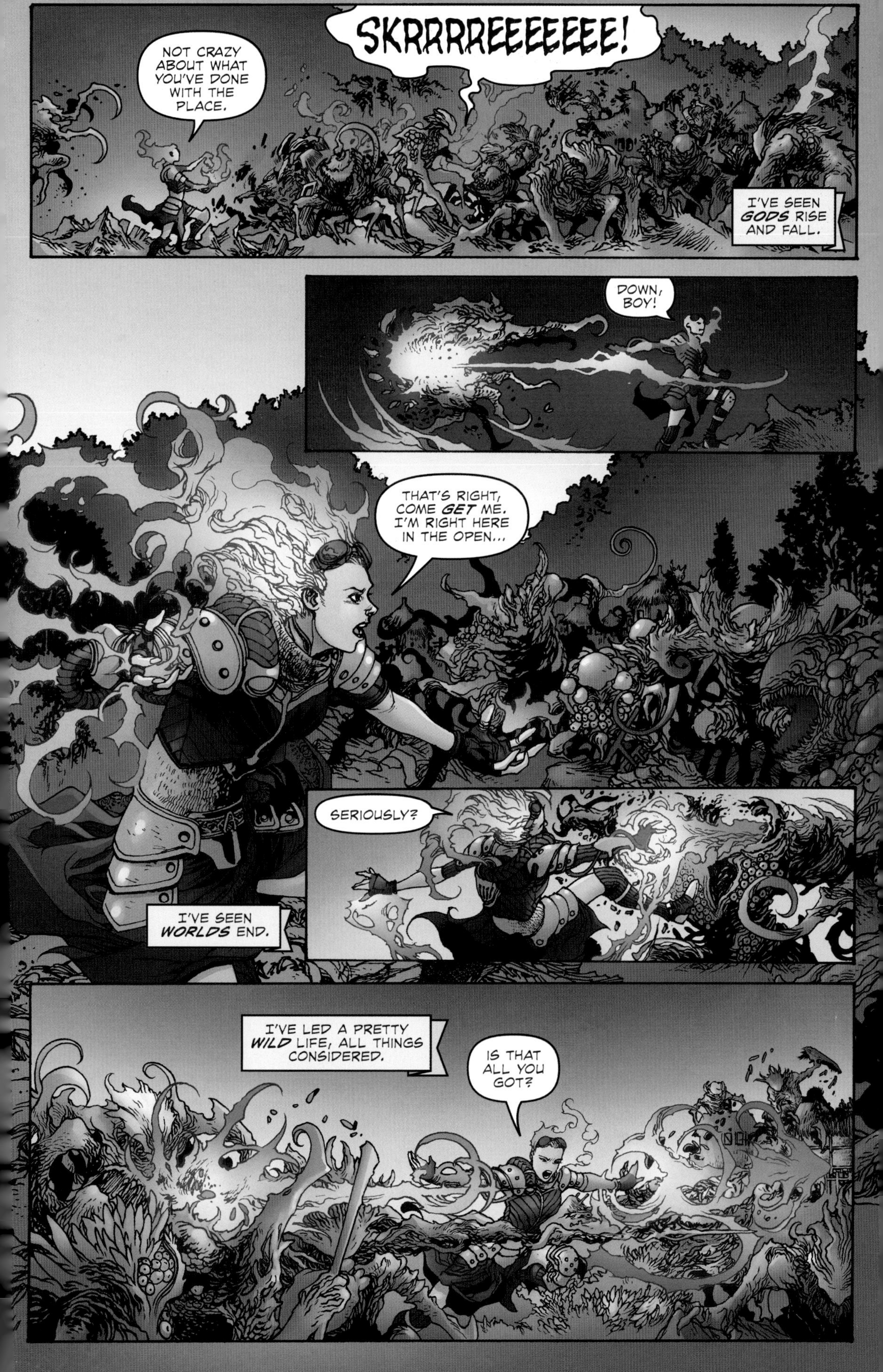
NOT CRAZY ABOUT WHAT YOU'VE DONE WITH THE PLACE.
SKRRRREEEEEEE!
I'VE SEEN GODS RISE AND FALL.
DOWN, BOY!
THAT'S RIGHT, COME GET ME. I'M RIGHT HERE IN THE OPEN...
SERIOUSLY?
I'VE SEEN WORLDS END.
I'VE LED A PRETTY WILD LIFE, ALL THINGS CONSIDERED.
IS THAT ALL YOU GOT?

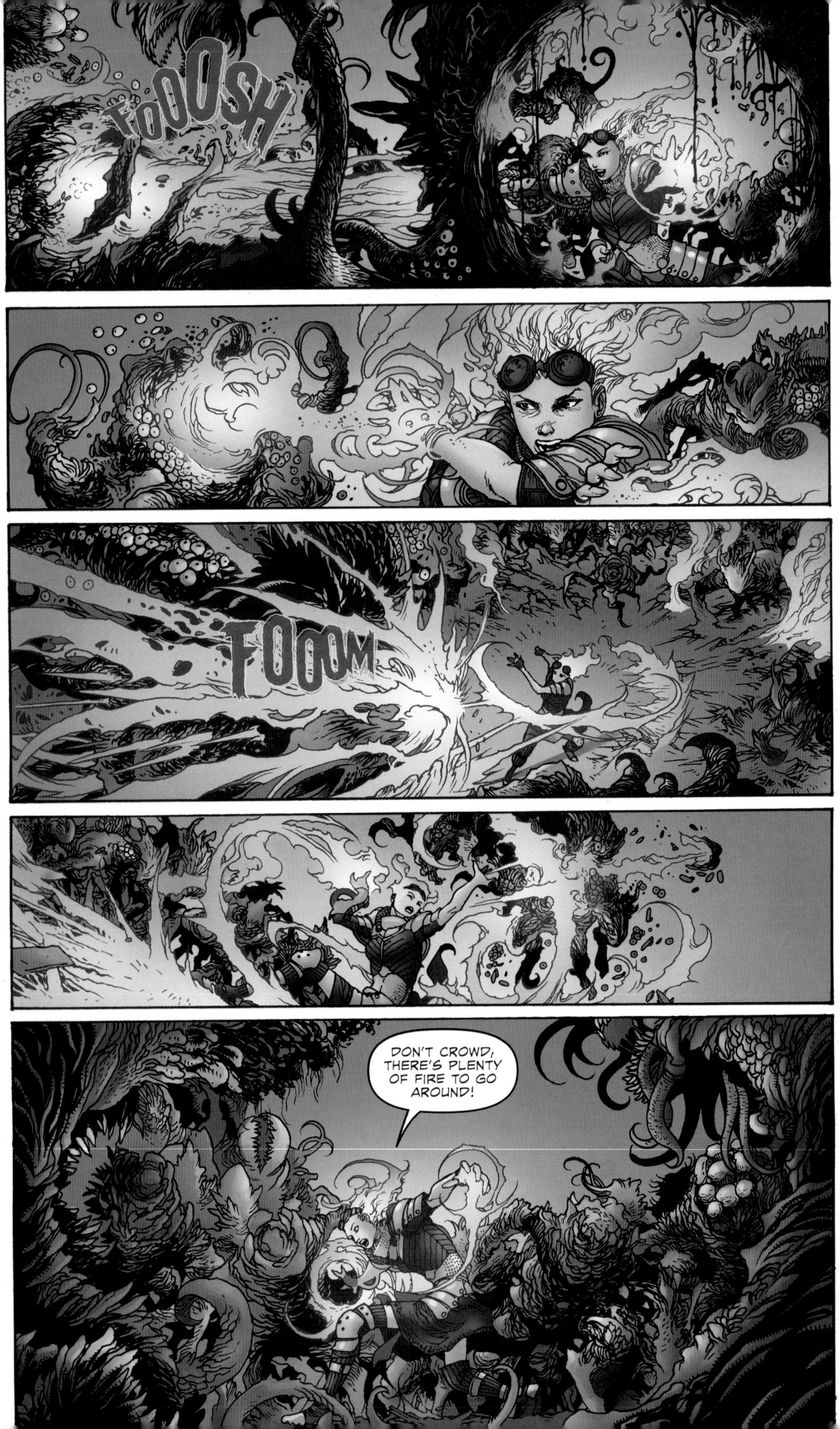
FOOOSH
FOOOM
DON'T CROWD, THERE'S PLENTY OF FIRE TO GO AROUND!

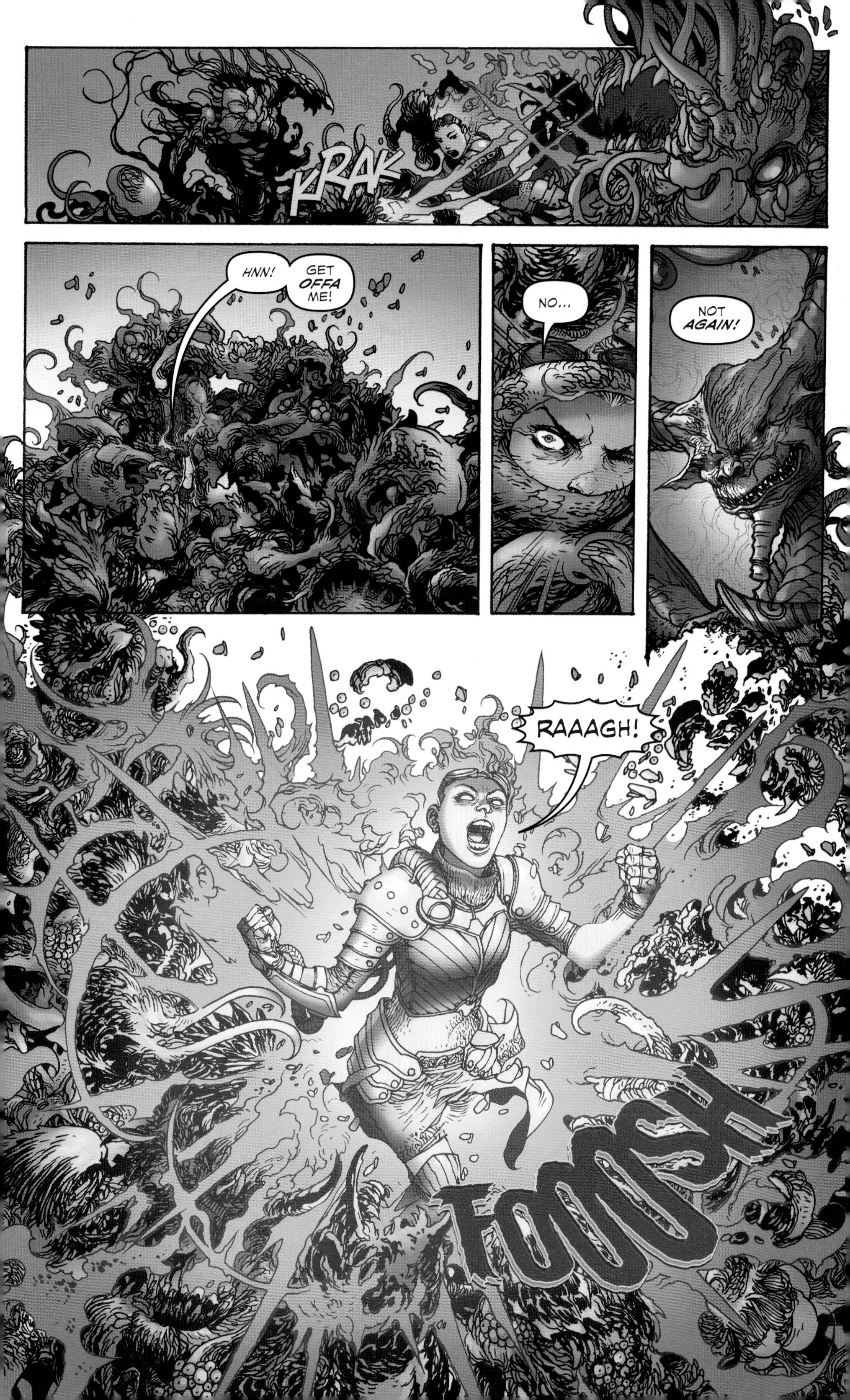
KRAK
HNN!
GET OFFA ME!
NO...
NOT AGAIN!
RAAAGH!
FOOOSH

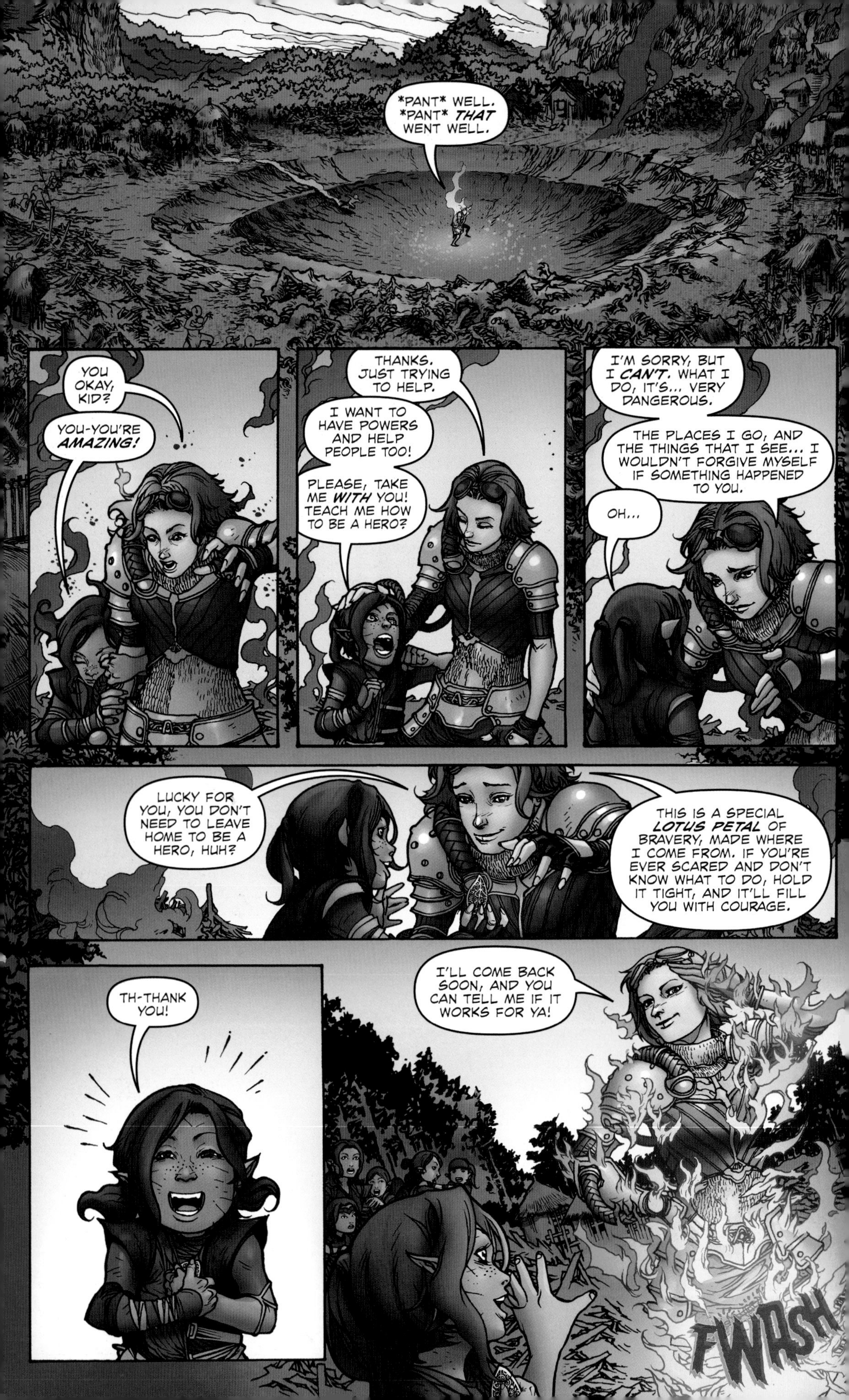
*PANT* WELL. *PANT* *THAT* WENT WELL.
YOU OKAY, KID?
YOU-YOU'RE **AMAZING!**
THANKS. JUST TRYING TO HELP.
I WANT TO HAVE POWERS AND HELP PEOPLE TOO!
PLEASE, TAKE ME **WITH** YOU! TEACH ME HOW TO BE A HERO?
I'M SORRY, BUT I **CAN'T.** WHAT I DO, IT'S... VERY DANGEROUS.
THE PLACES I GO, AND THE THINGS THAT I SEE... I WOULDN'T FORGIVE MYSELF IF SOMETHING HAPPENED TO YOU.
OH...
LUCKY FOR YOU, YOU DON'T NEED TO LEAVE HOME TO BE A HERO, HUH?
THIS IS A SPECIAL ***LOTUS PETAL*** OF BRAVERY, MADE WHERE I COME FROM. IF YOU'RE EVER SCARED AND DON'T KNOW WHAT TO DO, HOLD IT TIGHT, AND IT'LL FILL YOU WITH COURAGE.
TH-THANK YOU!
I'LL COME BACK SOON, AND YOU CAN TELL ME IF IT WORKS FOR YA!
FWASH

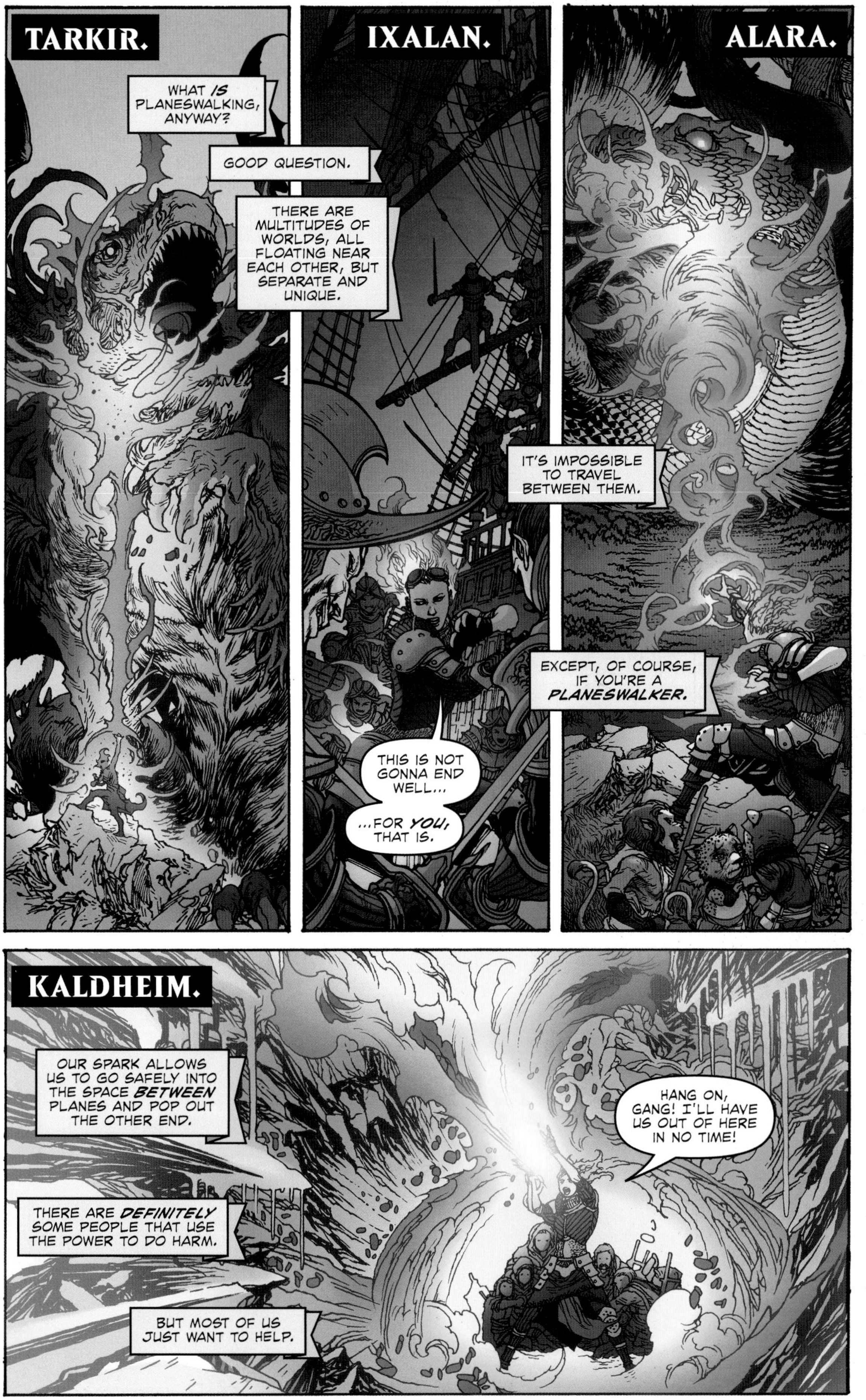
TARKIR.
WHAT IS PLANESWALKING, ANYWAY?
GOOD QUESTION.
THERE ARE MULTITUDES OF WORLDS, ALL FLOATING NEAR EACH OTHER, BUT SEPARATE AND UNIQUE.
IXALAN.
THIS IS NOT GONNA END WELL...
...FOR YOU, THAT IS.
ALARA.
IT'S IMPOSSIBLE TO TRAVEL BETWEEN THEM.
EXCEPT, OF COURSE, IF YOU'RE A PLANESWALKER.
KALDHEIM.
OUR SPARK ALLOWS US TO GO SAFELY INTO THE SPACE BETWEEN PLANES AND POP OUT THE OTHER END.
THERE ARE DEFINITELY SOME PEOPLE THAT USE THE POWER TO DO HARM.
BUT MOST OF US JUST WANT TO HELP.
HANG ON, GANG! I'LL HAVE US OUT OF HERE IN NO TIME!

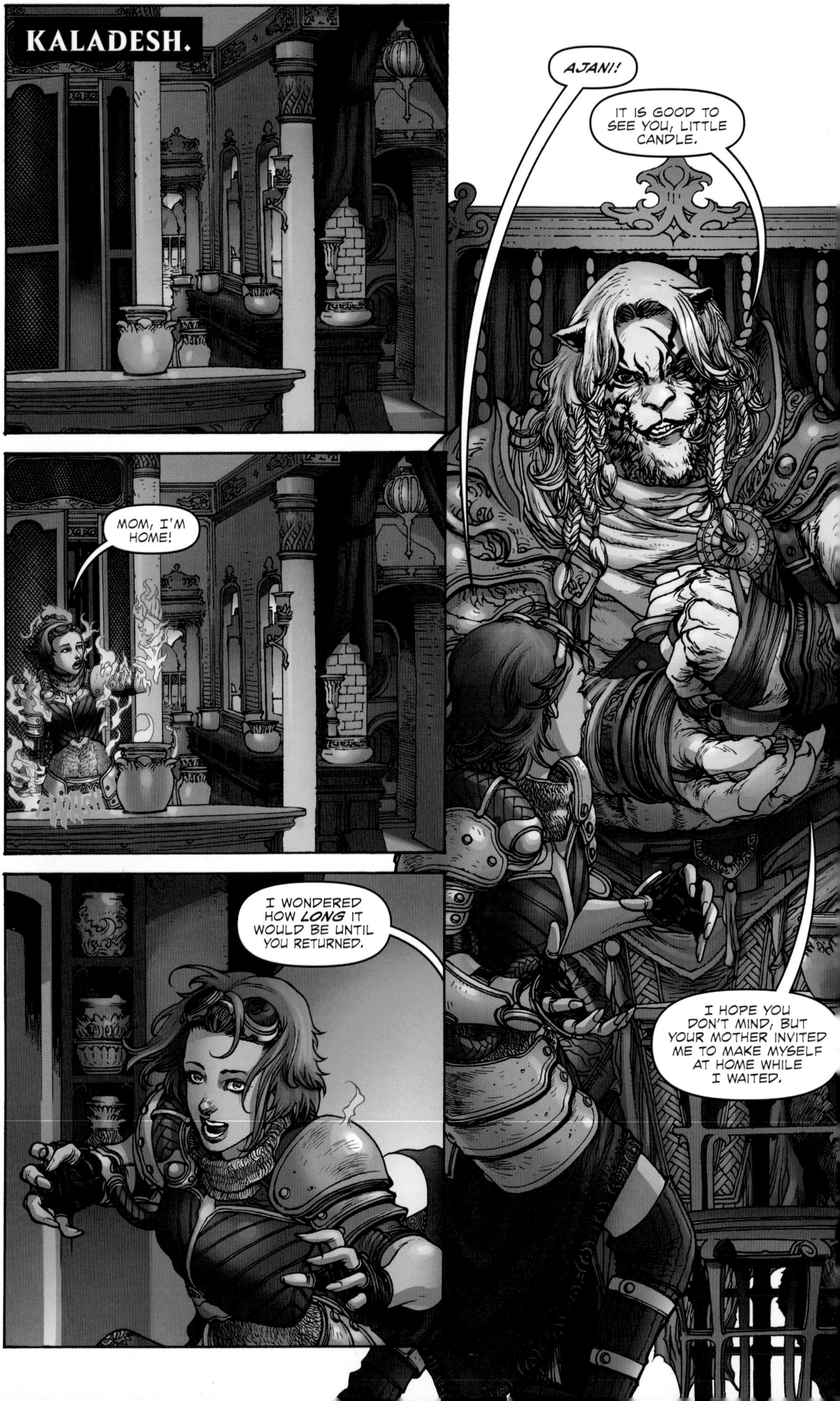
KALADESH.
MOM, I'M HOME!
FWASH
I WONDERED HOW LONG IT WOULD BE UNTIL YOU RETURNED.
AJANI!
IT IS GOOD TO SEE YOU, LITTLE CANDLE.
I HOPE YOU DON'T MIND, BUT YOUR MOTHER INVITED ME TO MAKE MYSELF AT HOME WHILE I WAITED.

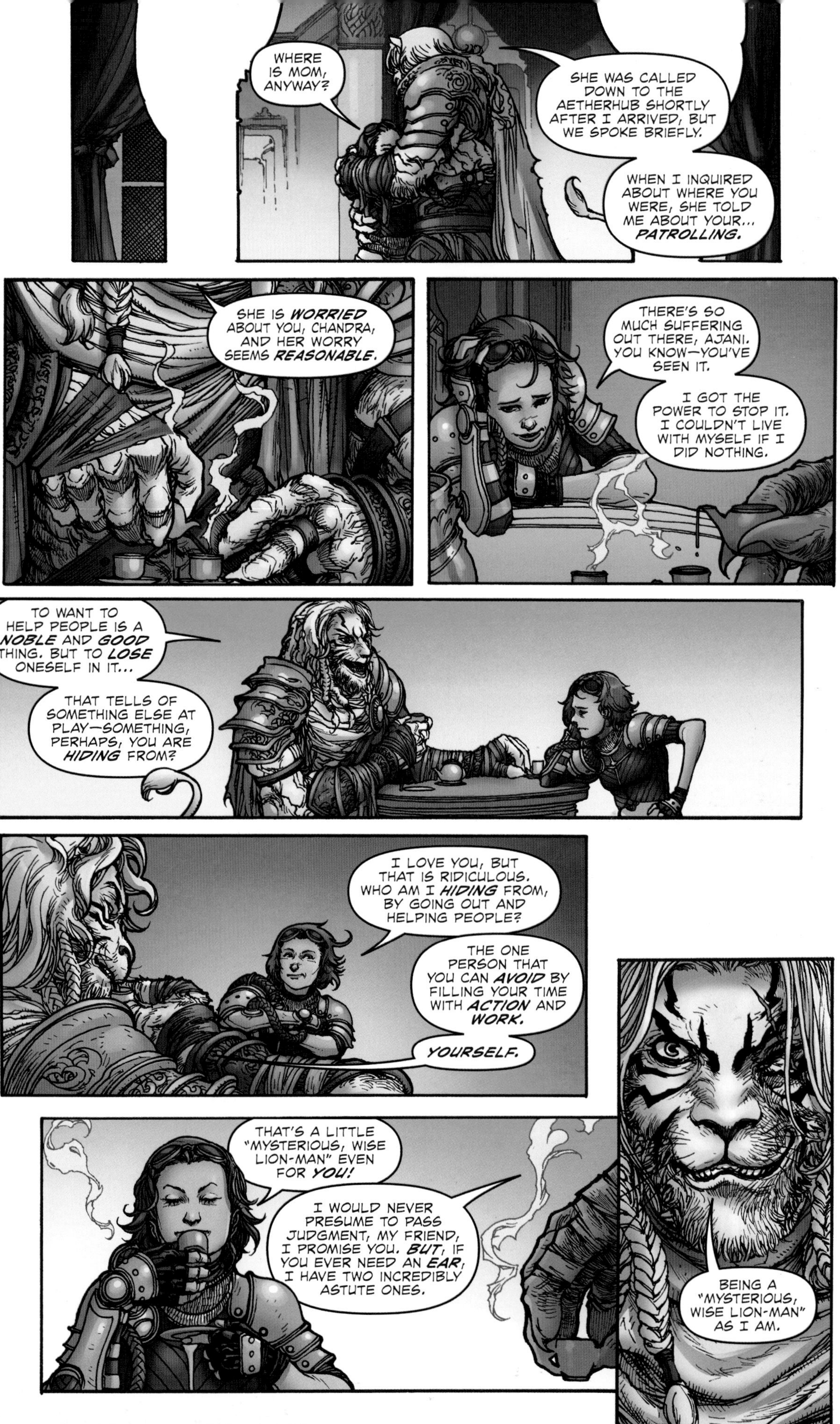
WHERE IS MOM, ANYWAY?
SHE WAS CALLED DOWN TO THE AETHERHUB SHORTLY AFTER I ARRIVED, BUT WE SPOKE BRIEFLY.
WHEN I INQUIRED ABOUT WHERE YOU WERE, SHE TOLD ME ABOUT YOUR... PATROLLING.
SHE IS WORRIED ABOUT YOU, CHANDRA, AND HER WORRY SEEMS REASONABLE.
THERE'S SO MUCH SUFFERING OUT THERE, AJANI. YOU KNOW—YOU'VE SEEN IT.
I GOT THE POWER TO STOP IT. I COULDN'T LIVE WITH MYSELF IF I DID NOTHING.
TO WANT TO HELP PEOPLE IS A NOBLE AND GOOD THING. BUT TO LOSE ONESELF IN IT...
THAT TELLS OF SOMETHING ELSE AT PLAY—SOMETHING, PERHAPS, YOU ARE HIDING FROM?
I LOVE YOU, BUT THAT IS RIDICULOUS. WHO AM I HIDING FROM, BY GOING OUT AND HELPING PEOPLE?
THE ONE PERSON THAT YOU CAN AVOID BY FILLING YOUR TIME WITH ACTION AND WORK.
YOURSELF.
THAT'S A LITTLE "MYSTERIOUS, WISE LION-MAN" EVEN FOR YOU!
I WOULD NEVER PRESUME TO PASS JUDGMENT, MY FRIEND, I PROMISE YOU. BUT, IF YOU EVER NEED AN EAR, I HAVE TWO INCREDIBLY ASTUTE ONES.
BEING A "MYSTERIOUS, WISE LION-MAN" AS I AM.

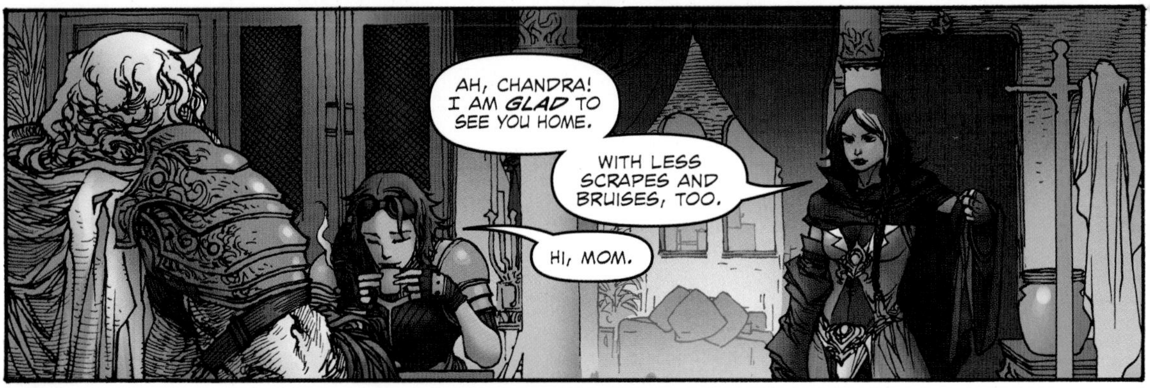
AH, CHANDRA! I AM GLAD TO SEE YOU HOME.
WITH LESS SCRAPES AND BRUISES, TOO.
HI, MOM.

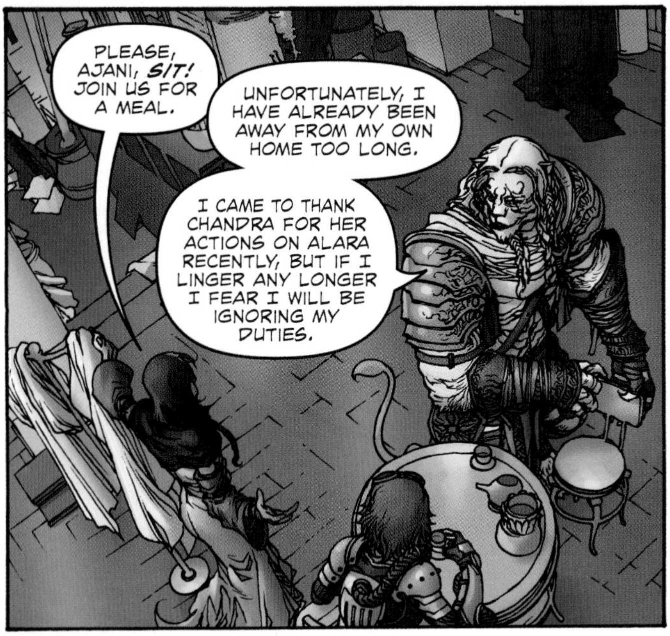
PLEASE, AJANI, SIT! JOIN US FOR A MEAL.
UNFORTUNATELY, I HAVE ALREADY BEEN AWAY FROM MY OWN HOME TOO LONG.
I CAME TO THANK CHANDRA FOR HER ACTIONS ON ALARA RECENTLY, BUT IF I LINGER ANY LONGER I FEAR I WILL BE IGNORING MY DUTIES.

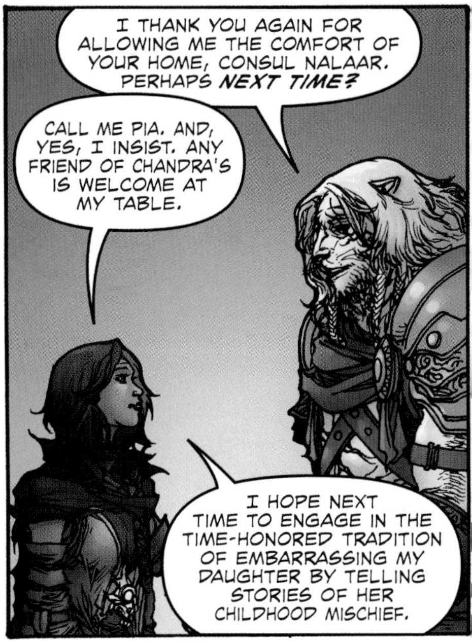
I THANK YOU AGAIN FOR ALLOWING ME THE COMFORT OF YOUR HOME, CONSUL NALAAR. PERHAPS NEXT TIME?
CALL ME PIA. AND, YES, I INSIST. ANY FRIEND OF CHANDRA'S IS WELCOME AT MY TABLE.
I HOPE NEXT TIME TO ENGAGE IN THE TIME-HONORED TRADITION OF EMBARRASSING MY DAUGHTER BY TELLING STORIES OF HER CHILDHOOD MISCHIEF.

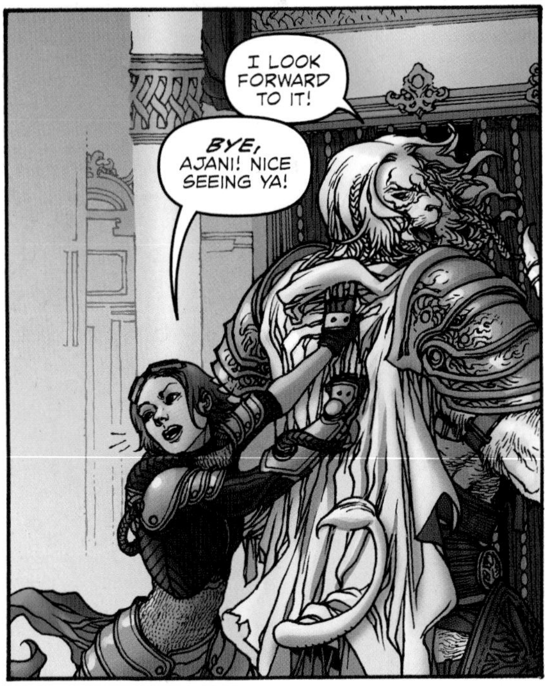
I LOOK FORWARD TO IT!
BYE, AJANI! NICE SEEING YA!

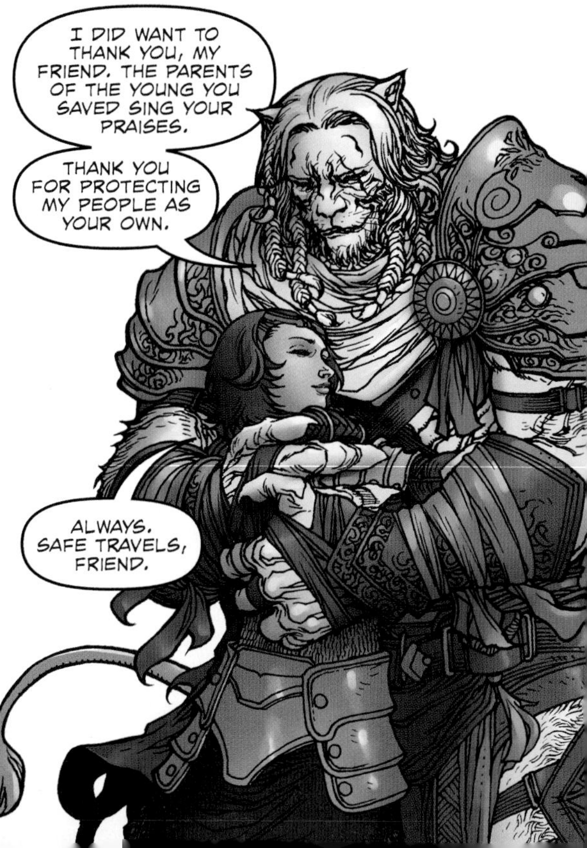
I DID WANT TO THANK YOU, MY FRIEND. THE PARENTS OF THE YOUNG YOU SAVED SING YOUR PRAISES.
THANK YOU FOR PROTECTING MY PEOPLE AS YOUR OWN.
ALWAYS. SAFE TRAVELS, FRIEND.

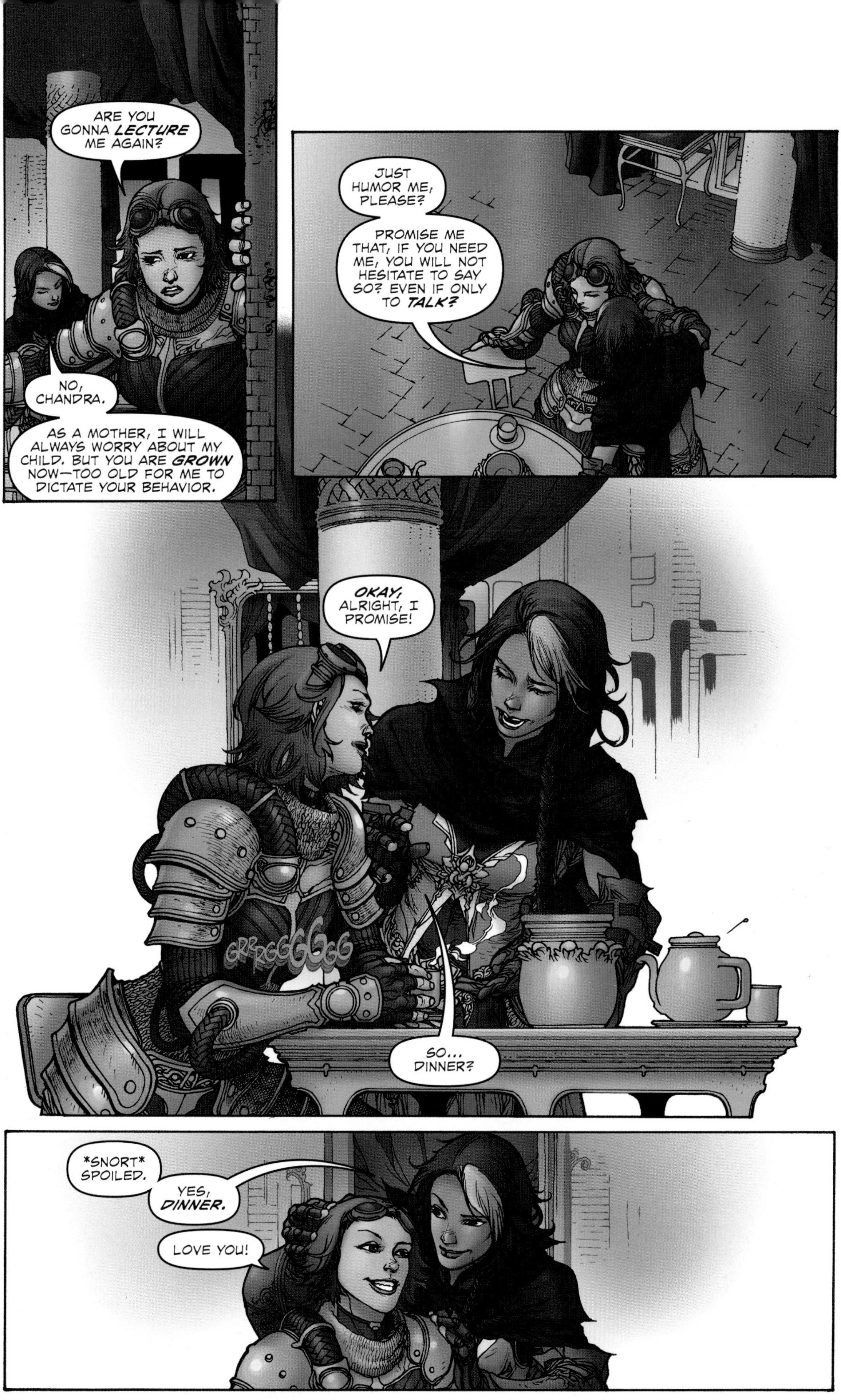
ARE YOU GONNA LECTURE ME AGAIN?
NO, CHANDRA.
AS A MOTHER, I WILL ALWAYS WORRY ABOUT MY CHILD. BUT YOU ARE GROWN NOW—TOO OLD FOR ME TO DICTATE YOUR BEHAVIOR.
JUST HUMOR ME, PLEASE?
PROMISE ME THAT, IF YOU NEED ME, YOU WILL NOT HESITATE TO SAY SO? EVEN IF ONLY TO TALK?
OKAY, ALRIGHT, I PROMISE!
GRRRGGGGGG
SO... DINNER?
*SNORT* SPOILED.
YES, DINNER.
LOVE YOU!

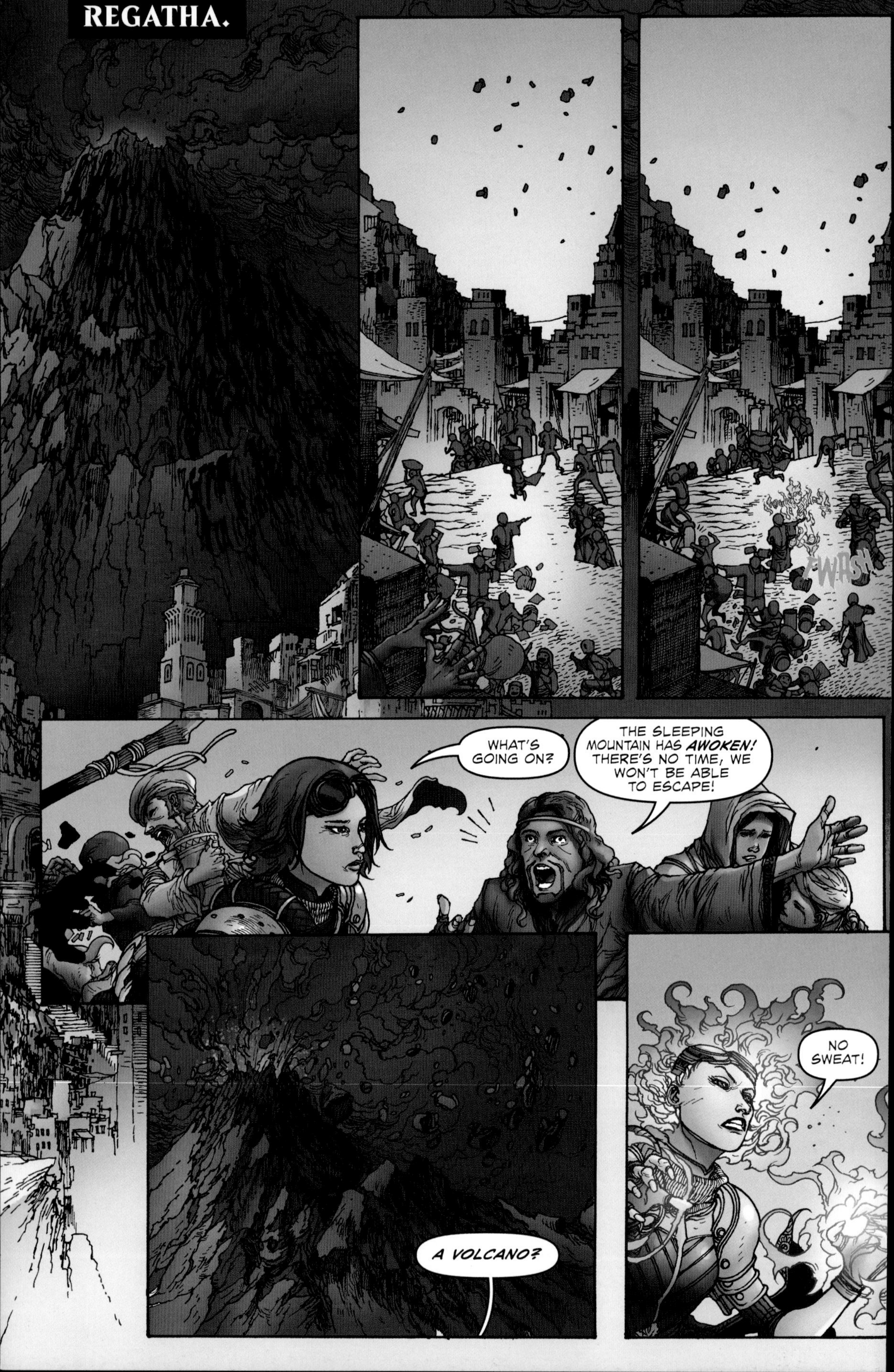
REGATHA.
FWASH
WHAT'S GOING ON?
THE SLEEPING MOUNTAIN HAS AWOKEN! THERE'S NO TIME, WE WON'T BE ABLE TO ESCAPE!
A VOLCANO?
NO SWEAT!

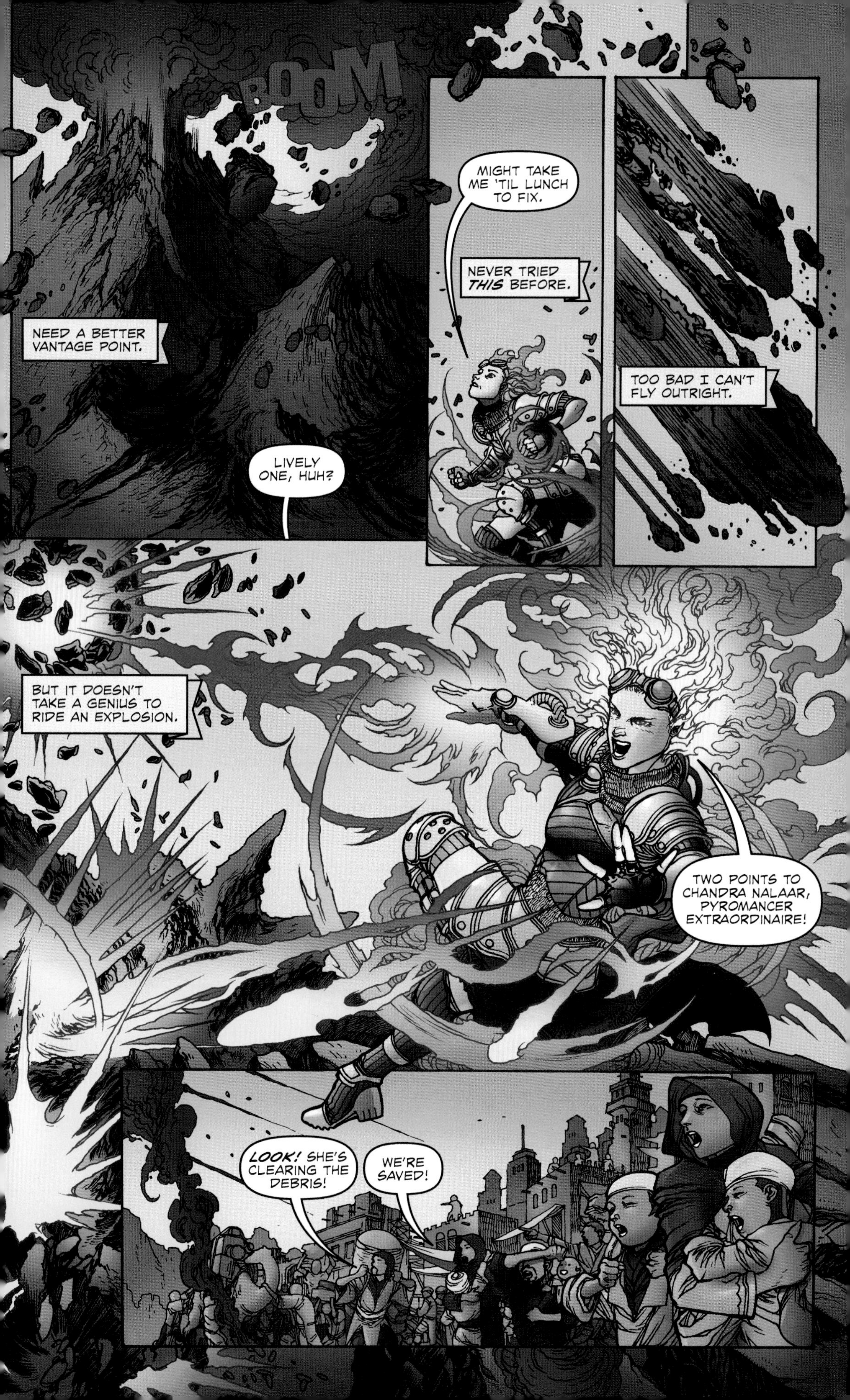
BOOM
NEED A BETTER VANTAGE POINT.
LIVELY ONE, HUH?
MIGHT TAKE ME 'TIL LUNCH TO FIX.
NEVER TRIED *THIS* BEFORE.
TOO BAD I CAN'T FLY OUTRIGHT.
BUT IT DOESN'T TAKE A GENIUS TO RIDE AN EXPLOSION.
TWO POINTS TO CHANDRA NALAAR, PYROMANCER EXTRAORDINAIRE!
*LOOK!* SHE'S CLEARING THE DEBRIS!
WE'RE SAVED!

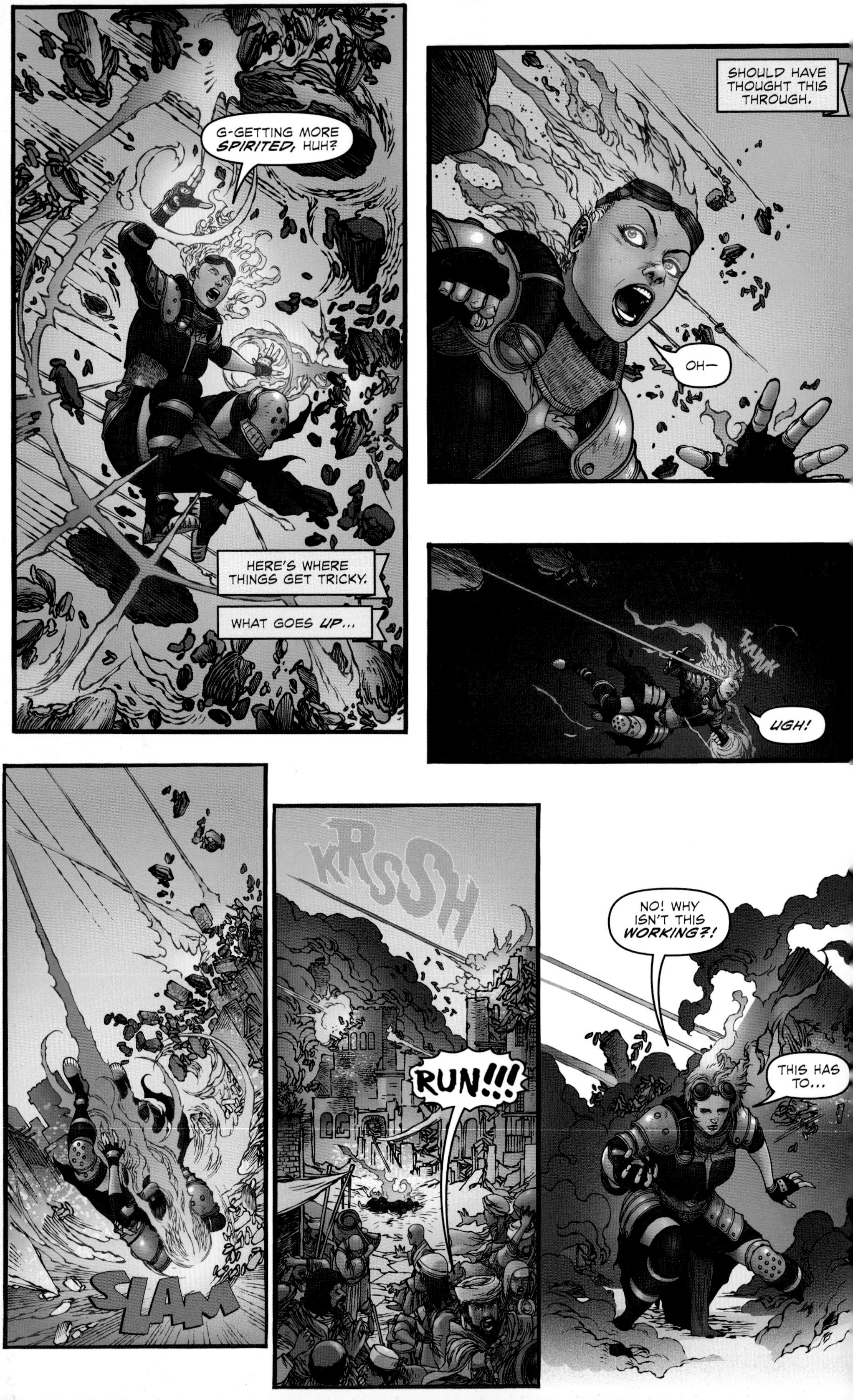
G-GETTING MORE SPIRITED, HUH?
HERE'S WHERE THINGS GET TRICKY.
WHAT GOES UP...
SHOULD HAVE THOUGHT THIS THROUGH.
OH—
THUNK
UGH!
SLAM
KRSSH
RUN!!!
NO! WHY ISN'T THIS WORKING?!
THIS HAS TO...

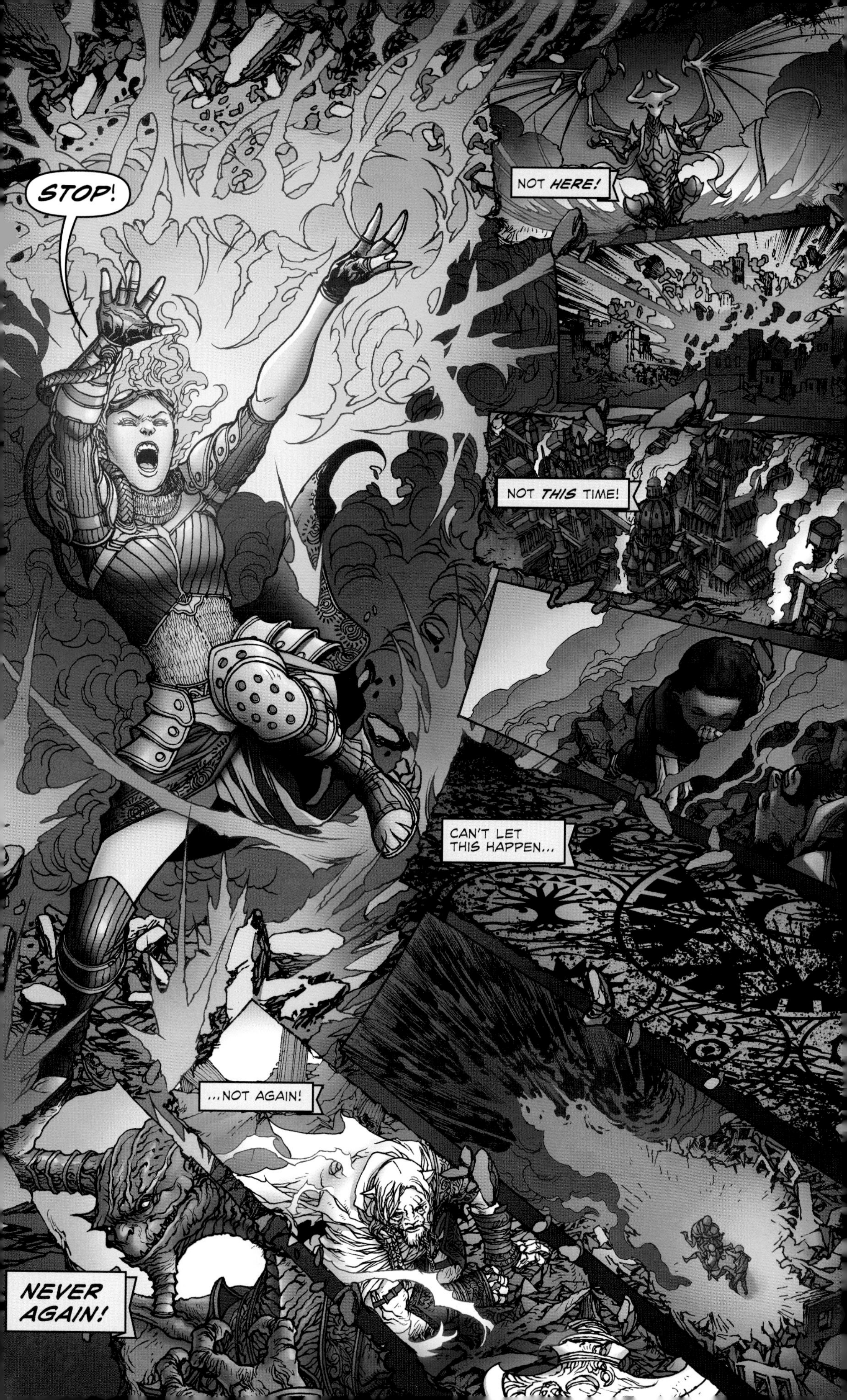
STOP!
NOT HERE!
NOT THIS TIME!
CAN'T LET THIS HAPPEN...
...NOT AGAIN!
NEVER AGAIN!

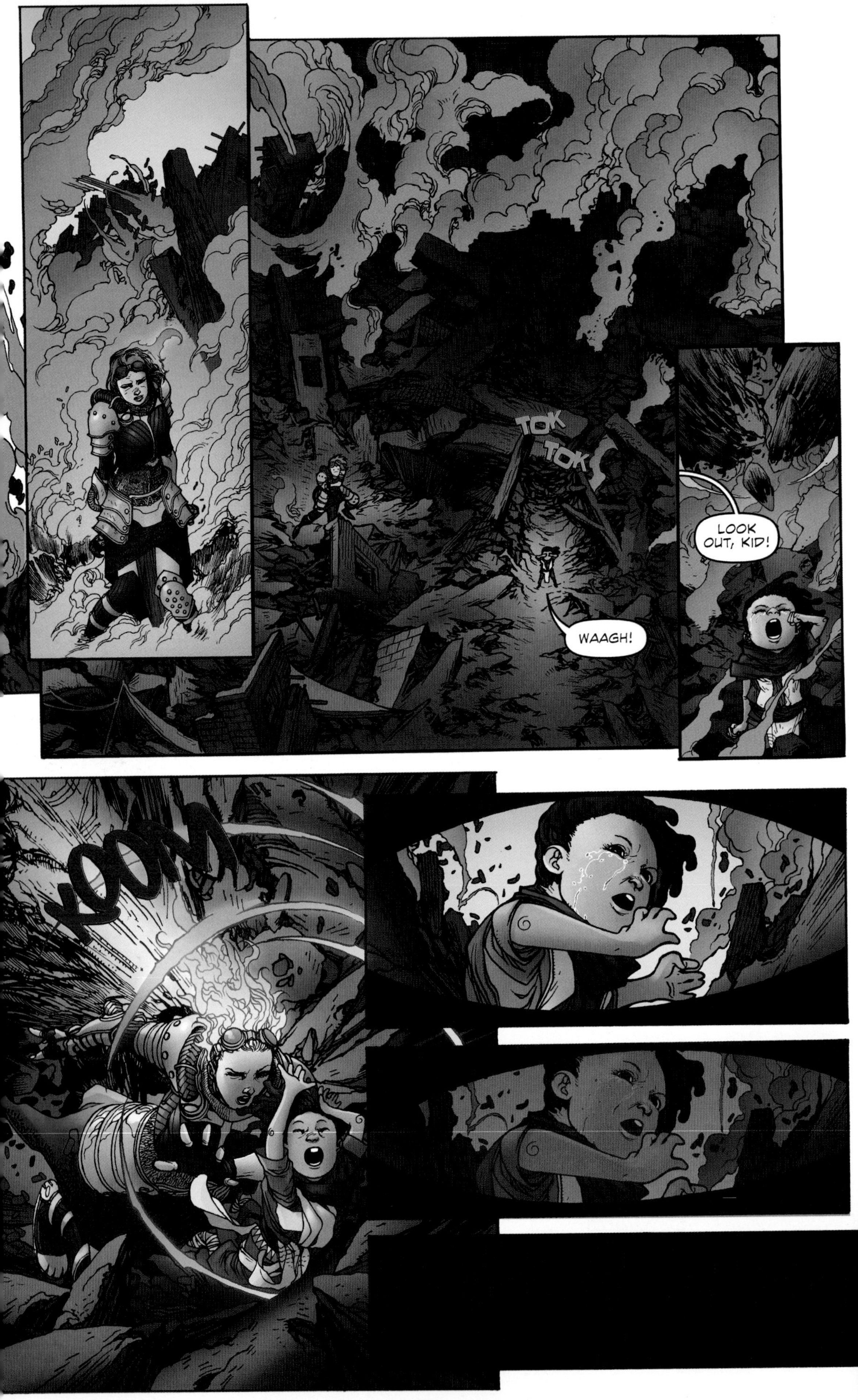
TOK
TOK
WAAGH!
LOOK OUT, KID!
KOOM

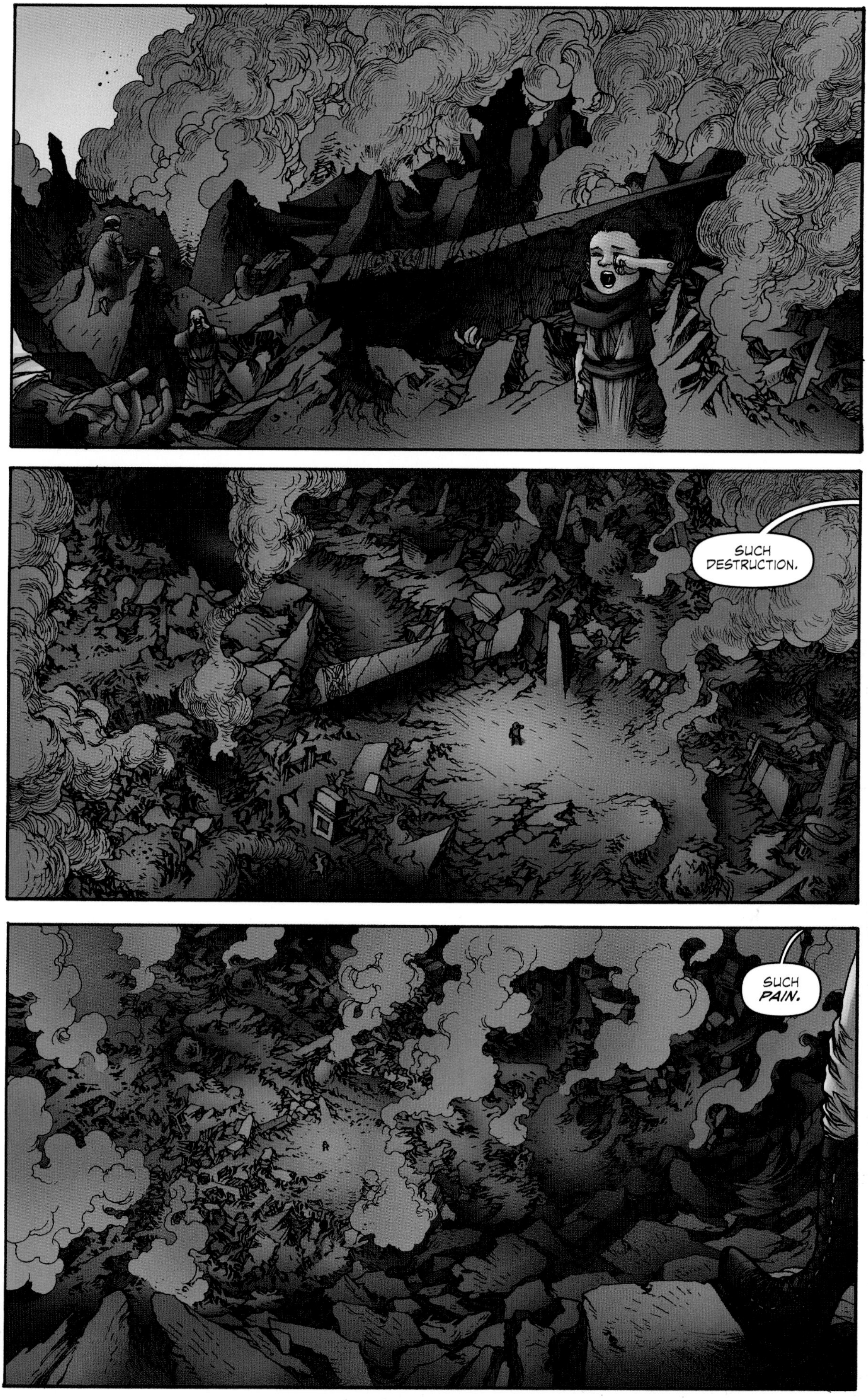
SUCH DESTRUCTION.
SUCH PAIN.

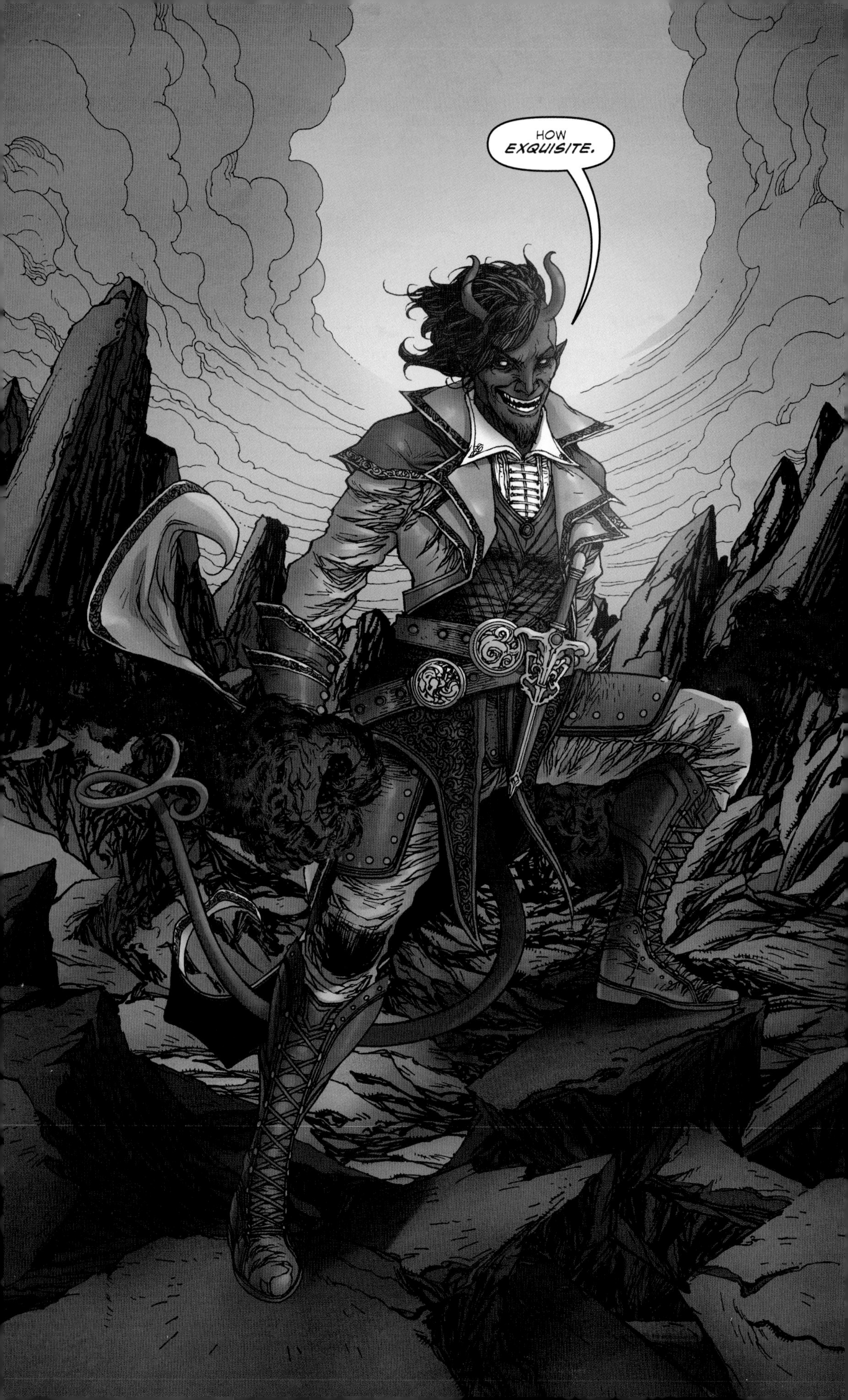
HOW *EXQUISITE.*

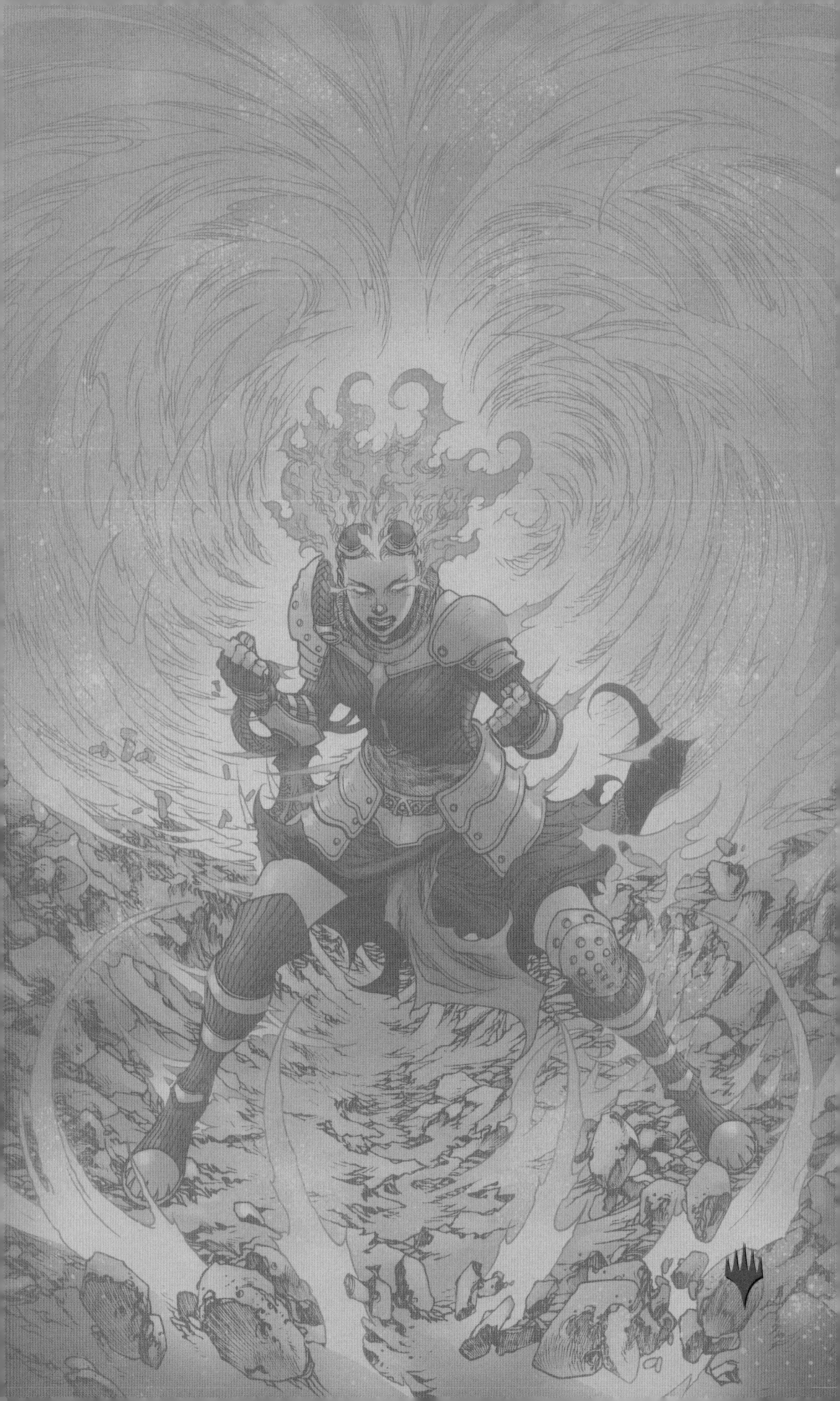

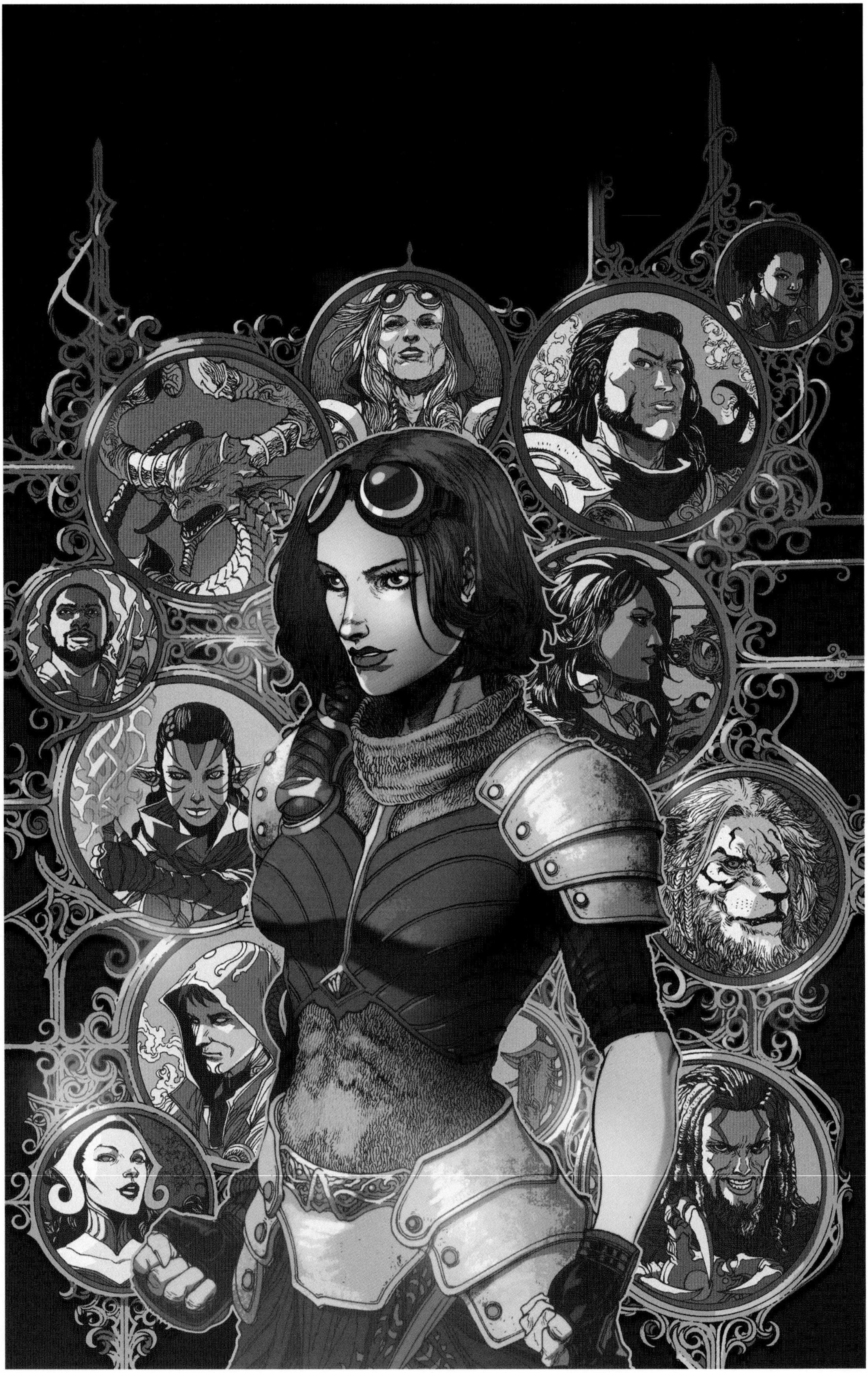

Art by Harvey Tolibao • Colors by Matt Herms

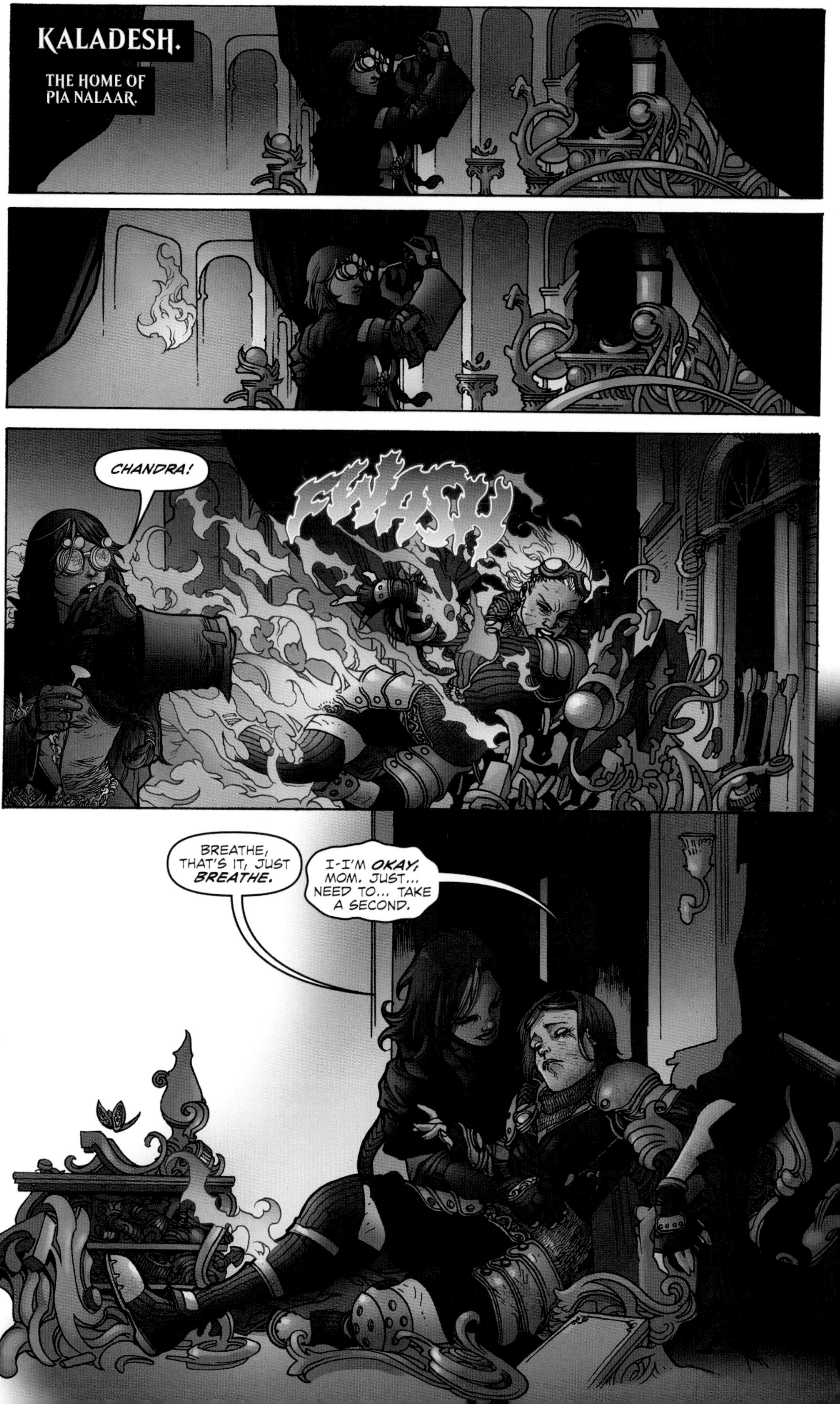

KALADESH.
THE HOME OF PIA NALAAR.
CHANDRA!
FWASH
BREATHE, THAT'S IT, JUST BREATHE.
I-I'M OKAY, MOM. JUST... NEED TO... TAKE A SECOND.

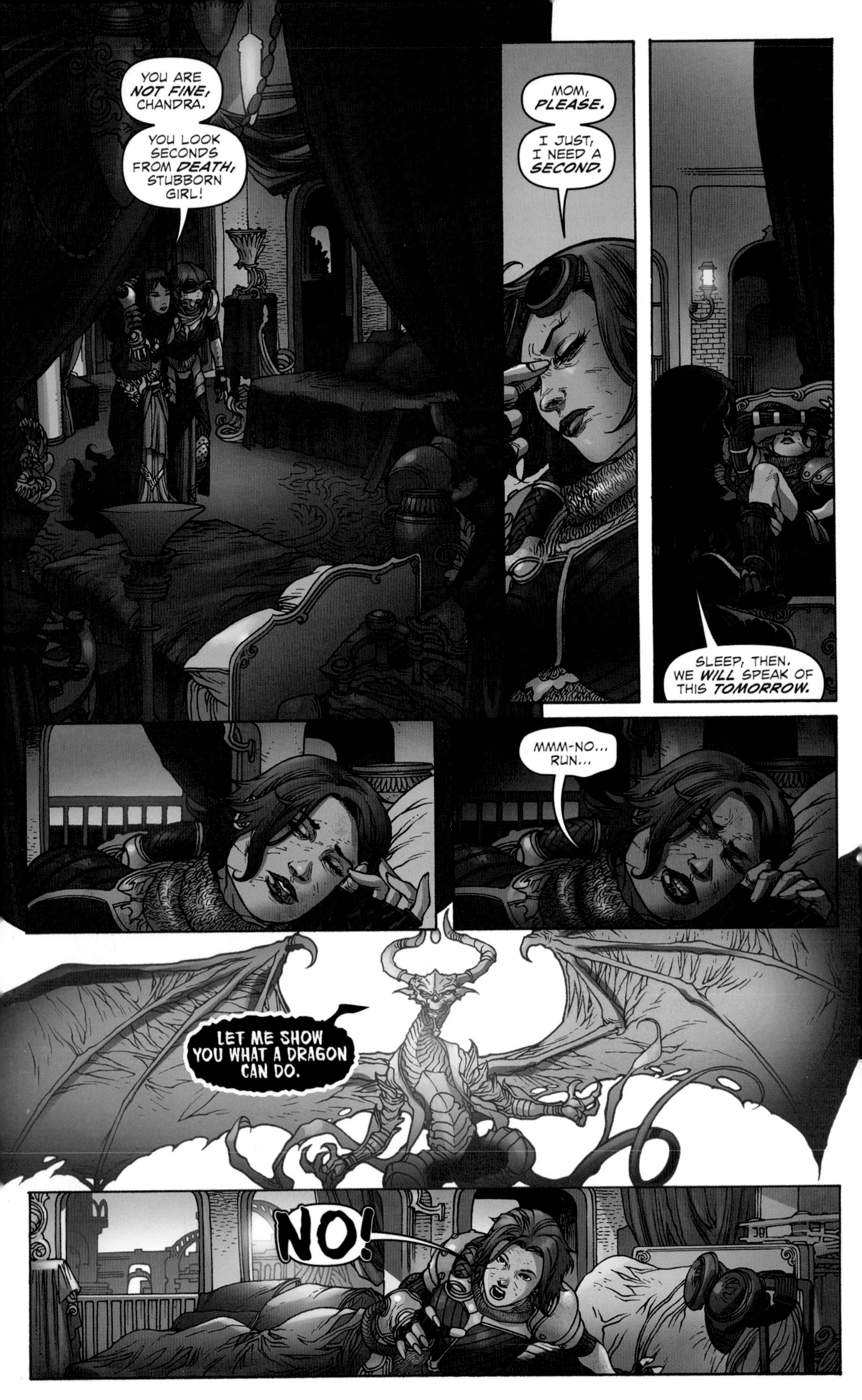
YOU ARE NOT FINE, CHANDRA.
YOU LOOK SECONDS FROM DEATH, STUBBORN GIRL!
MOM, PLEASE.
I JUST, I NEED A SECOND.
SLEEP, THEN. WE WILL SPEAK OF THIS TOMORROW.
MMM-NO... RUN...
LET ME SHOW YOU WHAT A DRAGON CAN DO.
NO!

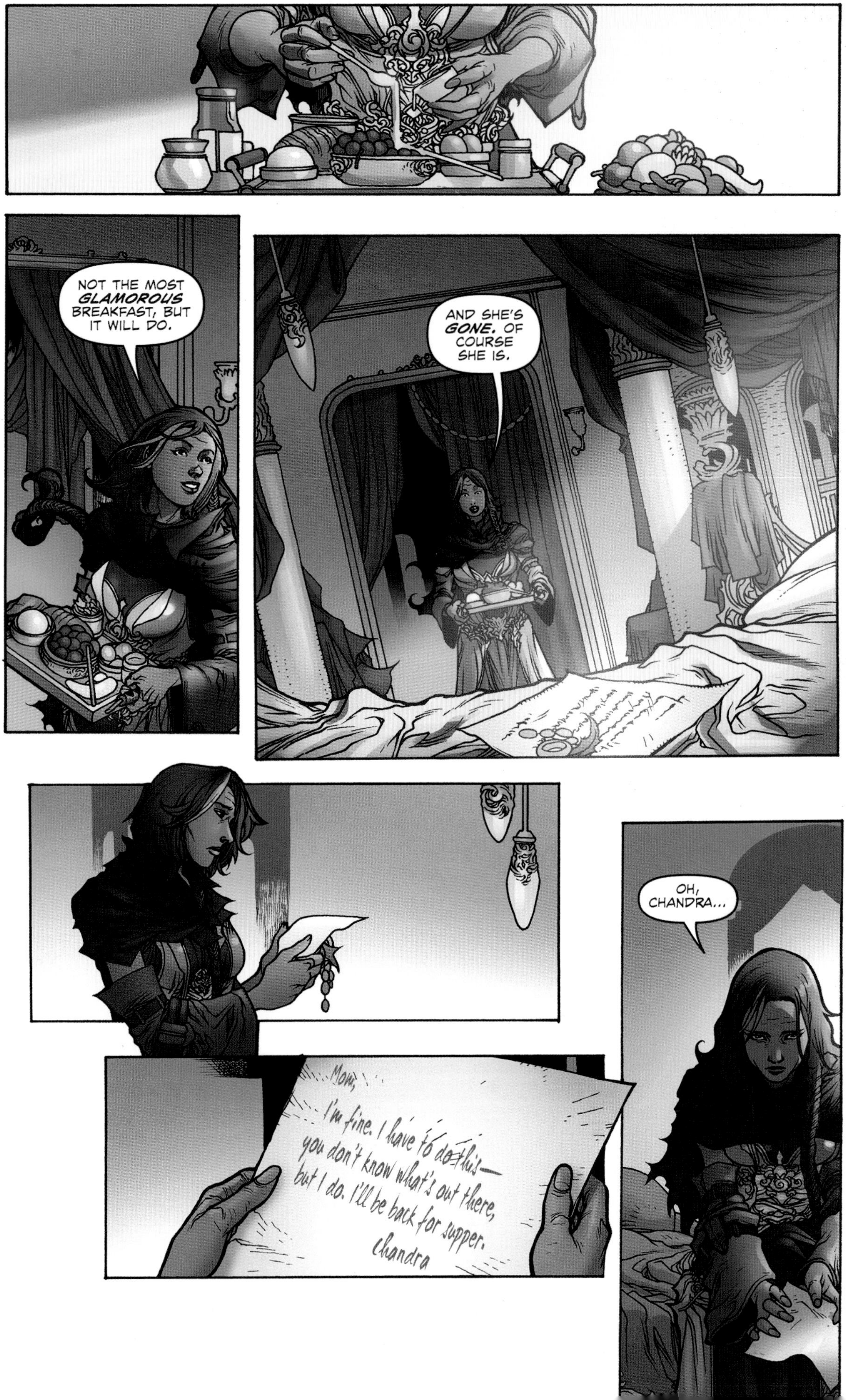
NOT THE MOST GLAMOROUS BREAKFAST, BUT IT WILL DO.
AND SHE'S GONE. OF COURSE SHE IS.
OH, CHANDRA...
Mom,
I'm fine. I have to do this— you don't know what's out there, but I do. I'll be back for supper.
Chandra

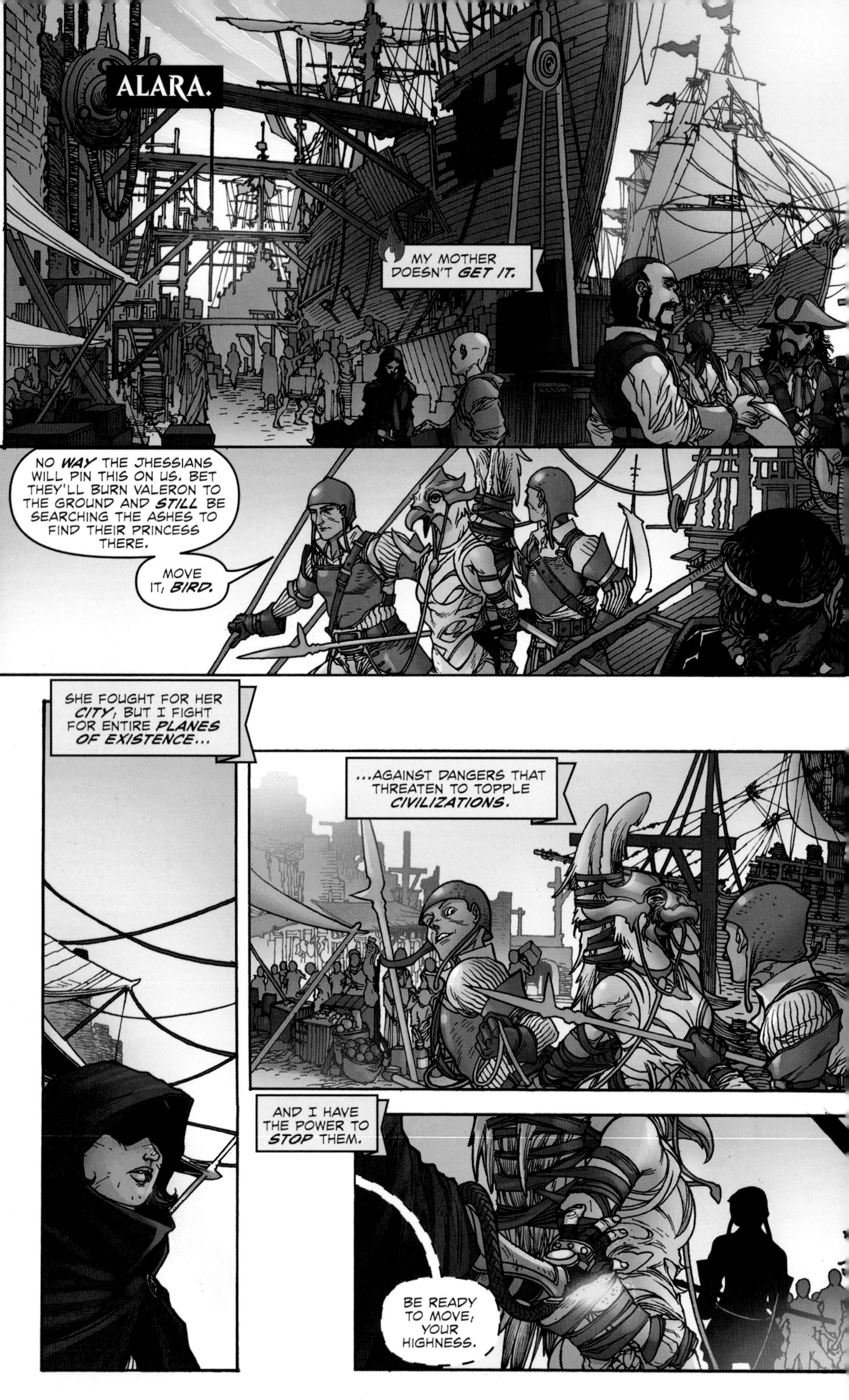
ALARA.
MY MOTHER DOESN'T GET IT.
NO WAY THE JHESSIANS WILL PIN THIS ON US. BET THEY'LL BURN VALERON TO THE GROUND AND STILL BE SEARCHING THE ASHES TO FIND THEIR PRINCESS THERE.
MOVE IT, BIRD.
SHE FOUGHT FOR HER CITY, BUT I FIGHT FOR ENTIRE PLANES OF EXISTENCE...
...AGAINST DANGERS THAT THREATEN TO TOPPLE CIVILIZATIONS.
AND I HAVE THE POWER TO STOP THEM.
BE READY TO MOVE, YOUR HIGHNESS.

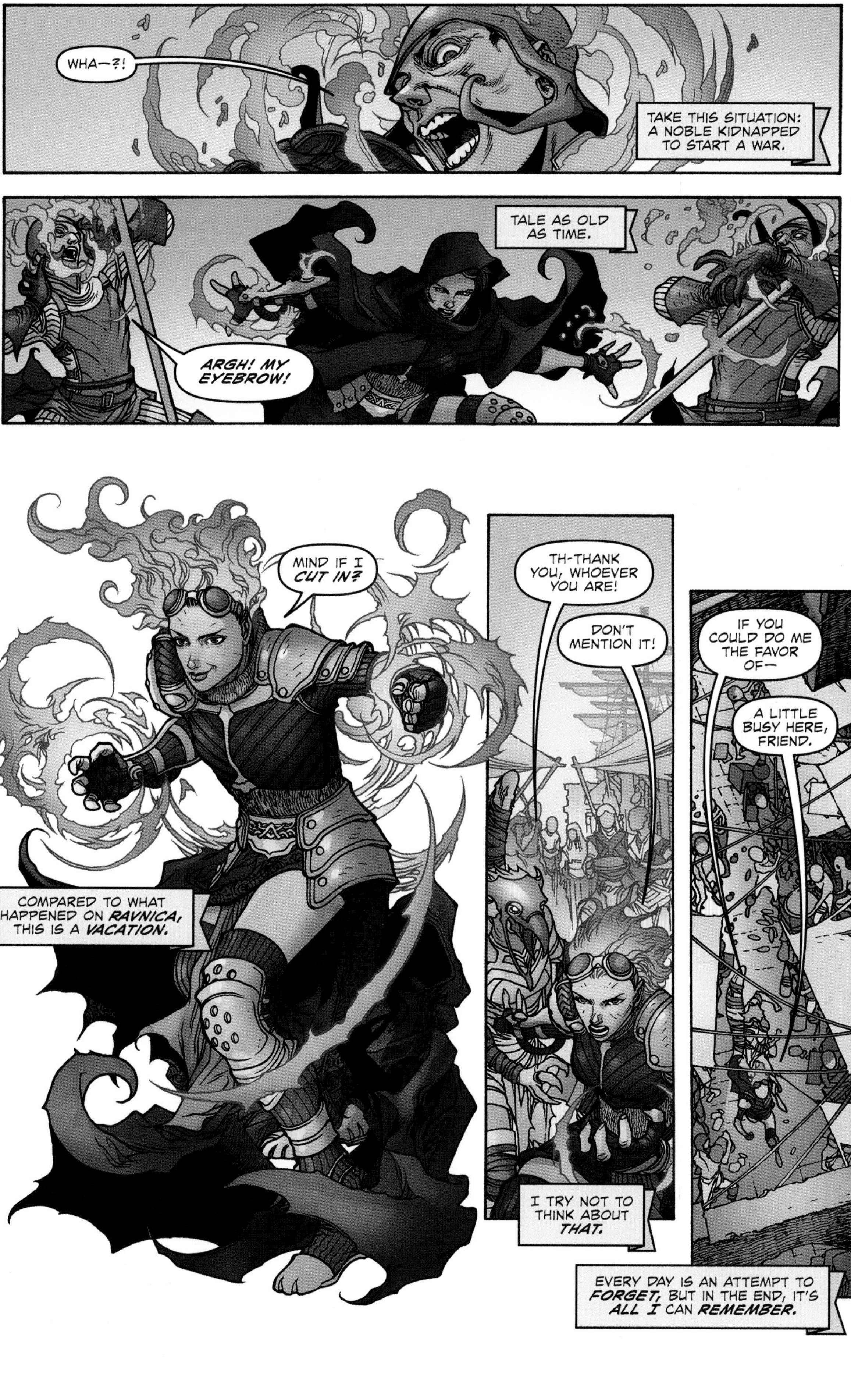
WHA—?!
TAKE THIS SITUATION: A NOBLE KIDNAPPED TO START A WAR.
TALE AS OLD AS TIME.
ARGH! MY EYEBROW!
MIND IF I CUT IN?
COMPARED TO WHAT HAPPENED ON RAVNICA, THIS IS A VACATION.
TH-THANK YOU, WHOEVER YOU ARE!
DON'T MENTION IT!
I TRY NOT TO THINK ABOUT THAT.
IF YOU COULD DO ME THE FAVOR OF—
A LITTLE BUSY HERE, FRIEND.
EVERY DAY IS AN ATTEMPT TO FORGET, BUT IN THE END, IT'S ALL I CAN REMEMBER.

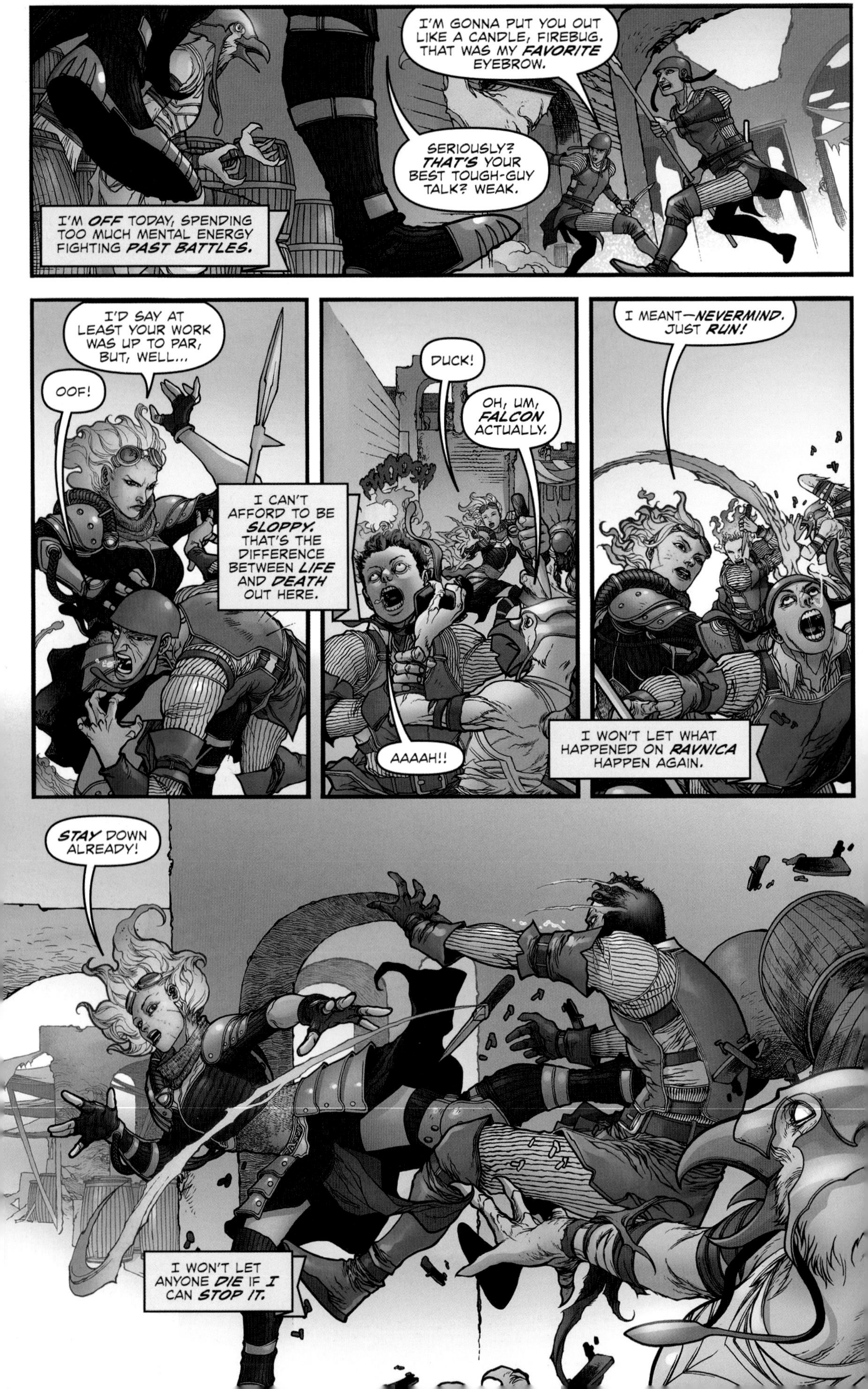

I'M OFF TODAY, SPENDING TOO MUCH MENTAL ENERGY FIGHTING PAST BATTLES.
I'M GONNA PUT YOU OUT LIKE A CANDLE, FIREBUG. THAT WAS MY FAVORITE EYEBROW.
SERIOUSLY? THAT'S YOUR BEST TOUGH-GUY TALK? WEAK.
I'D SAY AT LEAST YOUR WORK WAS UP TO PAR, BUT, WELL...
OOF!
I CAN'T AFFORD TO BE SLOPPY. THAT'S THE DIFFERENCE BETWEEN LIFE AND DEATH OUT HERE.
DUCK!
OH, UM, FALCON ACTUALLY.
AAAAH!!
I MEANT—NEVERMIND. JUST RUN!
I WON'T LET WHAT HAPPENED ON RAVNICA HAPPEN AGAIN.
STAY DOWN ALREADY!
I WON'T LET ANYONE DIE IF I CAN STOP IT.

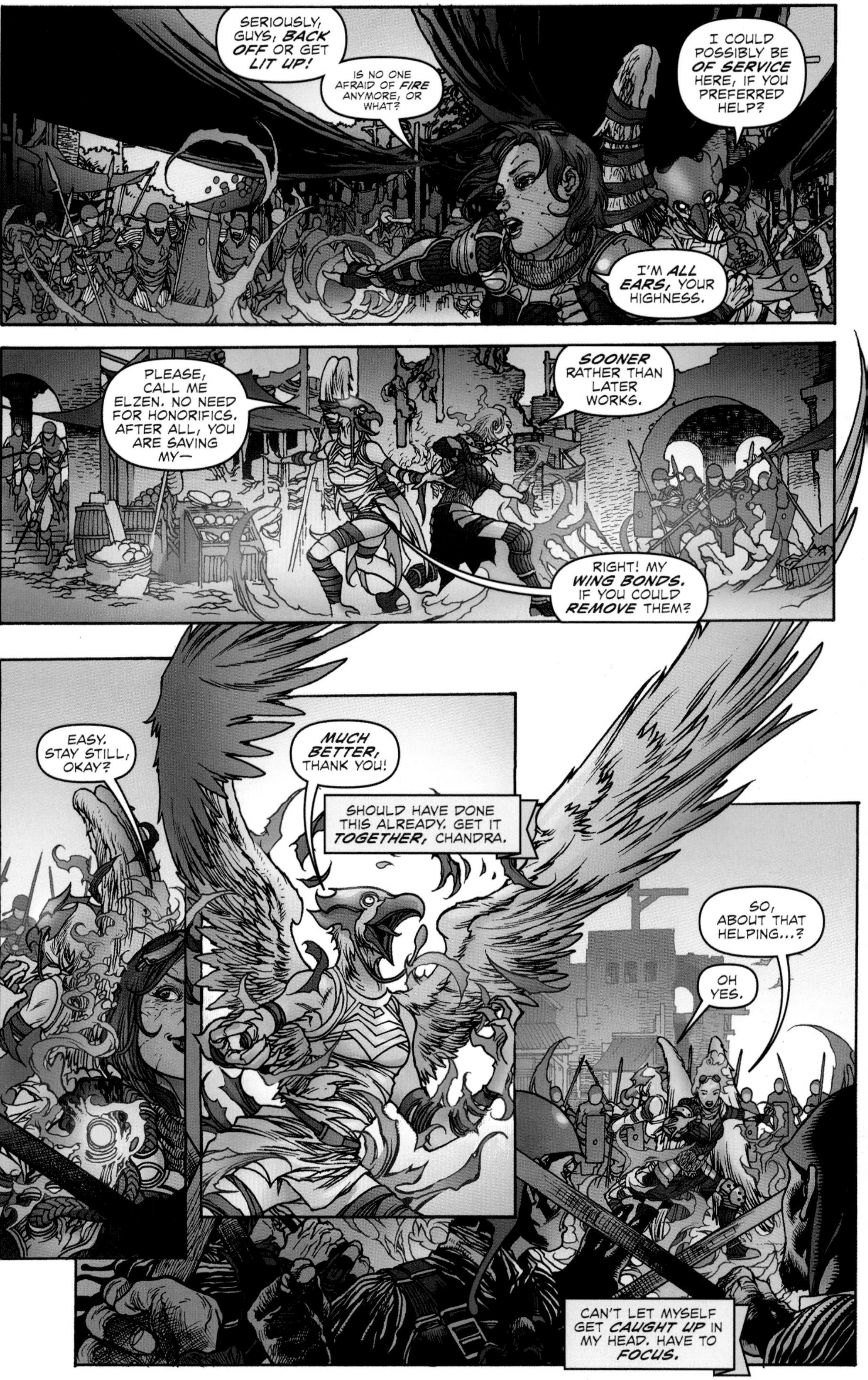
SERIOUSLY, GUYS, BACK OFF OR GET LIT UP!
IS NO ONE AFRAID OF FIRE ANYMORE, OR WHAT?
I COULD POSSIBLY BE OF SERVICE HERE, IF YOU PREFERRED HELP?
I'M ALL EARS, YOUR HIGHNESS.
PLEASE, CALL ME ELZEN. NO NEED FOR HONORIFICS. AFTER ALL, YOU ARE SAVING MY—
SOONER RATHER THAN LATER WORKS.
RIGHT! MY WING BONDS. IF YOU COULD REMOVE THEM?
EASY. STAY STILL, OKAY?
MUCH BETTER, THANK YOU!
SHOULD HAVE DONE THIS ALREADY. GET IT TOGETHER, CHANDRA.
SO, ABOUT THAT HELPING...?
OH YES.
CAN'T LET MYSELF GET CAUGHT UP IN MY HEAD. HAVE TO FOCUS.

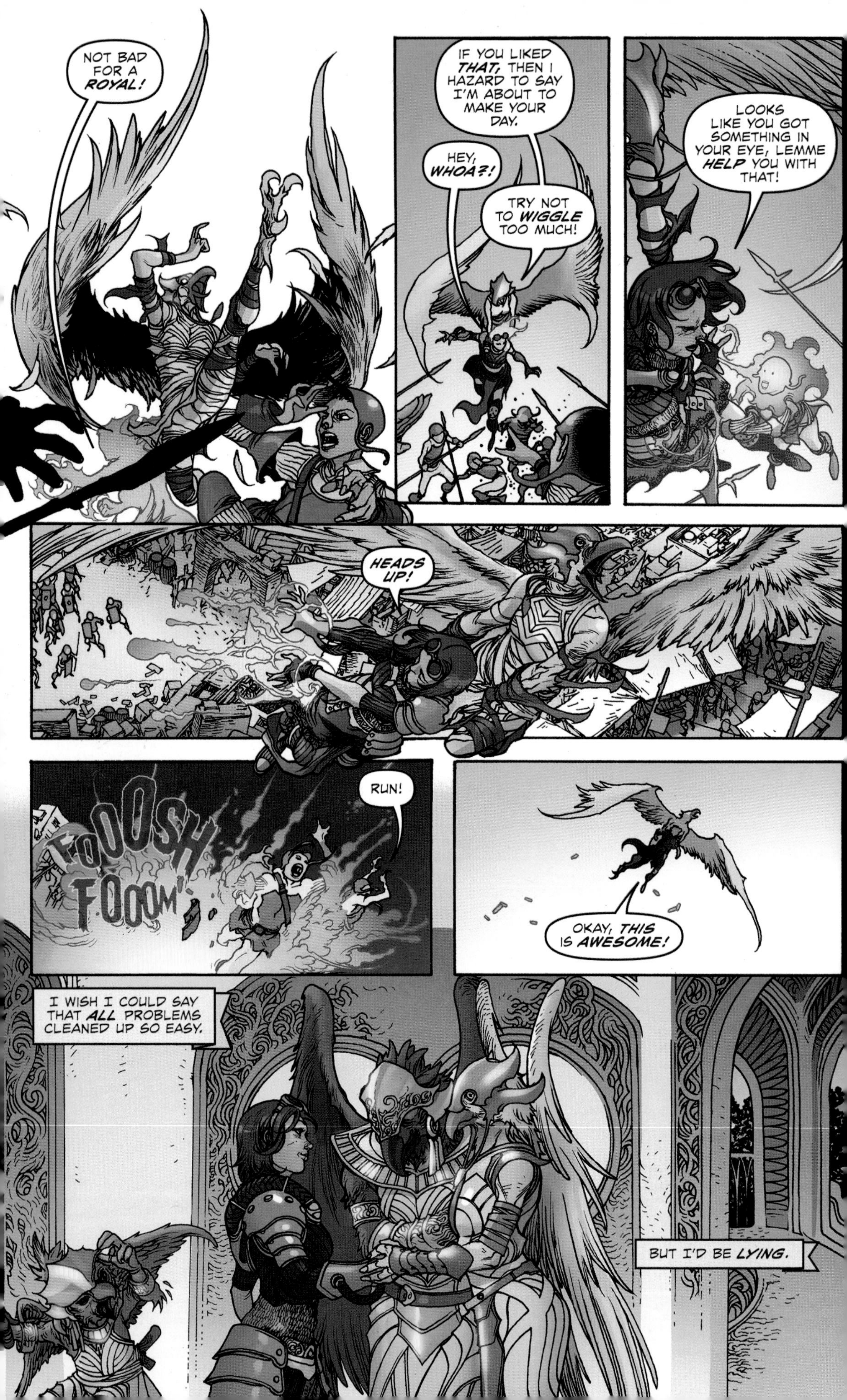
NOT BAD FOR A ROYAL!
IF YOU LIKED THAT, THEN I HAZARD TO SAY I'M ABOUT TO MAKE YOUR DAY.
HEY, WHOA?!
TRY NOT TO WIGGLE TOO MUCH!
LOOKS LIKE YOU GOT SOMETHING IN YOUR EYE, LEMME HELP YOU WITH THAT!
HEADS UP!
RUN!
FOOOSH
FOOOM
OKAY, THIS IS AWESOME!
I WISH I COULD SAY THAT ALL PROBLEMS CLEANED UP SO EASY.
BUT I'D BE LYING.

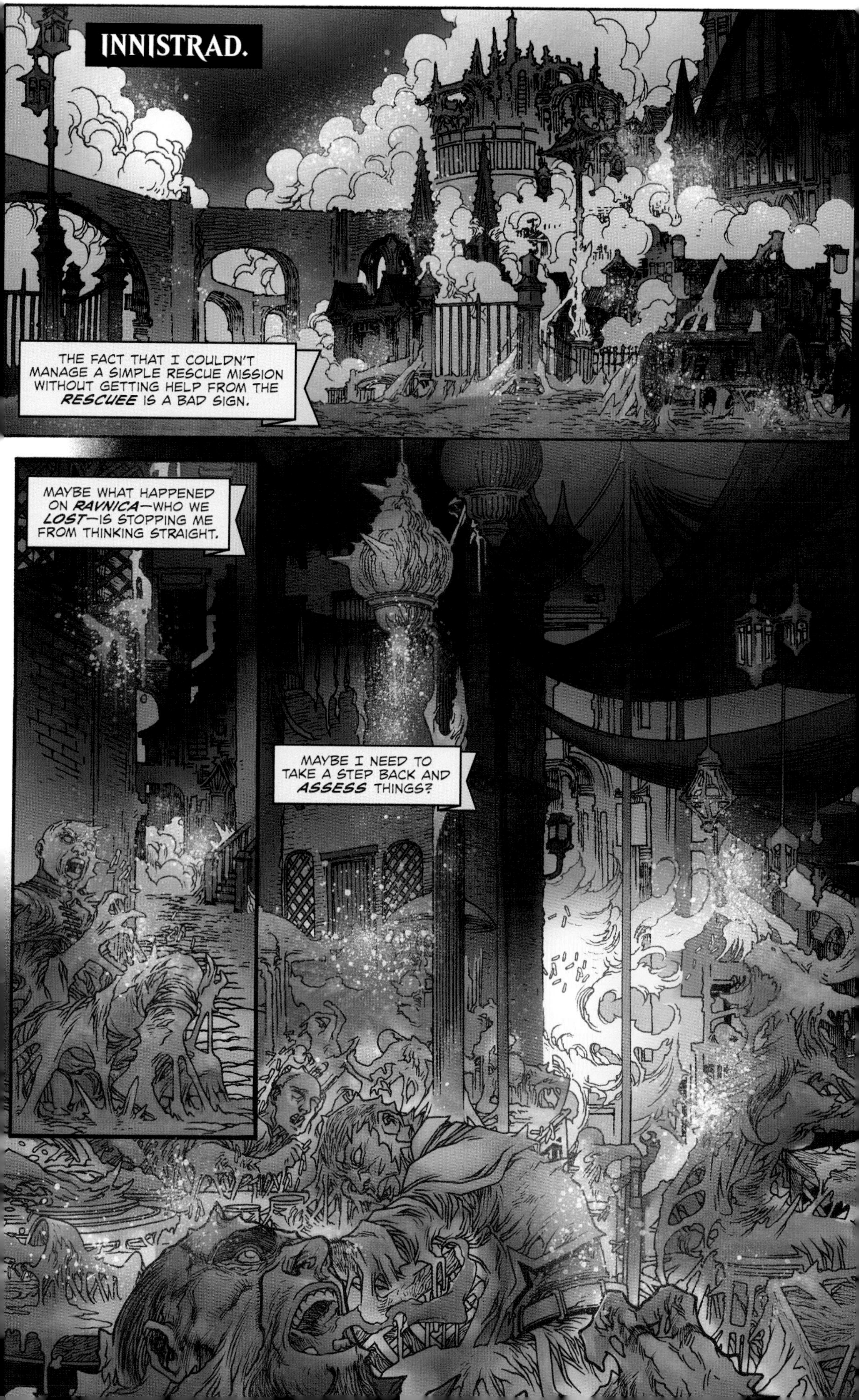
INNISTRAD.
THE FACT THAT I COULDN'T MANAGE A SIMPLE RESCUE MISSION WITHOUT GETTING HELP FROM THE RESCUEE IS A BAD SIGN.
MAYBE WHAT HAPPENED ON RAVNICA—WHO WE LOST—IS STOPPING ME FROM THINKING STRAIGHT.
MAYBE I NEED TO TAKE A STEP BACK AND ASSESS THINGS?

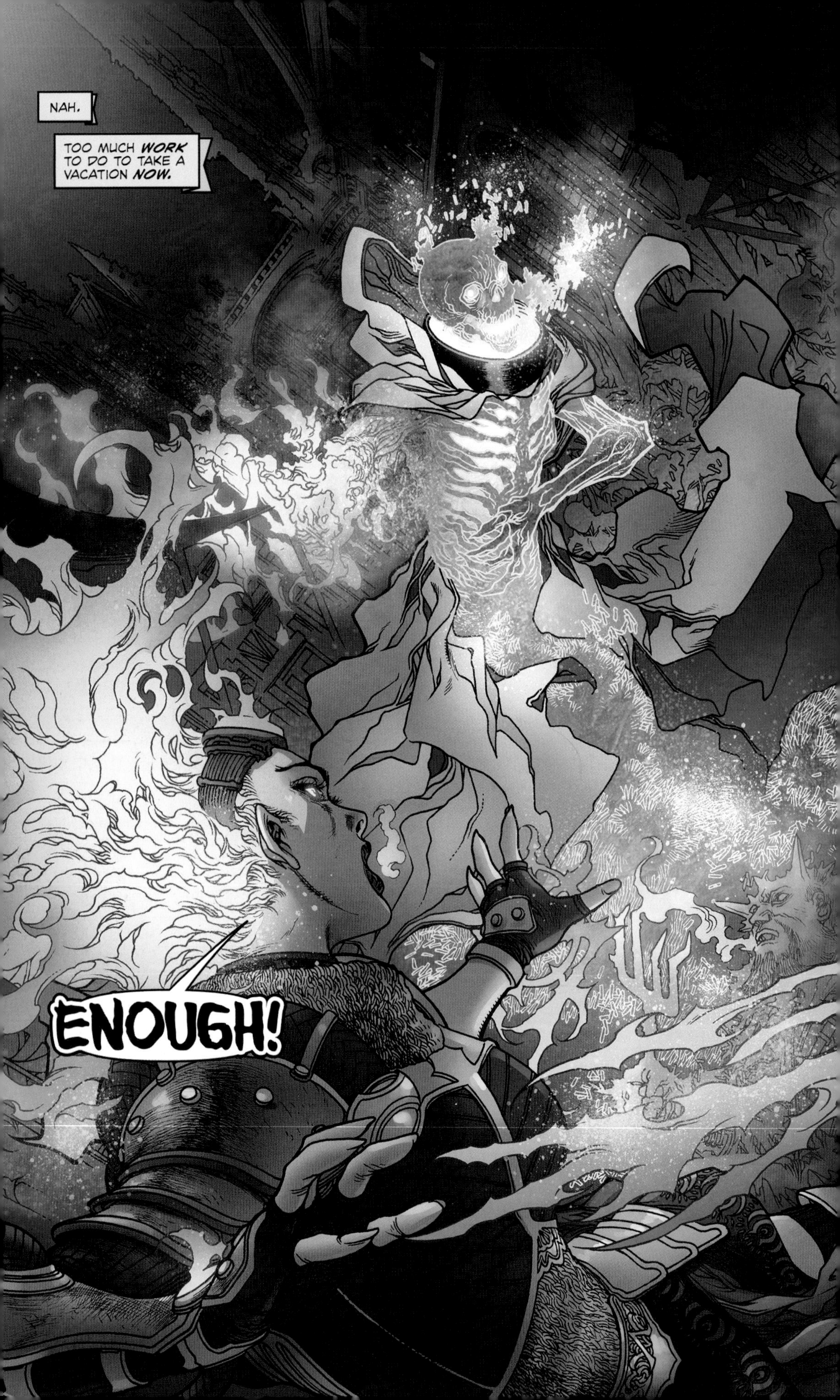
NAH.
TOO MUCH **WORK** TO DO TO TAKE A VACATION **NOW.**
ENOUGH!

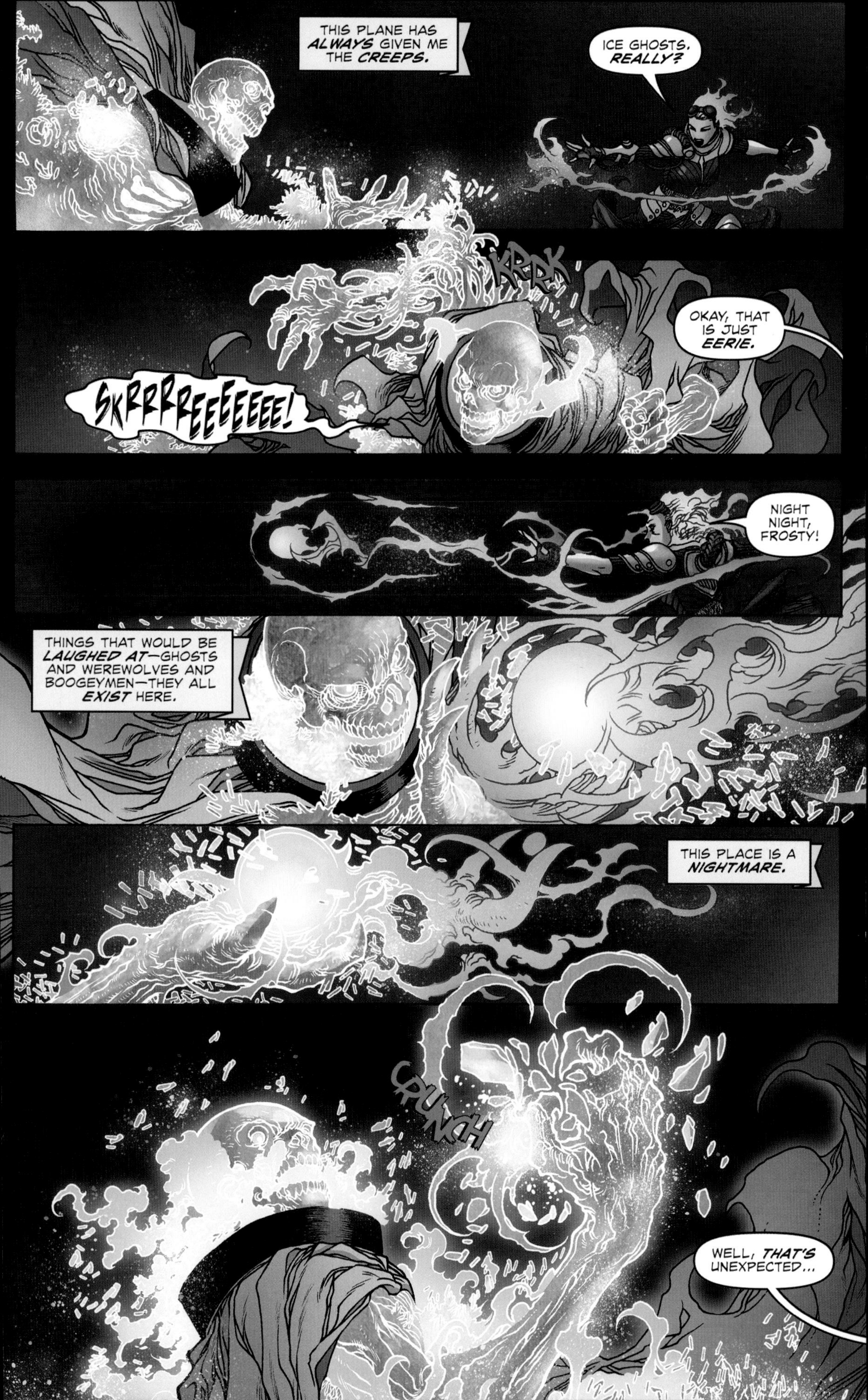
THIS PLANE HAS ALWAYS GIVEN ME THE CREEPS.
ICE GHOSTS. REALLY?
KRRK
OKAY, THAT IS JUST EERIE.
SKRRRREEEEEEE!
NIGHT NIGHT, FROSTY!
THINGS THAT WOULD BE LAUGHED AT—GHOSTS AND WEREWOLVES AND BOOGEYMEN—THEY ALL EXIST HERE.
THIS PLACE IS A NIGHTMARE.
CRUNCH
WELL, THAT'S UNEXPECTED...

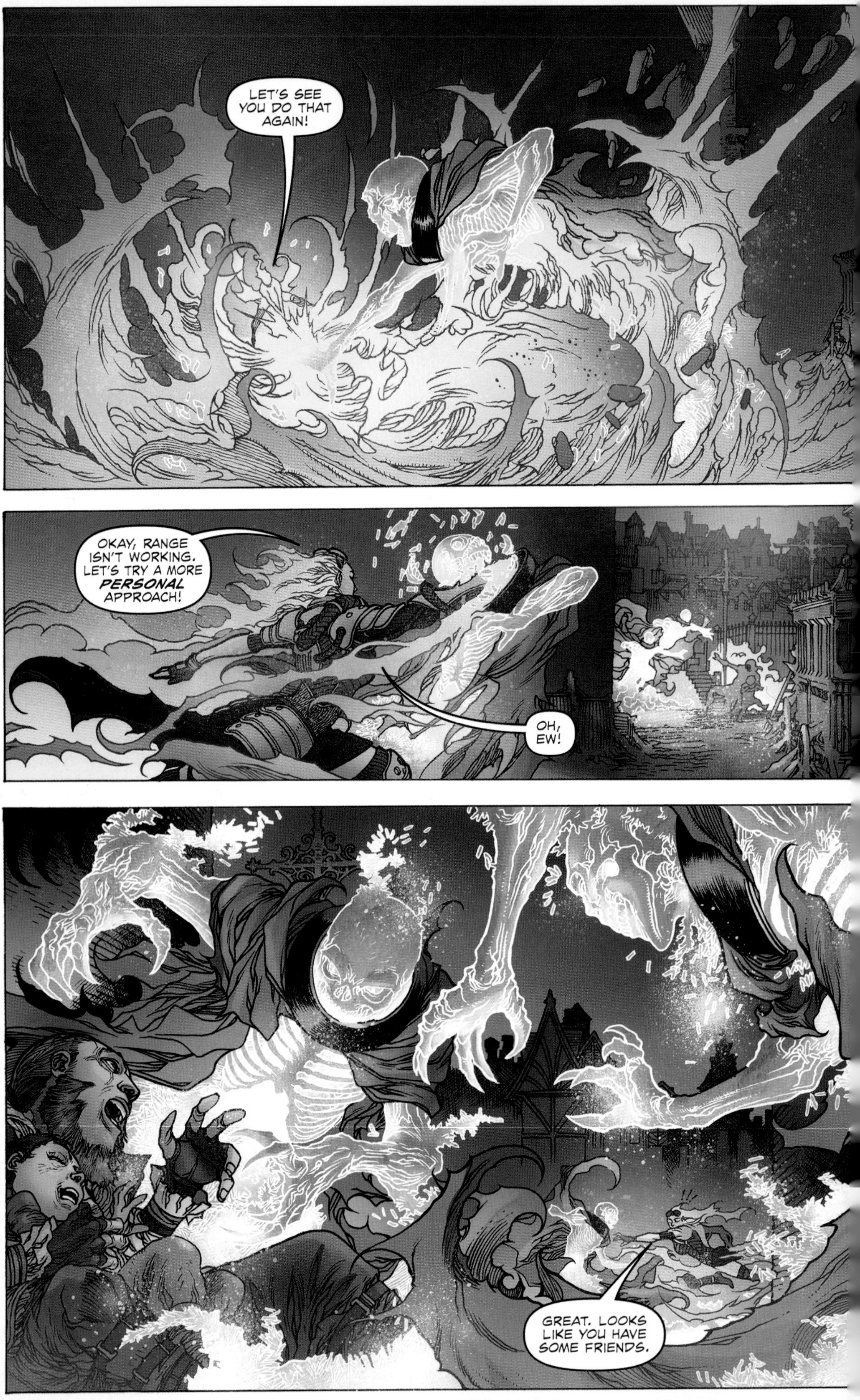
LET'S SEE YOU DO THAT AGAIN!
OKAY, RANGE ISN'T WORKING. LET'S TRY A MORE PERSONAL APPROACH!
OH, EW!
GREAT. LOOKS LIKE YOU HAVE SOME FRIENDS.

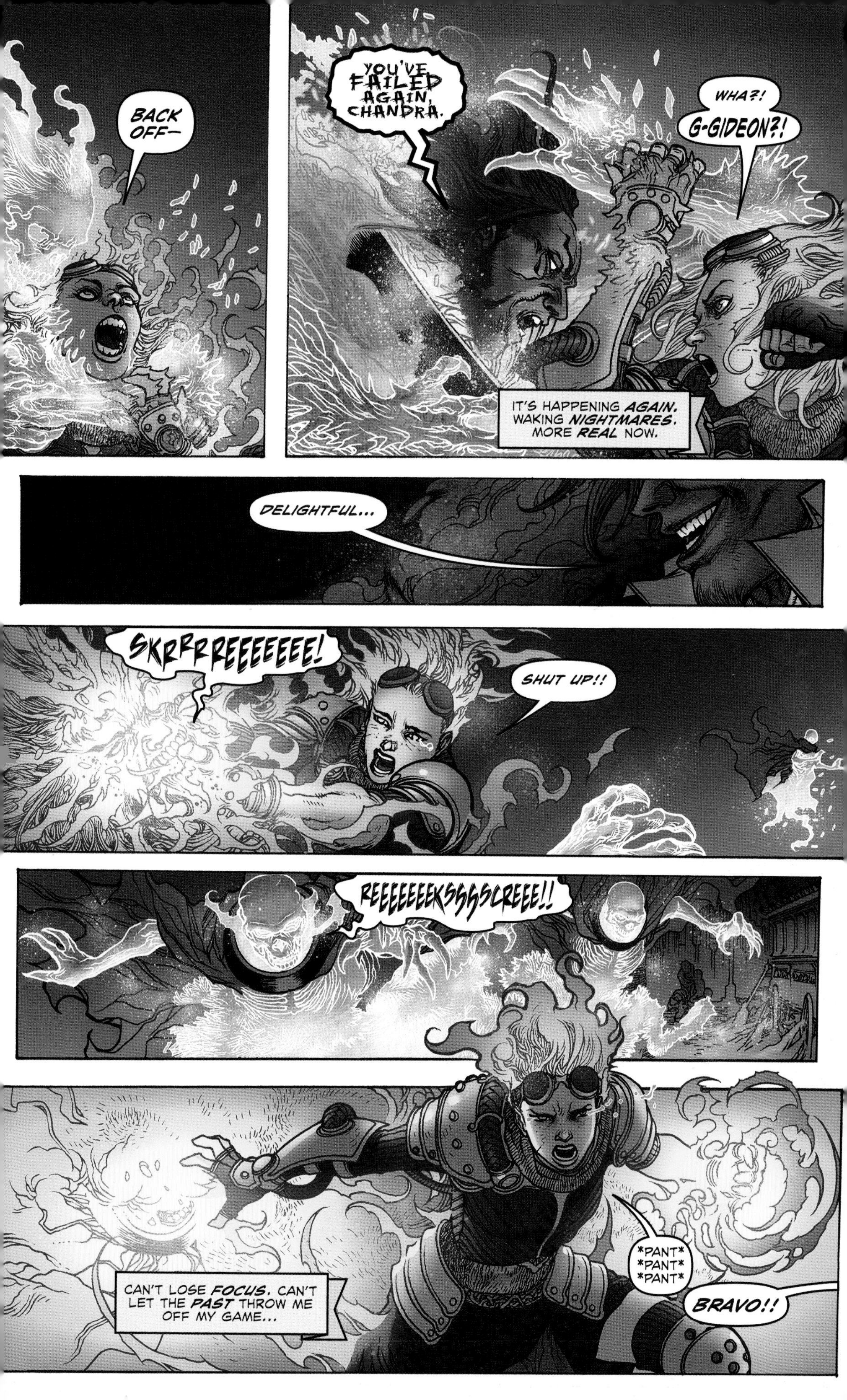
BACK OFF—
YOU'VE FAILED AGAIN, CHANDRA.
WHA?!
G-GIDEON?!
IT'S HAPPENING AGAIN. WAKING NIGHTMARES. MORE REAL NOW.
DELIGHTFUL...
SKRRRREEEEEEE!
SHUT UP!!
REEEEEEEKSSSSCREEE!!
CAN'T LOSE FOCUS. CAN'T LET THE PAST THROW ME OFF MY GAME...
*PANT* *PANT* *PANT*
BRAVO!!

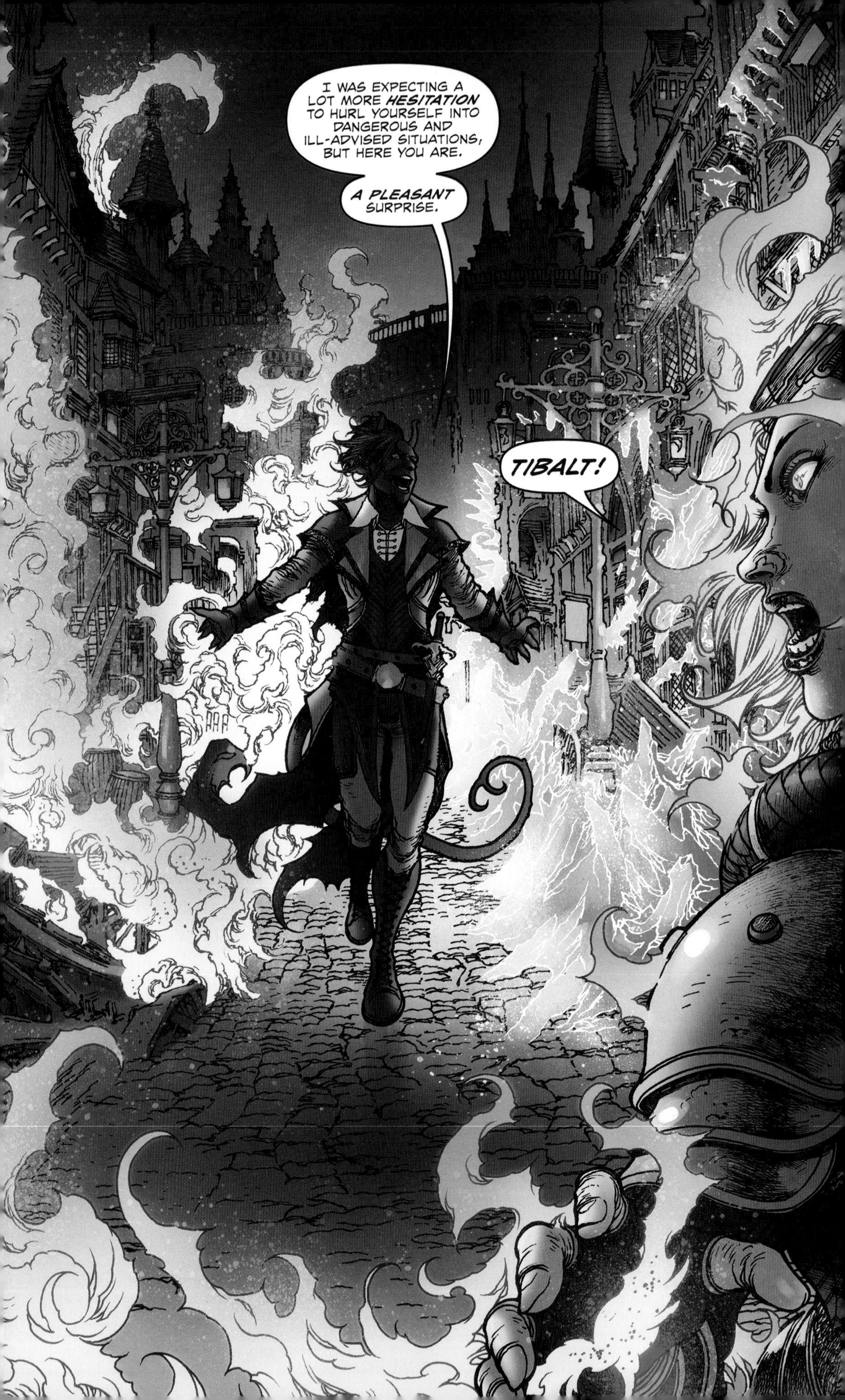
I WAS EXPECTING A LOT MORE HESITATION TO HURL YOURSELF INTO DANGEROUS AND ILL-ADVISED SITUATIONS, BUT HERE YOU ARE.
A PLEASANT SURPRISE.
TIBALT!

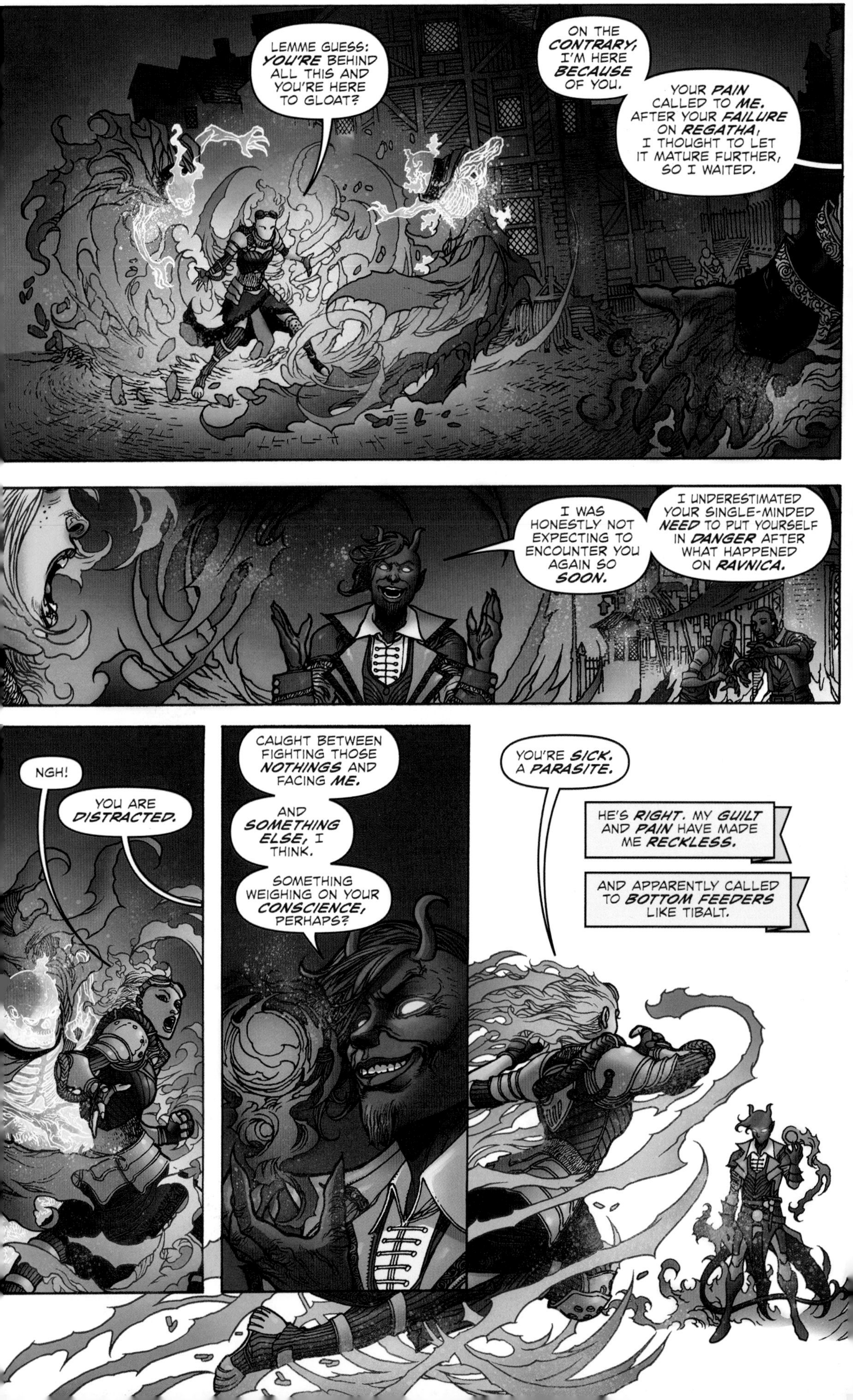
LEMME GUESS: YOU'RE BEHIND ALL THIS AND YOU'RE HERE TO GLOAT?
ON THE CONTRARY, I'M HERE BECAUSE OF YOU.
YOUR PAIN CALLED TO ME. AFTER YOUR FAILURE ON REGATHA, I THOUGHT TO LET IT MATURE FURTHER, SO I WAITED.
I WAS HONESTLY NOT EXPECTING TO ENCOUNTER YOU AGAIN SO SOON.
I UNDERESTIMATED YOUR SINGLE-MINDED NEED TO PUT YOURSELF IN DANGER AFTER WHAT HAPPENED ON RAVNICA.
NGH!
YOU ARE DISTRACTED.
CAUGHT BETWEEN FIGHTING THOSE NOTHINGS AND FACING ME.
AND SOMETHING ELSE, I THINK.
SOMETHING WEIGHING ON YOUR CONSCIENCE, PERHAPS?
YOU'RE SICK. A PARASITE.
HE'S RIGHT. MY GUILT AND PAIN HAVE MADE ME RECKLESS.
AND APPARENTLY CALLED TO BOTTOM FEEDERS LIKE TIBALT.

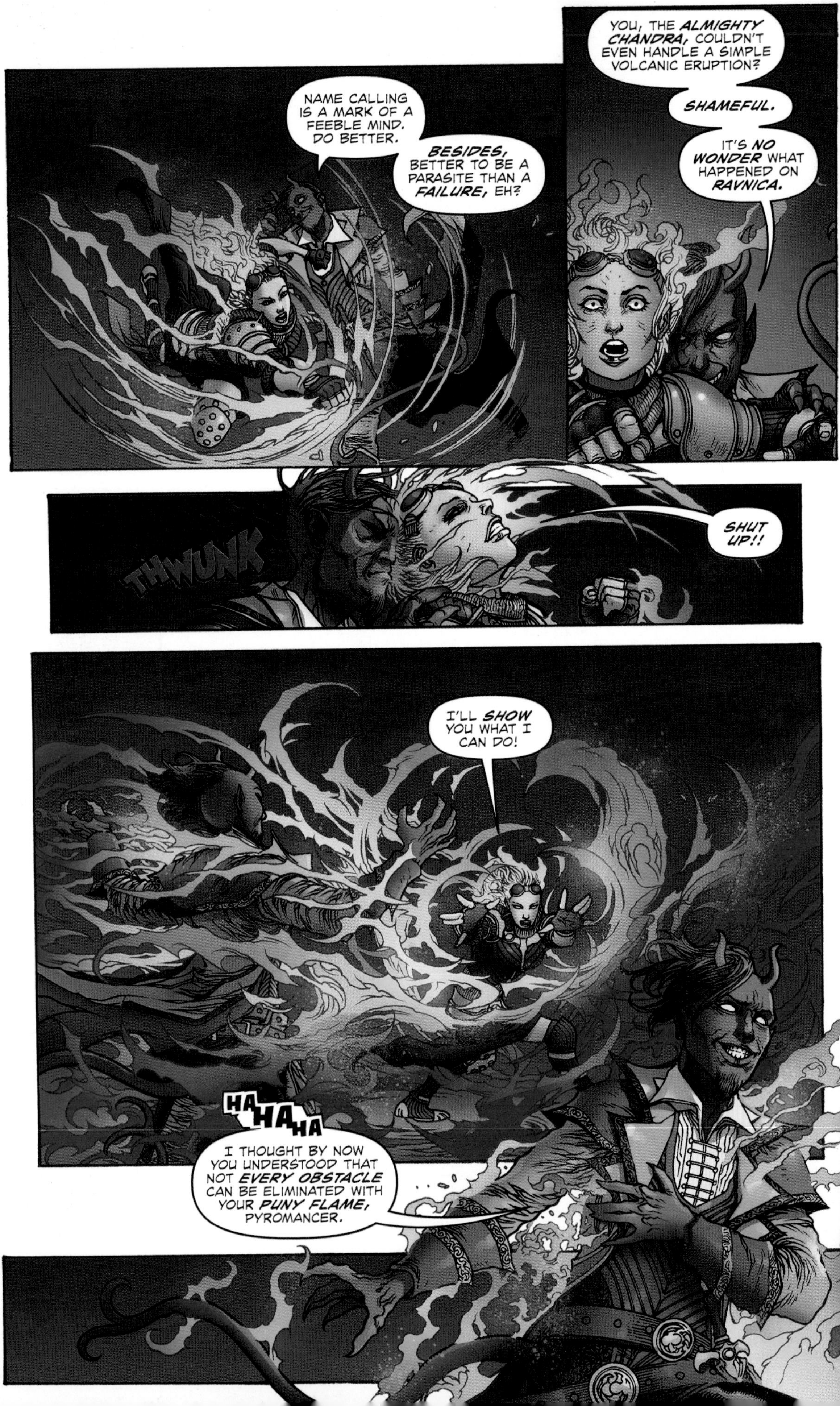
NAME CALLING IS A MARK OF A FEEBLE MIND. DO BETTER.
BESIDES, BETTER TO BE A PARASITE THAN A FAILURE, EH?
YOU, THE ALMIGHTY CHANDRA, COULDN'T EVEN HANDLE A SIMPLE VOLCANIC ERUPTION?
SHAMEFUL.
IT'S NO WONDER WHAT HAPPENED ON RAVNICA.
THWUNK
SHUT UP!!
I'LL SHOW YOU WHAT I CAN DO!
HA HA HA
I THOUGHT BY NOW YOU UNDERSTOOD THAT NOT EVERY OBSTACLE CAN BE ELIMINATED WITH YOUR PUNY FLAME, PYROMANCER.

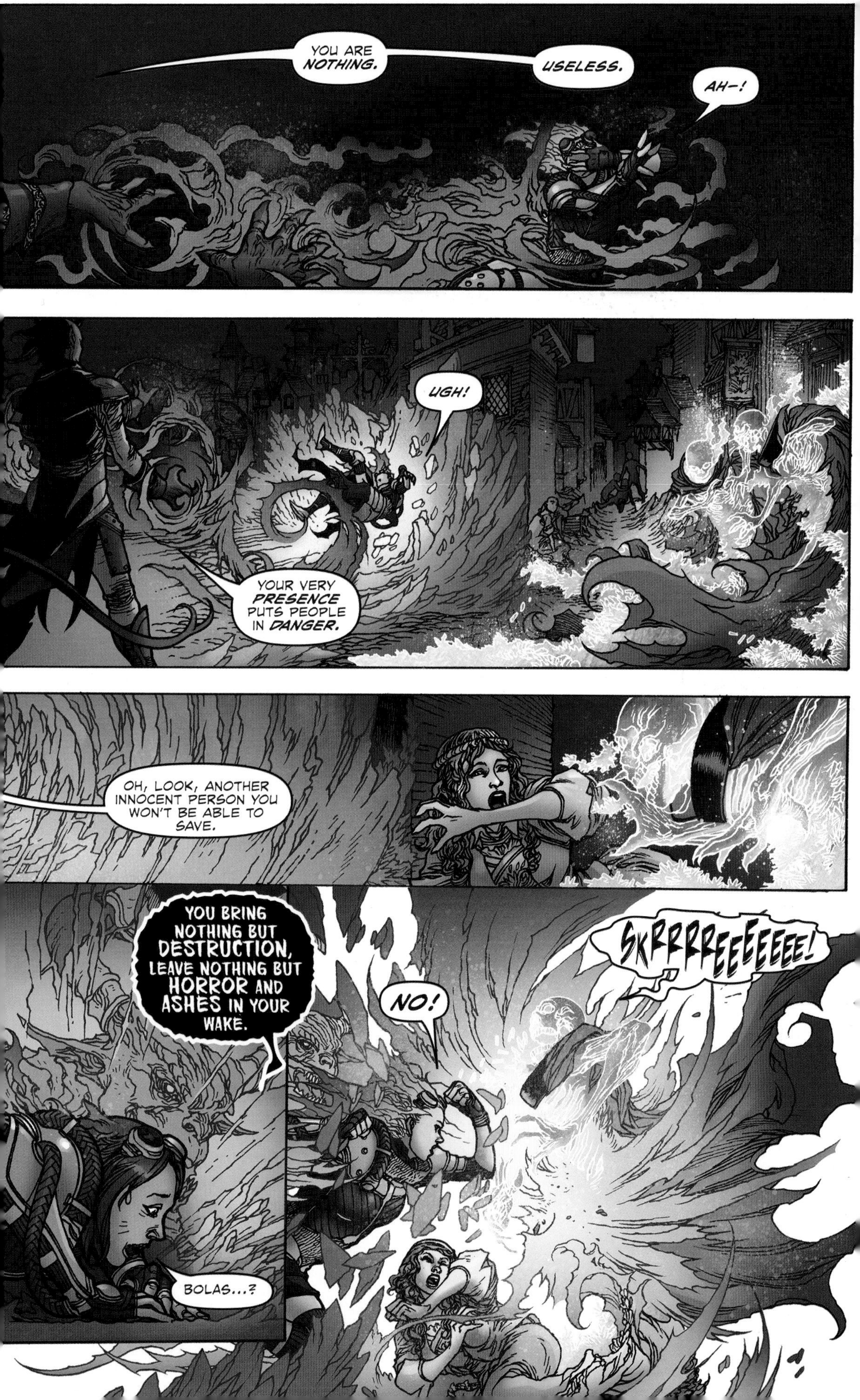
YOU ARE NOTHING.
USELESS.
AH-!
UGH!
YOUR VERY PRESENCE PUTS PEOPLE IN DANGER.
OH, LOOK, ANOTHER INNOCENT PERSON YOU WON'T BE ABLE TO SAVE.
YOU BRING NOTHING BUT DESTRUCTION, LEAVE NOTHING BUT HORROR AND ASHES IN YOUR WAKE.
NO!
SKRRRREEEEEEE!
BOLAS...?

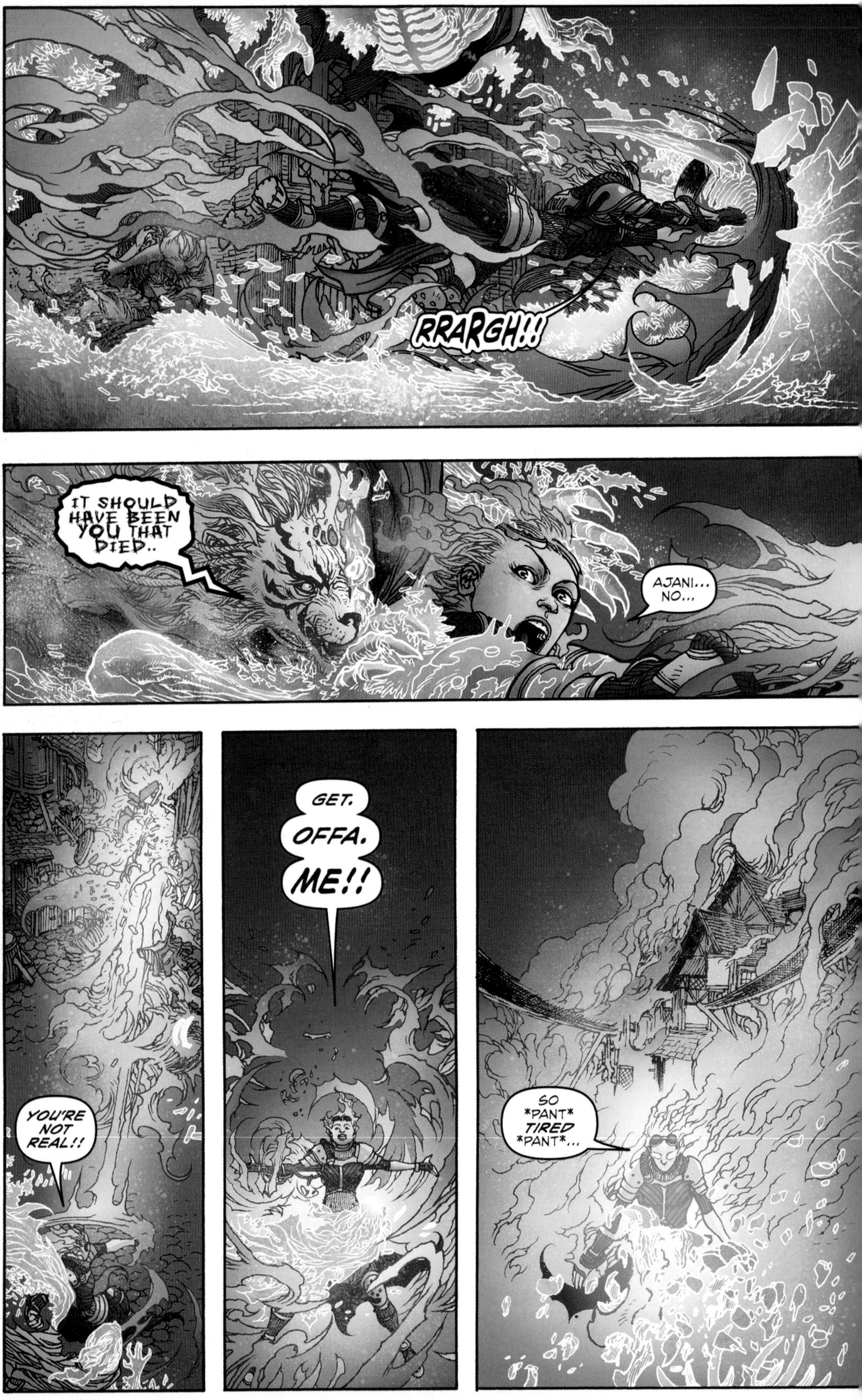
RRARGH!!
IT SHOULD HAVE BEEN YOU THAT DIED..
AJANI... NO...
YOU'RE NOT REAL!!
GET.
OFFA.
ME!!
SO *PANT* TIRED *PANT*...

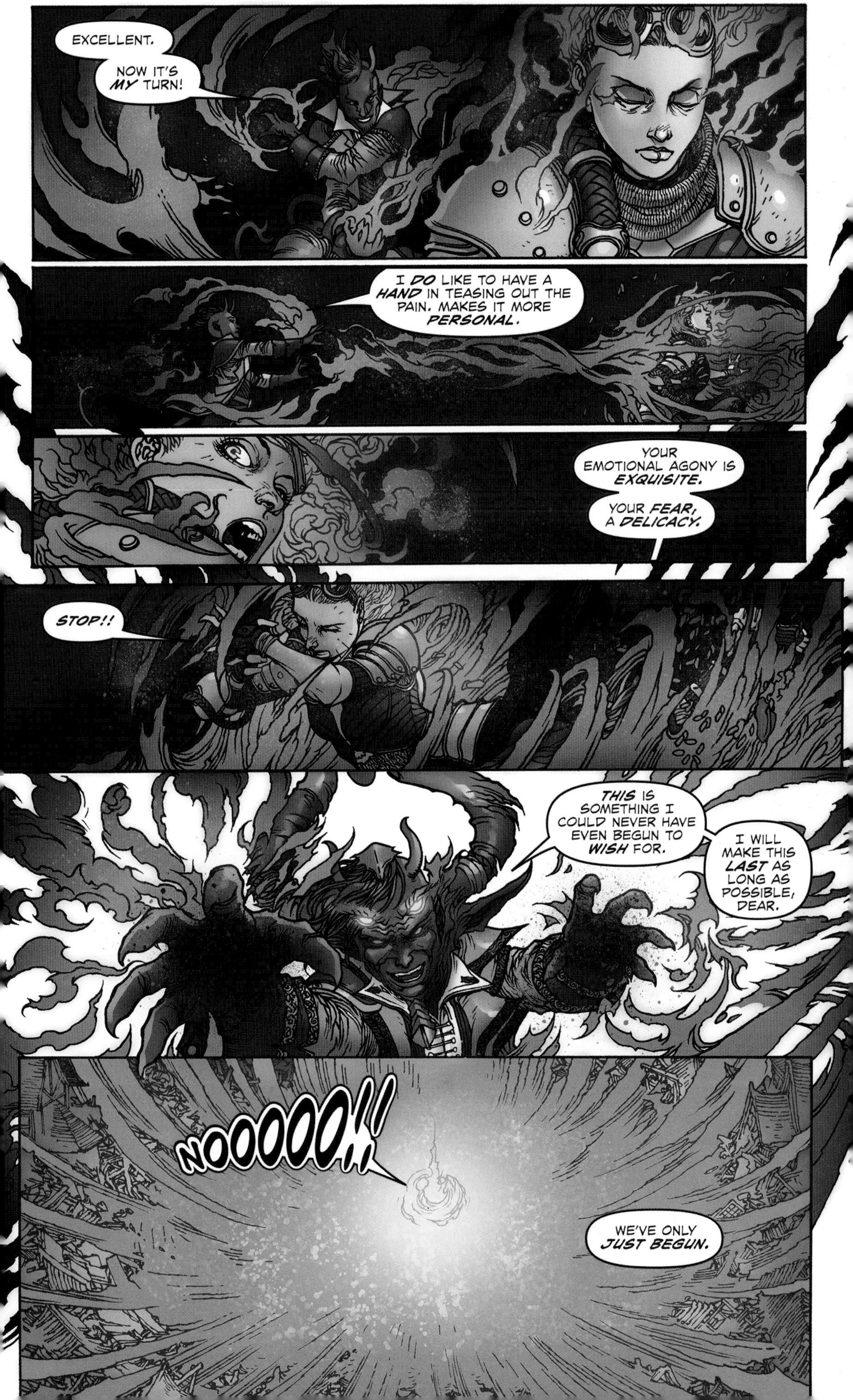
EXCELLENT.
NOW IT'S MY TURN!
I DO LIKE TO HAVE A HAND IN TEASING OUT THE PAIN. MAKES IT MORE PERSONAL.
YOUR EMOTIONAL AGONY IS EXQUISITE.
YOUR FEAR, A DELICACY.
STOP!!
THIS IS SOMETHING I COULD NEVER HAVE EVEN BEGUN TO WISH FOR.
I WILL MAKE THIS LAST AS LONG AS POSSIBLE, DEAR.
NOOOOO!!!
WE'VE ONLY JUST BEGUN.

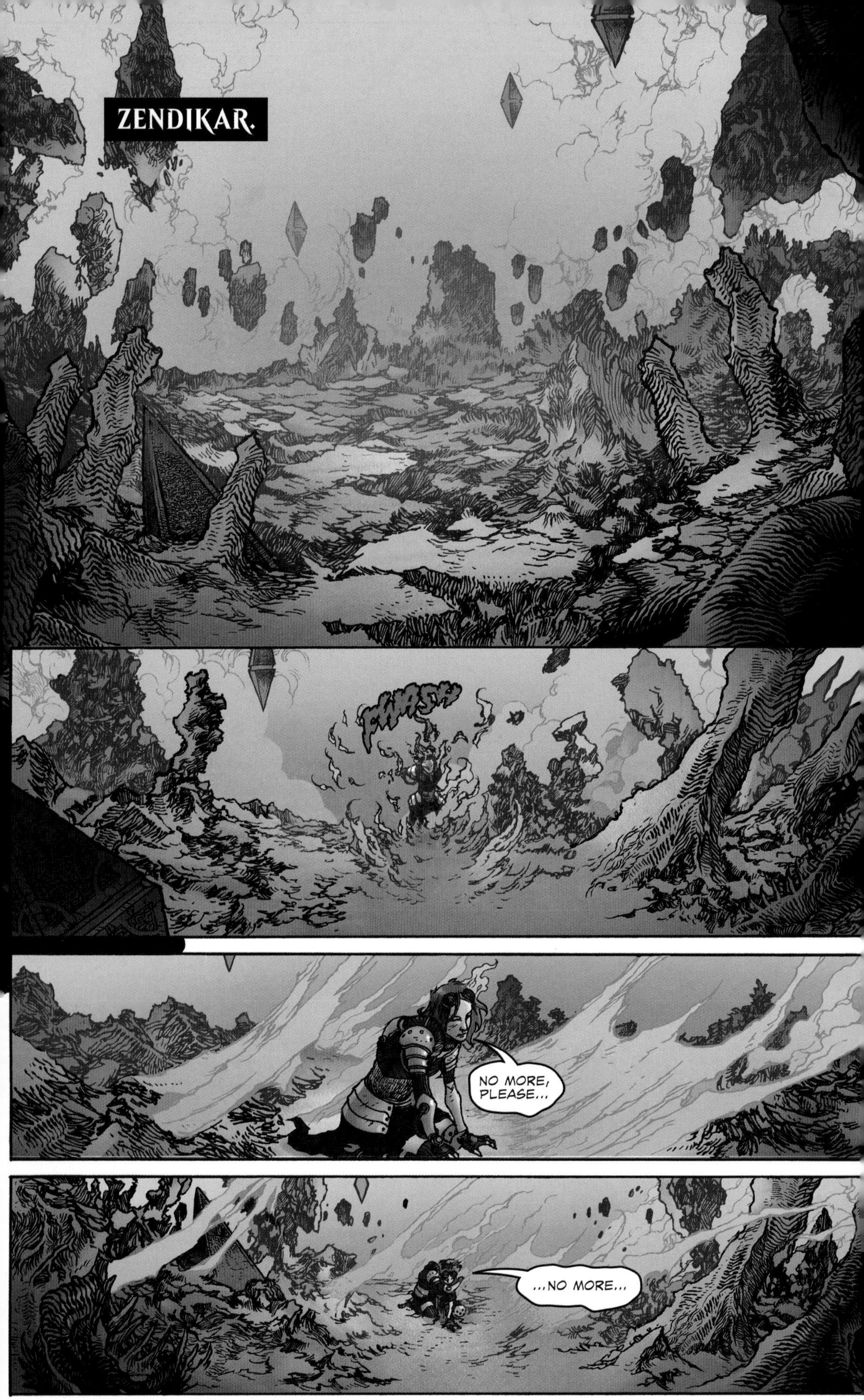
ZENDIKAR.
FWASH
NO MORE, PLEASE...
...NO MORE...

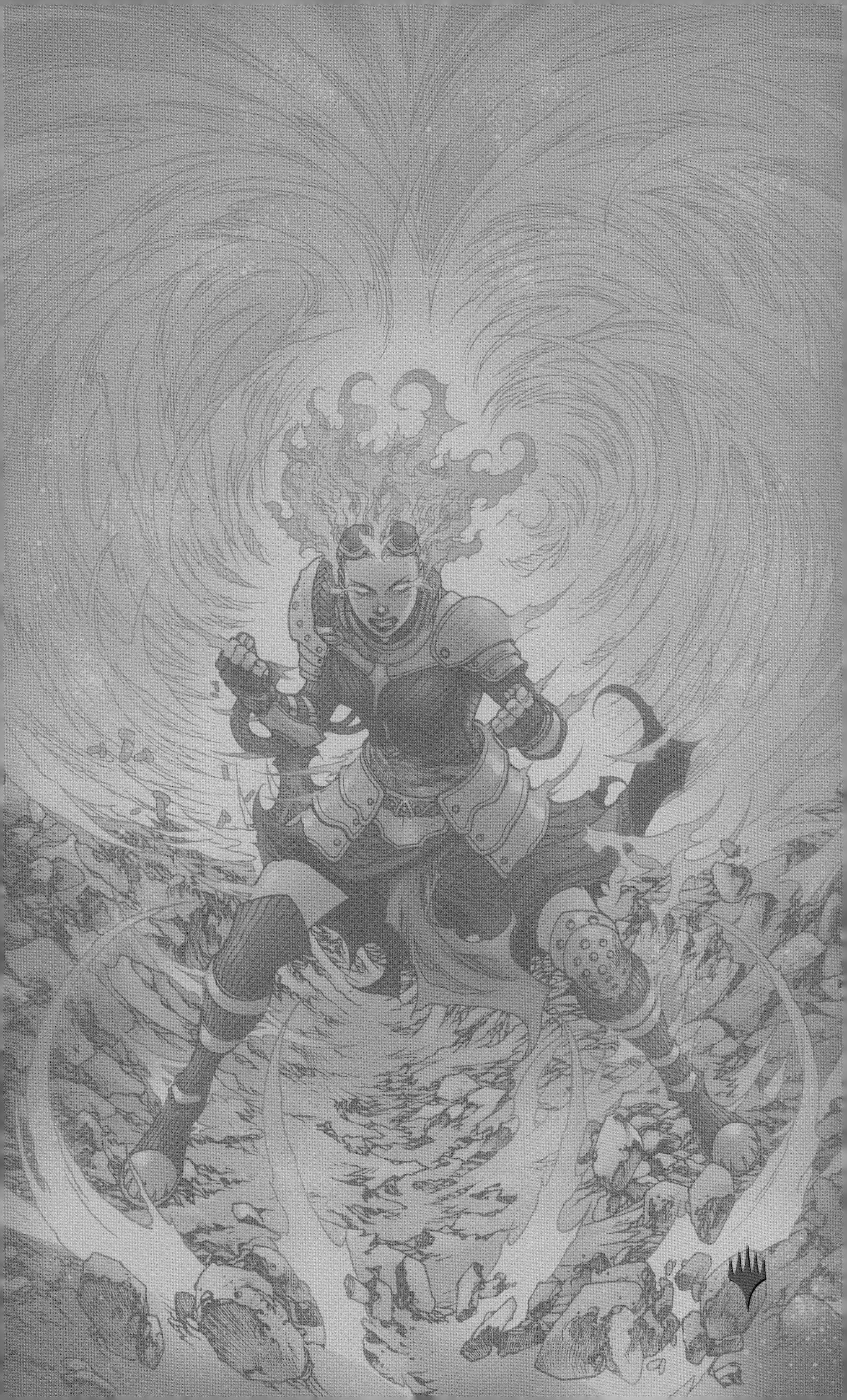

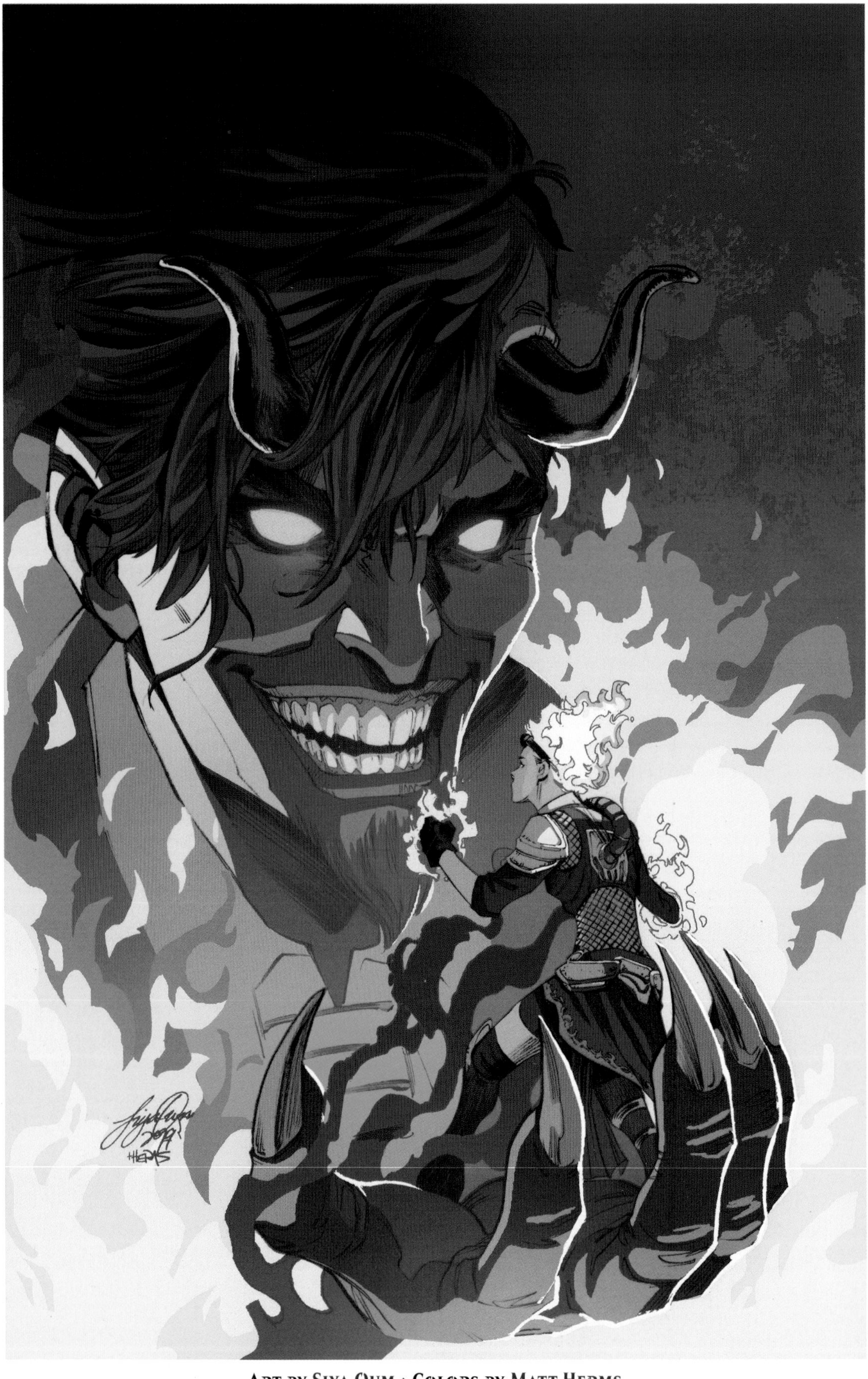

Art by Siya Oum • Colors by Matt Herms

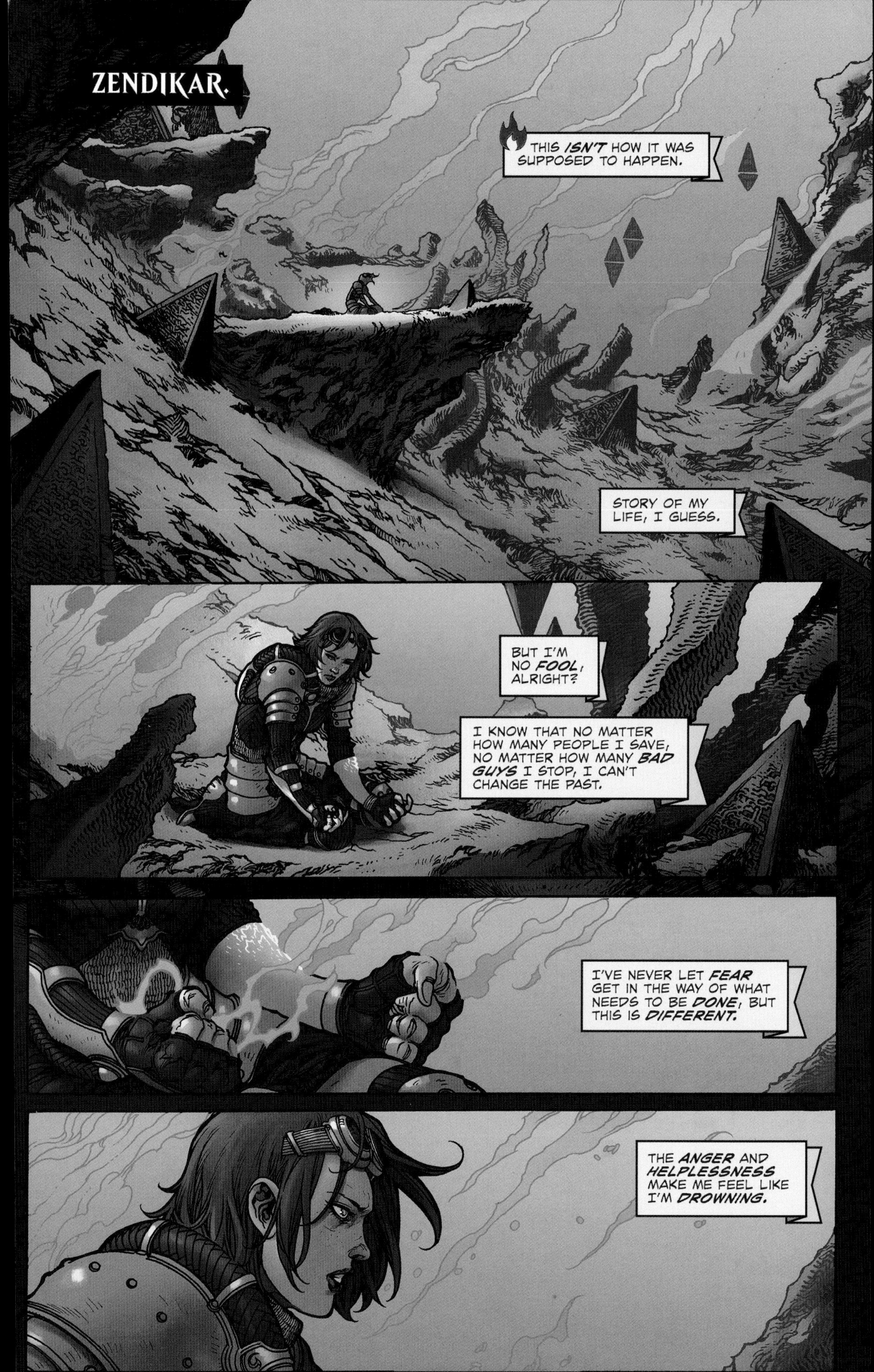
ZENDIKAR.
THIS ISN'T HOW IT WAS SUPPOSED TO HAPPEN.
STORY OF MY LIFE, I GUESS.
BUT I'M NO FOOL, ALRIGHT?
I KNOW THAT NO MATTER HOW MANY PEOPLE I SAVE, NO MATTER HOW MANY BAD GUYS I STOP, I CAN'T CHANGE THE PAST.
I'VE NEVER LET FEAR GET IN THE WAY OF WHAT NEEDS TO BE DONE, BUT THIS IS DIFFERENT.
THE ANGER AND HELPLESSNESS MAKE ME FEEL LIKE I'M DROWNING.

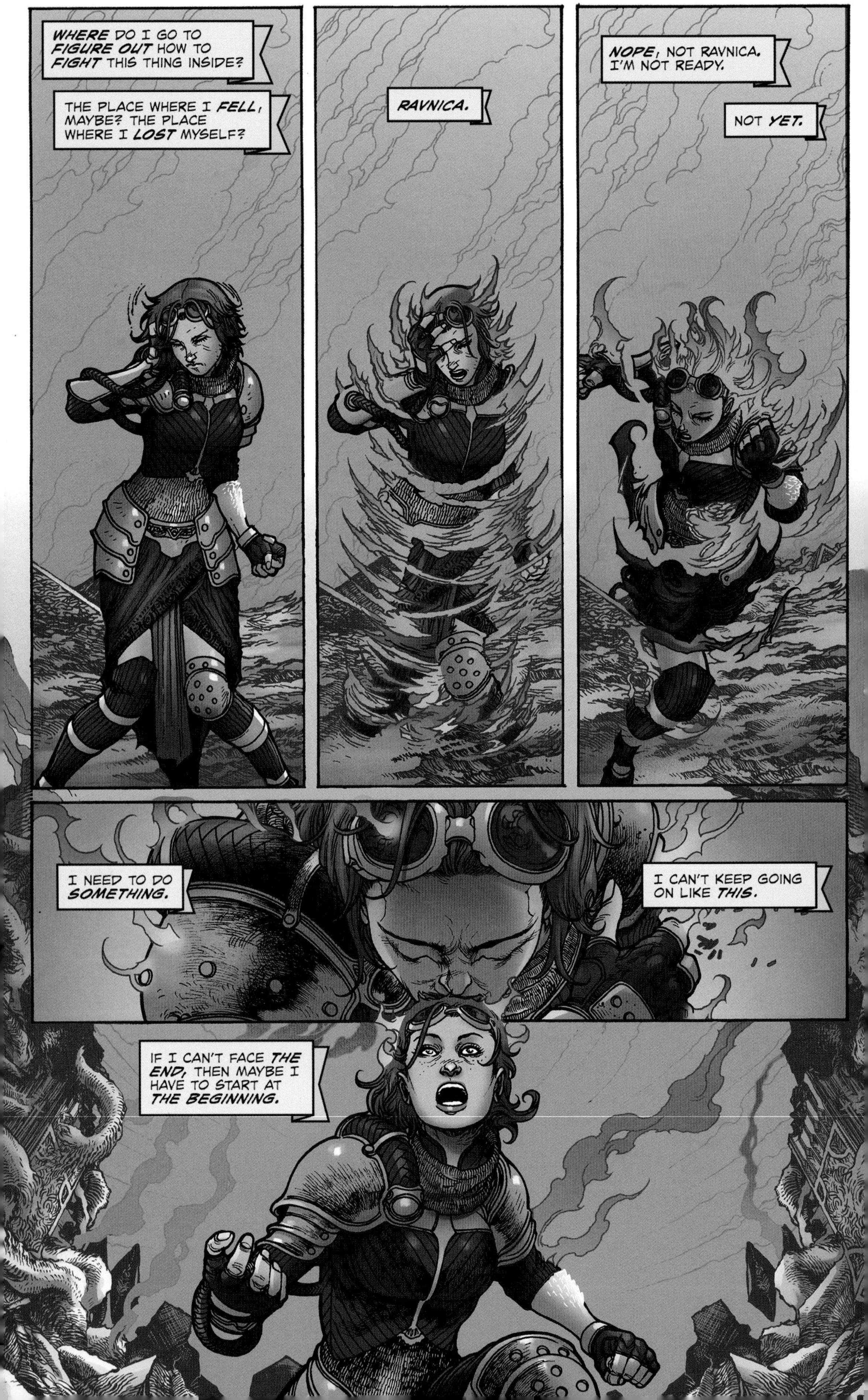
WHERE DO I GO TO FIGURE OUT HOW TO FIGHT THIS THING INSIDE?
THE PLACE WHERE I FELL, MAYBE? THE PLACE WHERE I LOST MYSELF?
RAVNICA.
NOPE, NOT RAVNICA. I'M NOT READY.
NOT YET.
I NEED TO DO SOMETHING.
I CAN'T KEEP GOING ON LIKE THIS.
IF I CAN'T FACE THE END, THEN MAYBE I HAVE TO START AT THE BEGINNING.

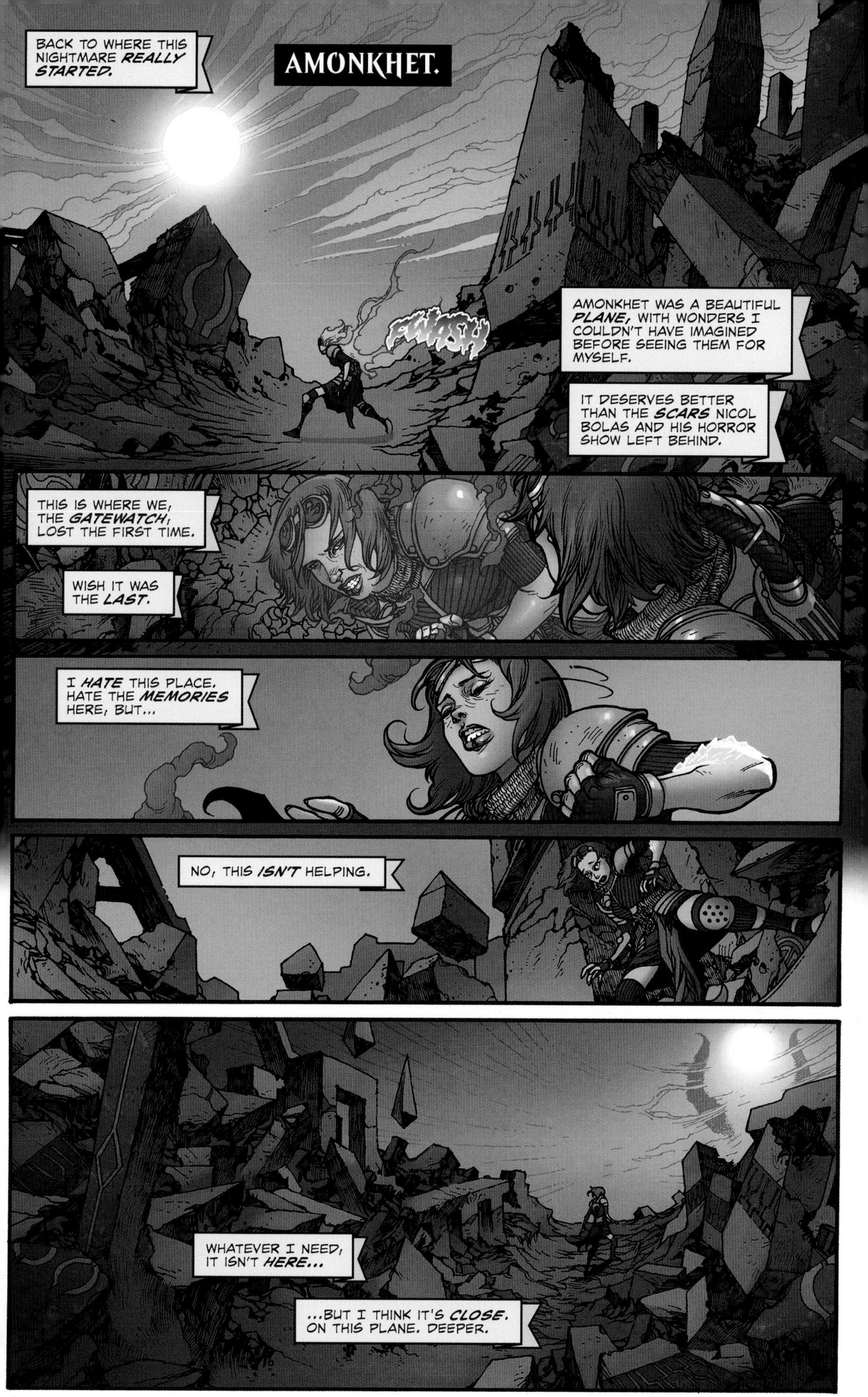

BACK TO WHERE THIS NIGHTMARE REALLY STARTED.
AMONKHET.
FLASH
AMONKHET WAS A BEAUTIFUL PLANE, WITH WONDERS I COULDN'T HAVE IMAGINED BEFORE SEEING THEM FOR MYSELF.
IT DESERVES BETTER THAN THE SCARS NICOL BOLAS AND HIS HORROR SHOW LEFT BEHIND.
THIS IS WHERE WE, THE GATEWATCH, LOST THE FIRST TIME.
WISH IT WAS THE LAST.
I HATE THIS PLACE. HATE THE MEMORIES HERE, BUT...
NO, THIS ISN'T HELPING.
WHATEVER I NEED, IT ISN'T HERE...
...BUT I THINK IT'S CLOSE. ON THIS PLANE. DEEPER.

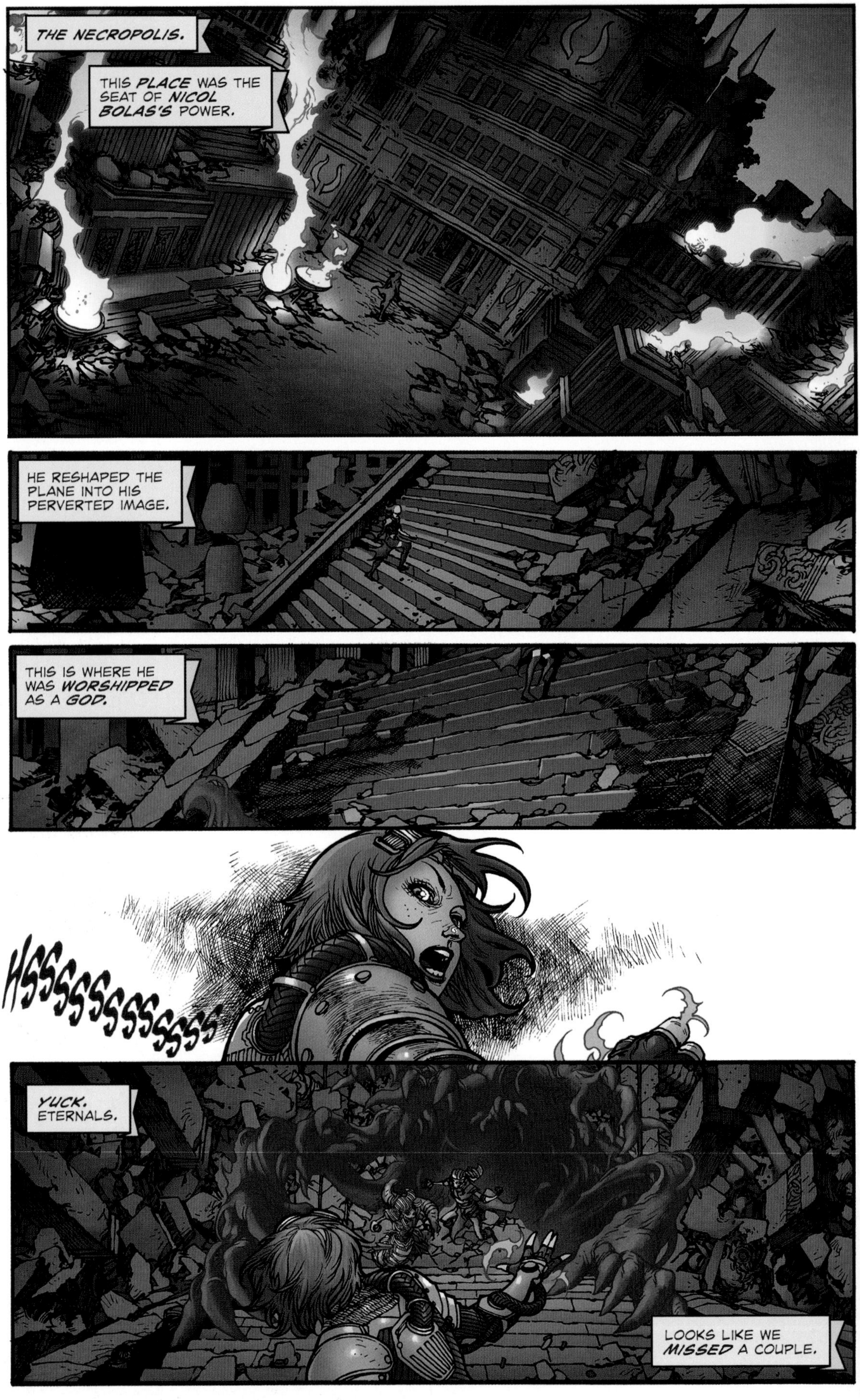
THE NECROPOLIS.
THIS PLACE WAS THE SEAT OF NICOL BOLAS'S POWER.
HE RESHAPED THE PLANE INTO HIS PERVERTED IMAGE.
THIS IS WHERE HE WAS WORSHIPPED AS A GOD.
HSSSSSSSSSSSS
YUCK. ETERNALS.
LOOKS LIKE WE MISSED A COUPLE.

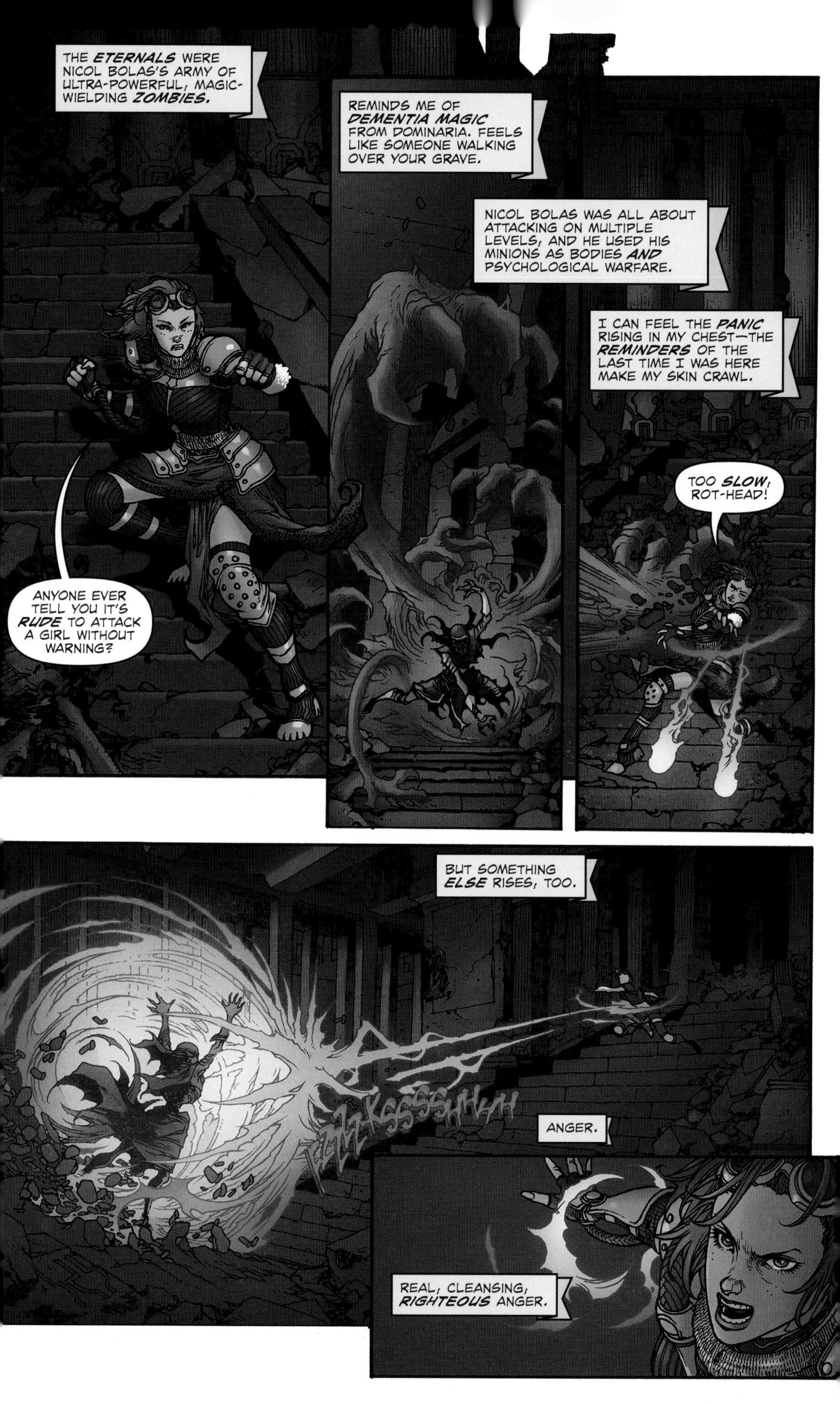
THE ETERNALS WERE NICOL BOLAS'S ARMY OF ULTRA-POWERFUL, MAGIC-WIELDING ZOMBIES.
ANYONE EVER TELL YOU IT'S RUDE TO ATTACK A GIRL WITHOUT WARNING?
REMINDS ME OF DEMENTIA MAGIC FROM DOMINARIA. FEELS LIKE SOMEONE WALKING OVER YOUR GRAVE.
NICOL BOLAS WAS ALL ABOUT ATTACKING ON MULTIPLE LEVELS, AND HE USED HIS MINIONS AS BODIES AND PSYCHOLOGICAL WARFARE.
I CAN FEEL THE PANIC RISING IN MY CHEST—THE REMINDERS OF THE LAST TIME I WAS HERE MAKE MY SKIN CRAWL.
TOO SLOW, ROT-HEAD!
BUT SOMETHING ELSE RISES, TOO.
ZZZKSSSSHHHH
ANGER.
REAL, CLEANSING, RIGHTEOUS ANGER.

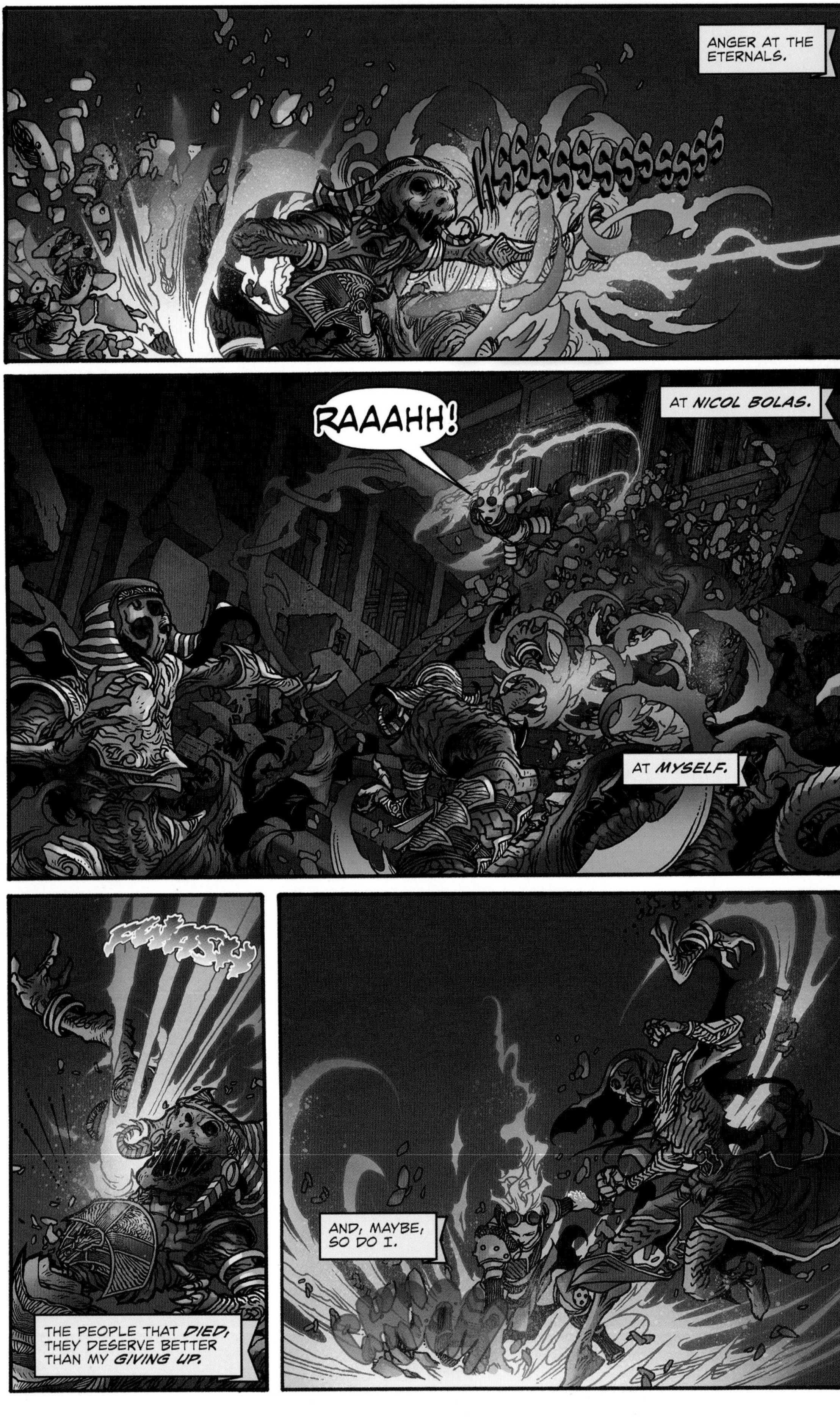
ANGER AT THE ETERNALS.
HSSSSSSSSSSSS
AT *NICOL BOLAS.*
RAAAHH!
AT *MYSELF.*
THE PEOPLE THAT *DIED,* THEY DESERVE BETTER THAN MY *GIVING UP.*
AND, MAYBE, SO DO I.

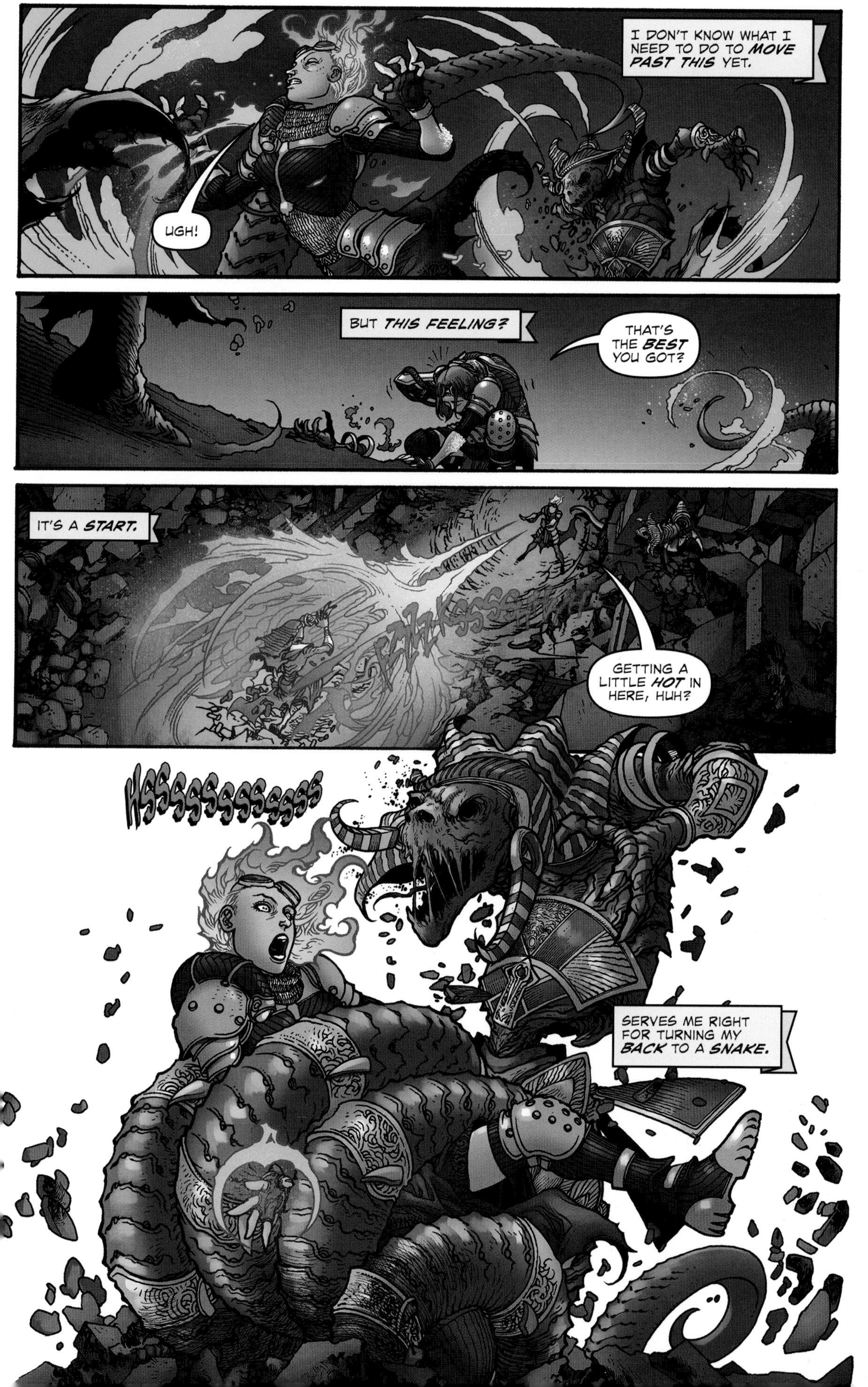
I DON'T KNOW WHAT I NEED TO DO TO MOVE PAST THIS YET.
UGH!
BUT THIS FEELING?
THAT'S THE BEST YOU GOT?
IT'S A START.
GETTING A LITTLE HOT IN HERE, HUH?
HSSSSSSSSSSS
SERVES ME RIGHT FOR TURNING MY BACK TO A SNAKE.

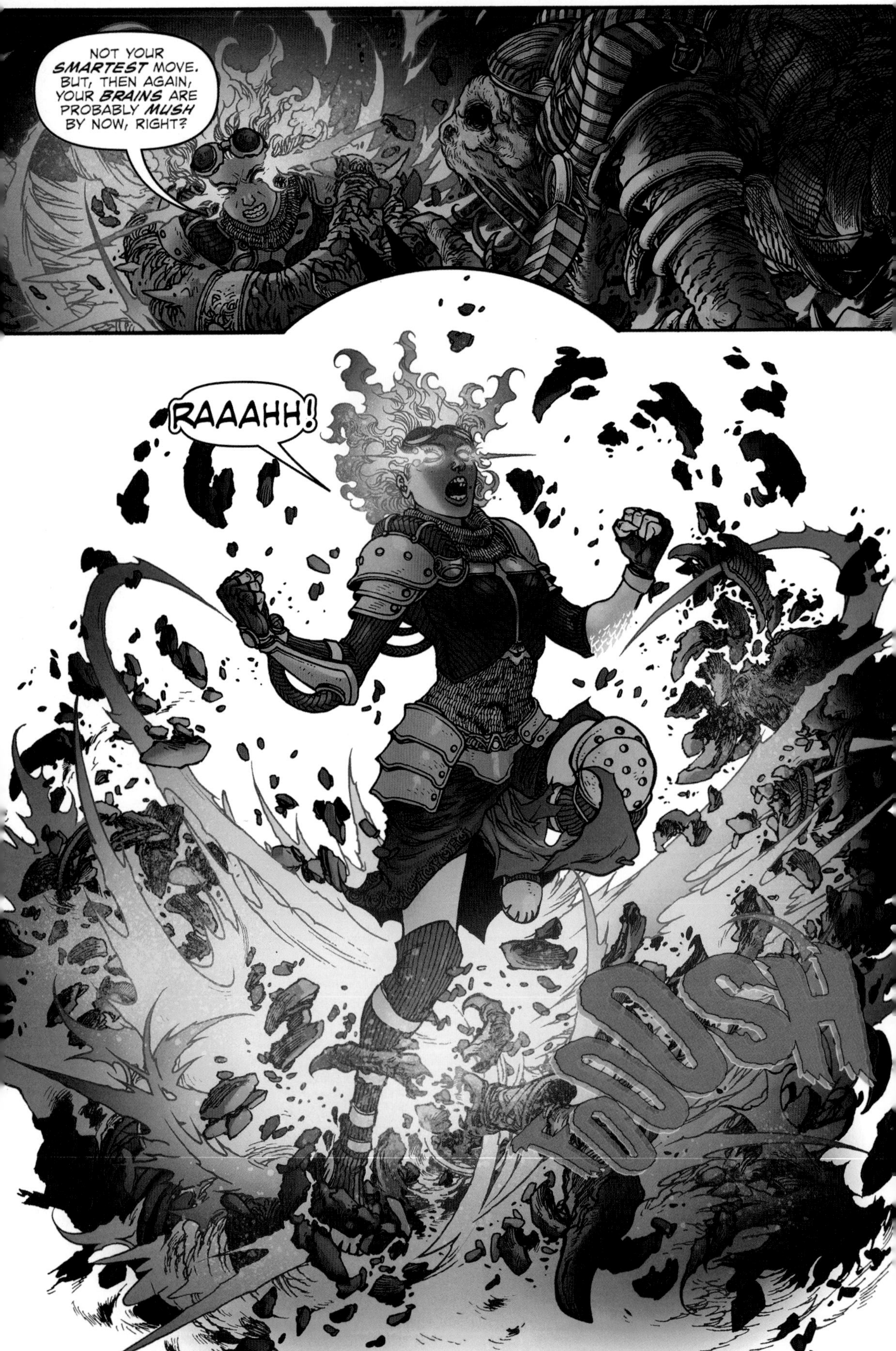
NOT YOUR SMARTEST MOVE. BUT, THEN AGAIN, YOUR BRAINS ARE PROBABLY MUSH BY NOW, RIGHT?
RAAAHH!

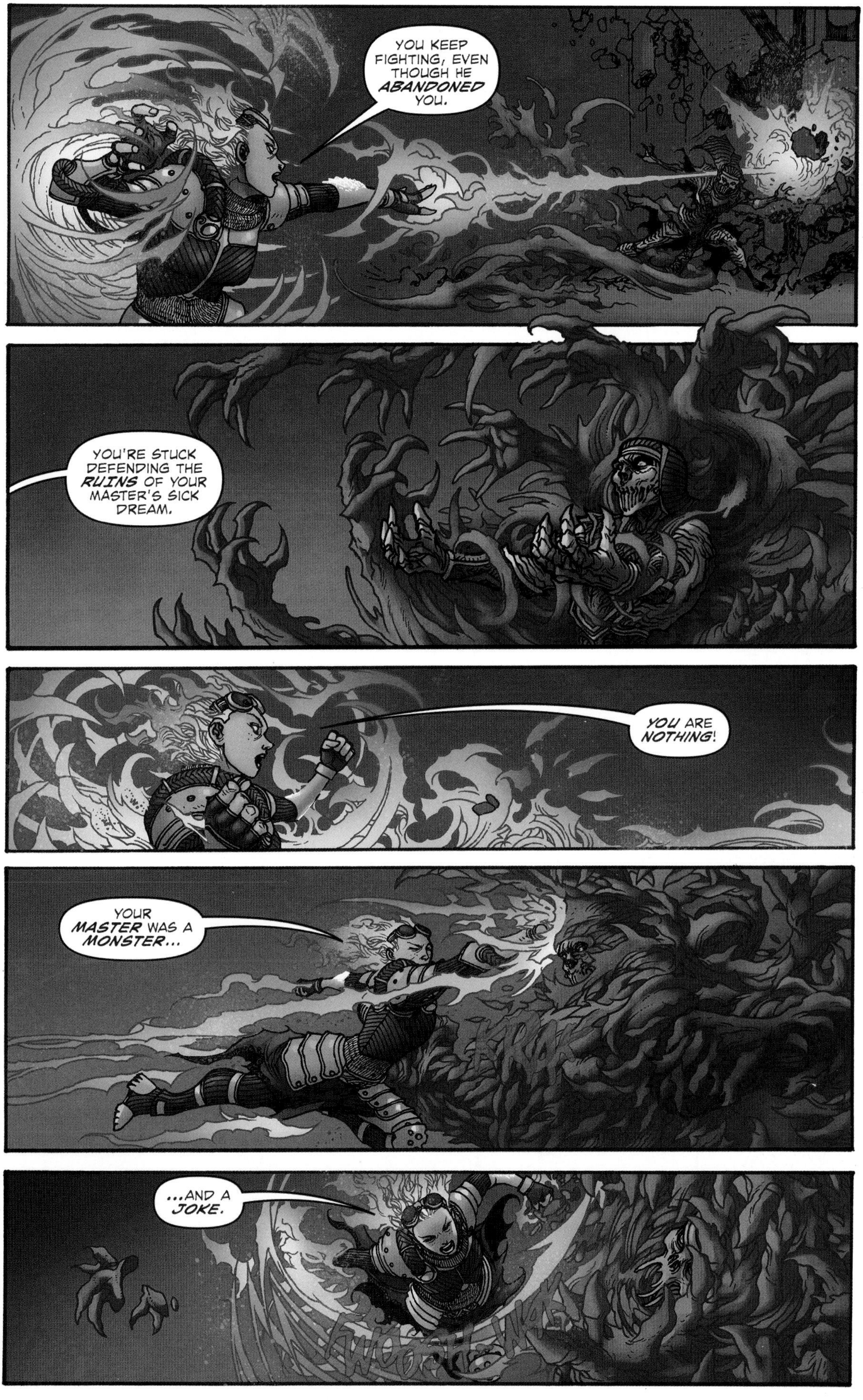
YOU KEEP FIGHTING, EVEN THOUGH HE *ABANDONED* YOU.
YOU'RE STUCK DEFENDING THE *RUINS* OF YOUR MASTER'S SICK DREAM.
*YOU* ARE *NOTHING*!
YOUR *MASTER* WAS A *MONSTER*...
...AND A *JOKE*.

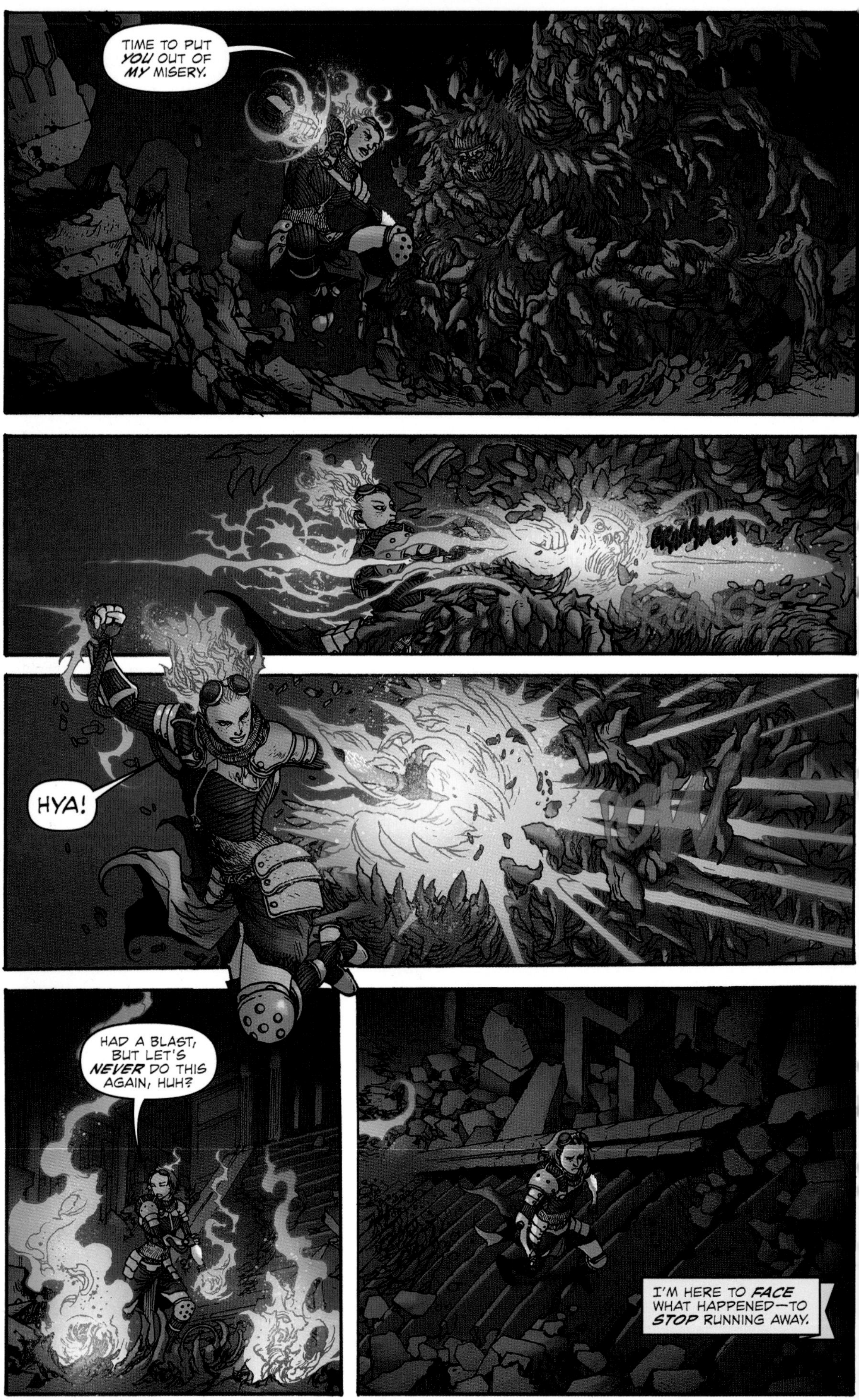
TIME TO PUT YOU OUT OF MY MISERY.
KRONG
HYA!
POW
HAD A BLAST, BUT LET'S NEVER DO THIS AGAIN, HUH?
I'M HERE TO FACE WHAT HAPPENED—TO STOP RUNNING AWAY.

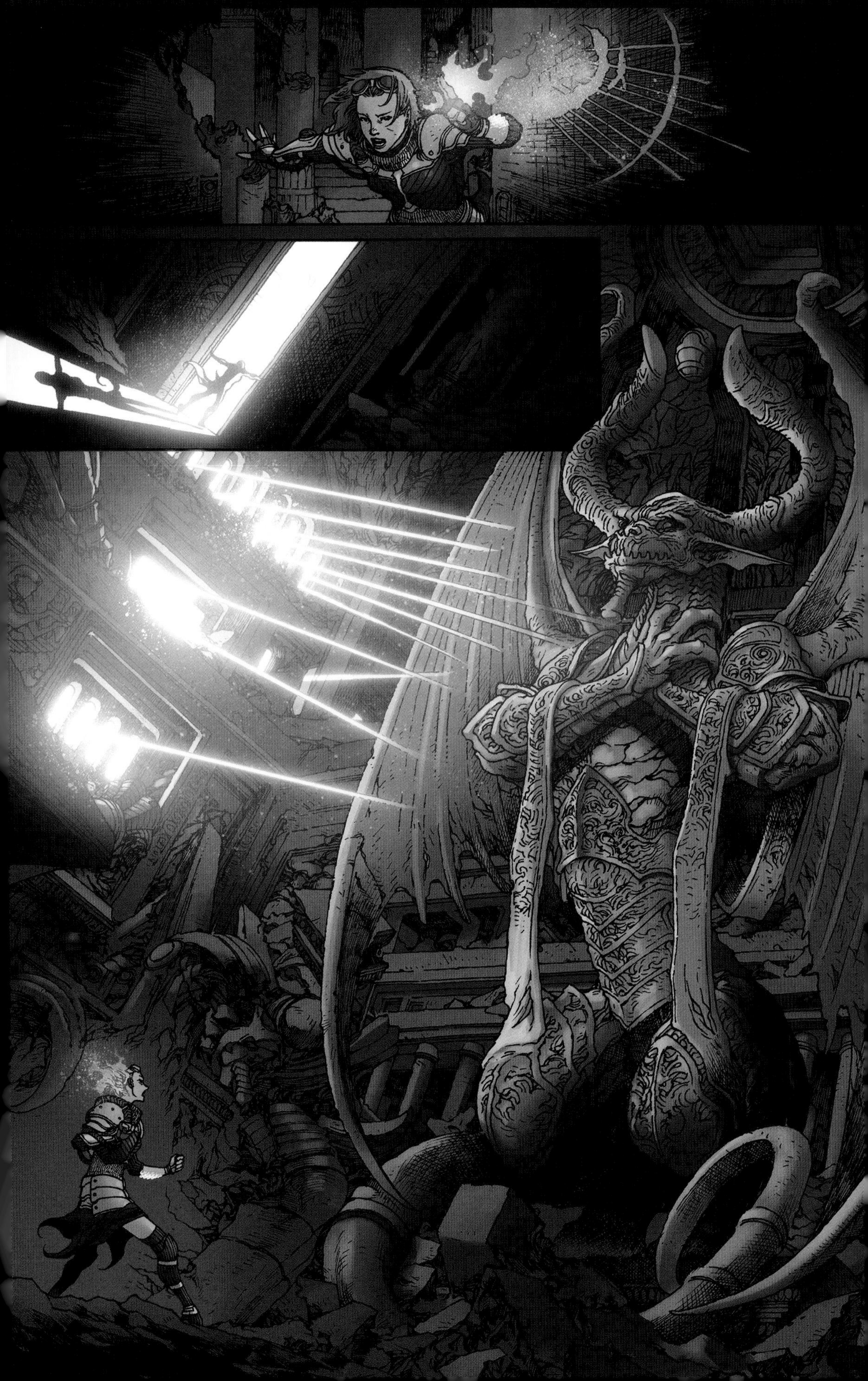

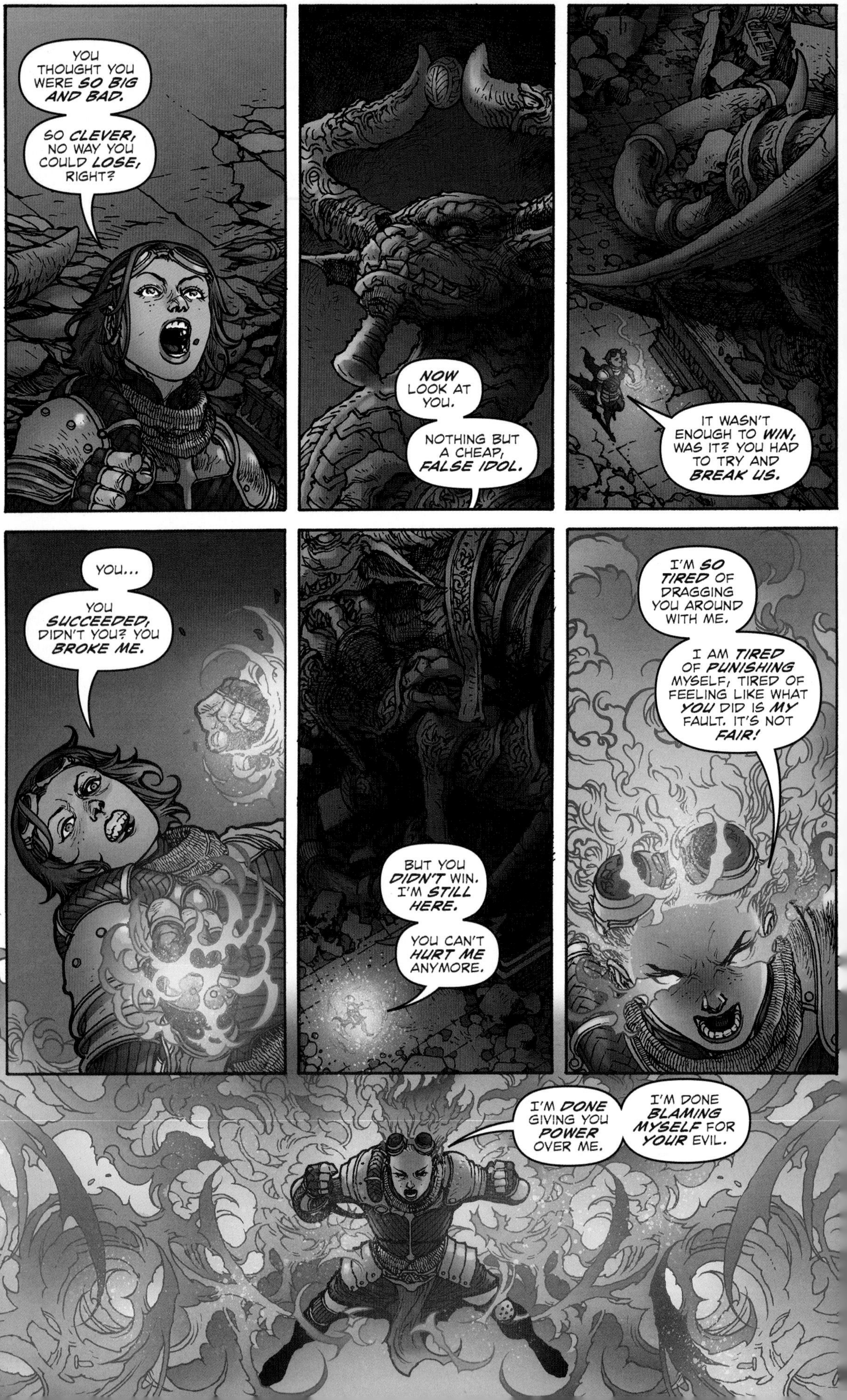
YOU THOUGHT YOU WERE SO BIG AND BAD.
SO CLEVER, NO WAY YOU COULD LOSE, RIGHT?
NOW LOOK AT YOU.
NOTHING BUT A CHEAP, FALSE IDOL.
IT WASN'T ENOUGH TO WIN, WAS IT? YOU HAD TO TRY AND BREAK US.
YOU...
YOU SUCCEEDED, DIDN'T YOU? YOU BROKE ME.
BUT YOU DIDN'T WIN. I'M STILL HERE.
YOU CAN'T HURT ME ANYMORE.
I'M SO TIRED OF DRAGGING YOU AROUND WITH ME.
I AM TIRED OF PUNISHING MYSELF, TIRED OF FEELING LIKE WHAT YOU DID IS MY FAULT. IT'S NOT FAIR!
I'M DONE GIVING YOU POWER OVER ME.
I'M DONE BLAMING MYSELF FOR YOUR EVIL.

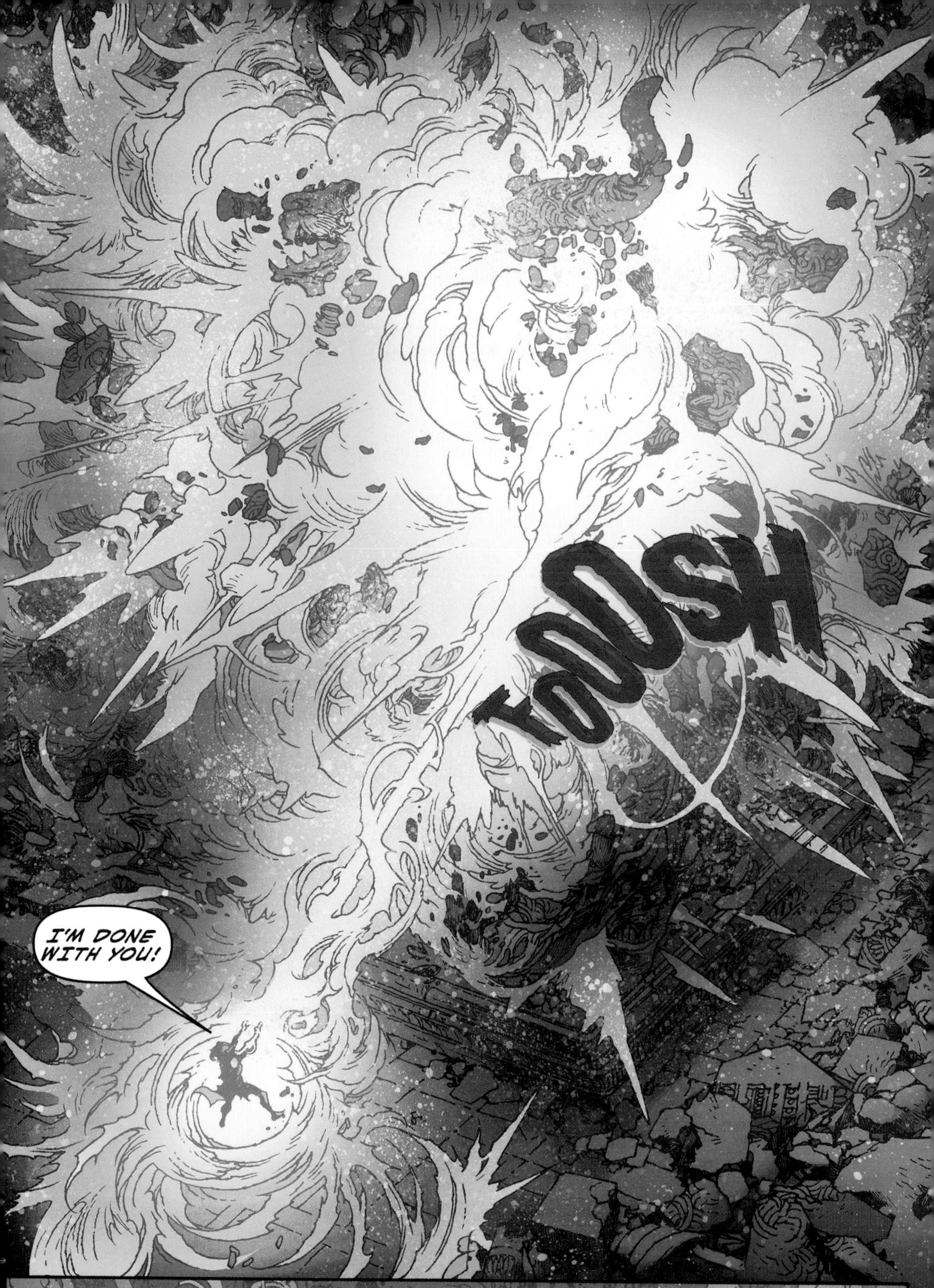
TOOOSH
I'M DONE WITH YOU!
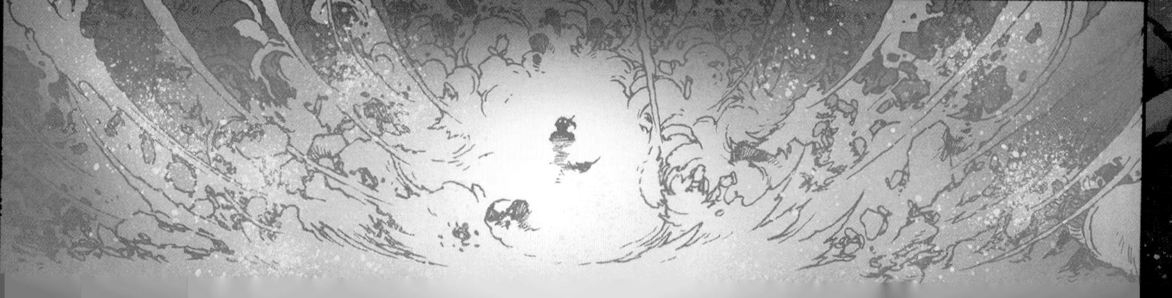

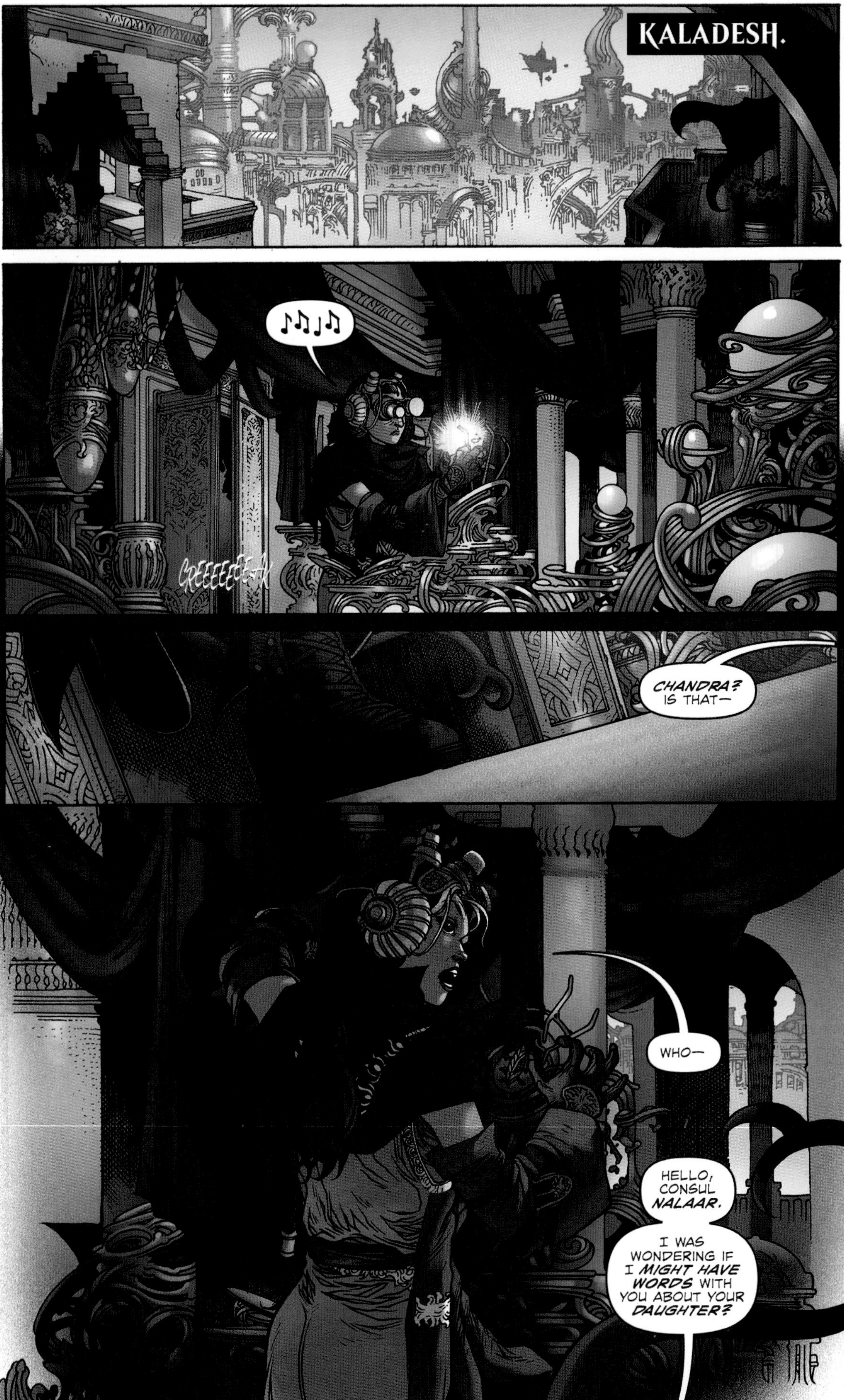
KALADESH.
♪♫♪♫
CREEEEEEEAK
CHANDRA? IS THAT—
WHO—
HELLO, CONSUL NALAAR.
I WAS WONDERING IF I MIGHT HAVE WORDS WITH YOU ABOUT YOUR DAUGHTER?

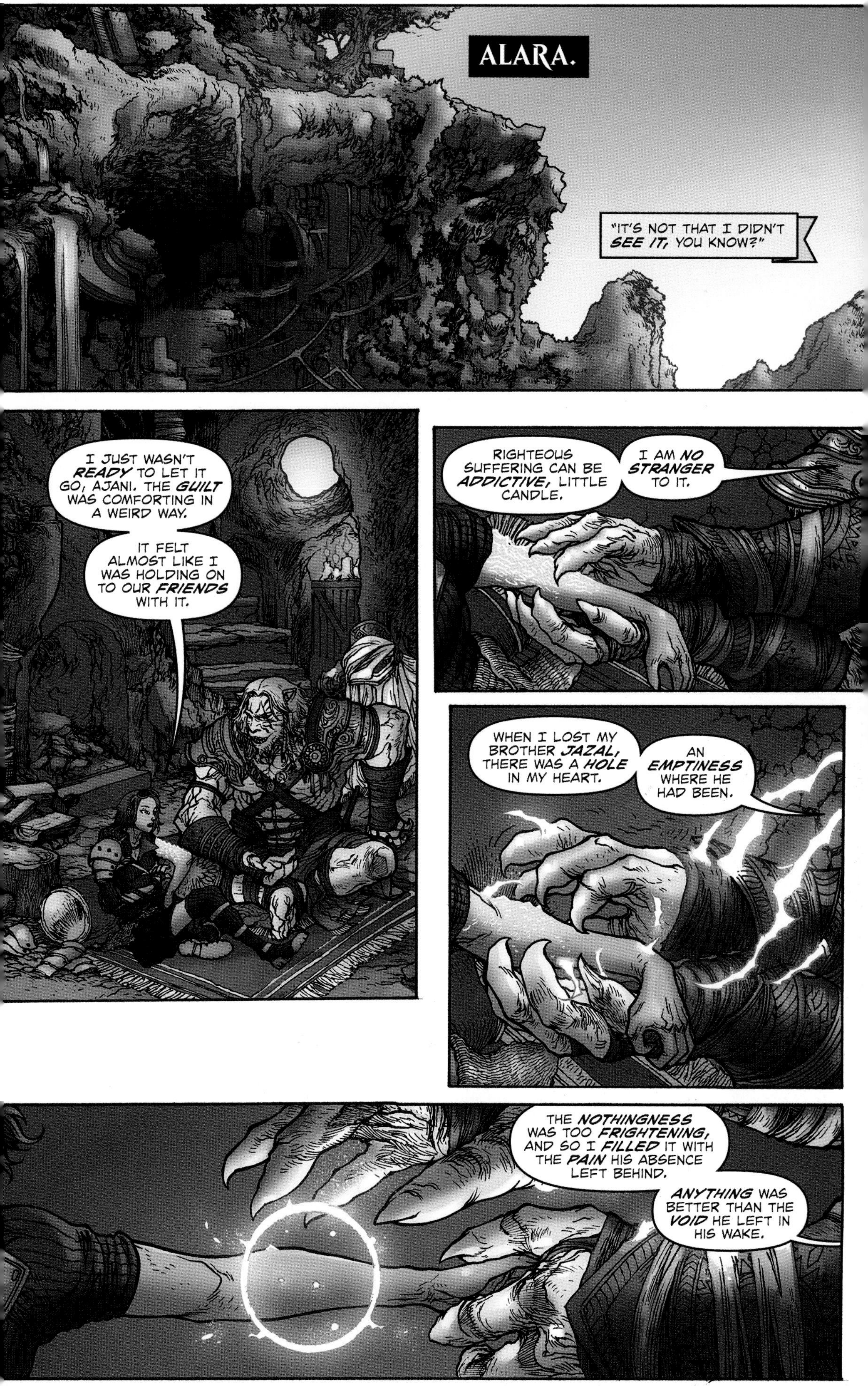
ALARA.
"IT'S NOT THAT I DIDN'T SEE IT, YOU KNOW?"
I JUST WASN'T READY TO LET IT GO, AJANI. THE GUILT WAS COMFORTING IN A WEIRD WAY.
IT FELT ALMOST LIKE I WAS HOLDING ON TO OUR FRIENDS WITH IT.
RIGHTEOUS SUFFERING CAN BE ADDICTIVE, LITTLE CANDLE.
I AM NO STRANGER TO IT.
WHEN I LOST MY BROTHER JAZAL, THERE WAS A HOLE IN MY HEART.
AN EMPTINESS WHERE HE HAD BEEN.
THE NOTHINGNESS WAS TOO FRIGHTENING, AND SO I FILLED IT WITH THE PAIN HIS ABSENCE LEFT BEHIND.
ANYTHING WAS BETTER THAN THE VOID HE LEFT IN HIS WAKE.

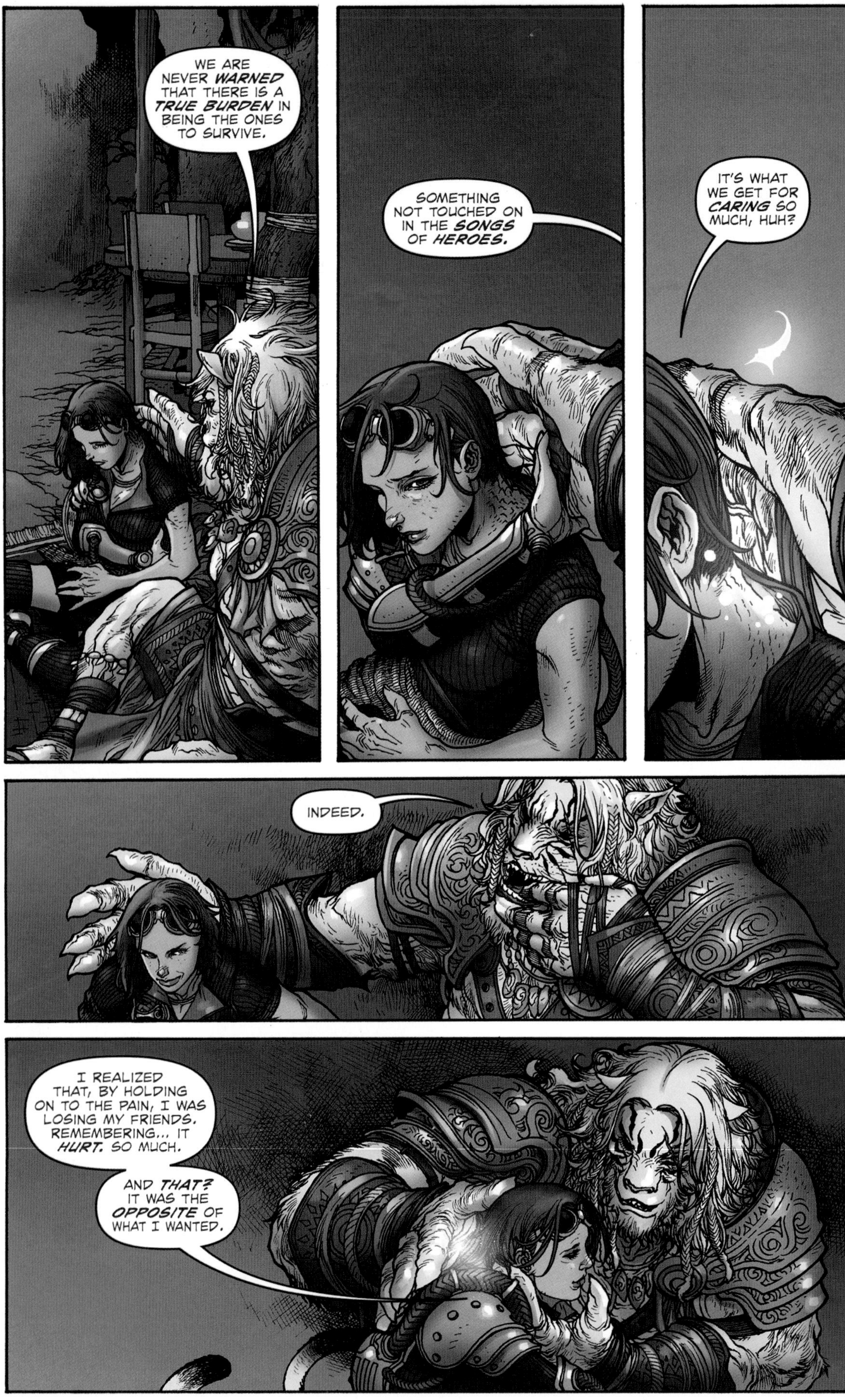
WE ARE NEVER WARNED THAT THERE IS A TRUE BURDEN IN BEING THE ONES TO SURVIVE.
SOMETHING NOT TOUCHED ON IN THE SONGS OF HEROES.
IT'S WHAT WE GET FOR CARING SO MUCH, HUH?
INDEED.
I REALIZED THAT, BY HOLDING ON TO THE PAIN, I WAS LOSING MY FRIENDS. REMEMBERING... IT HURT. SO MUCH.
AND THAT? IT WAS THE OPPOSITE OF WHAT I WANTED.

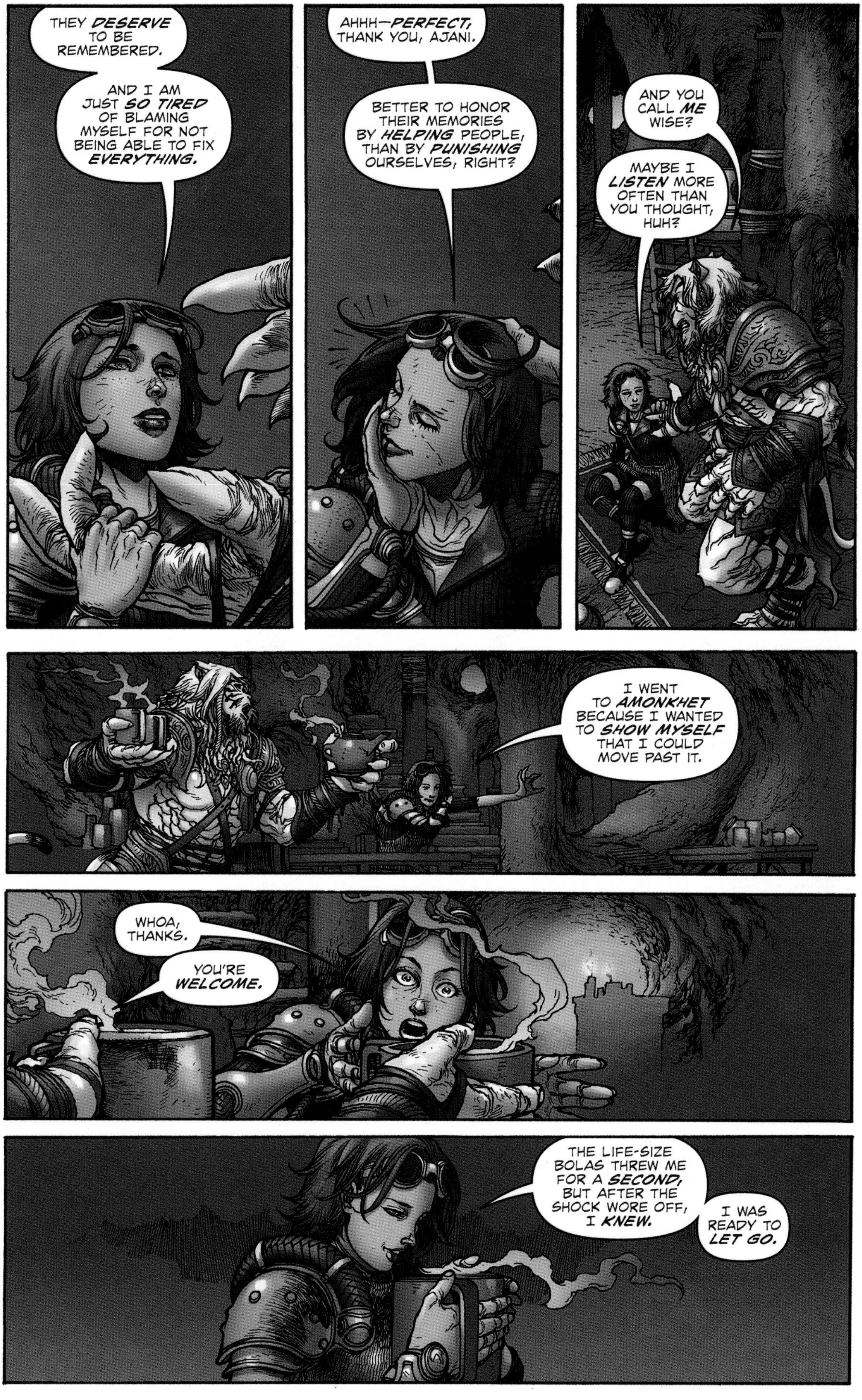
THEY DESERVE TO BE REMEMBERED.
AND I AM JUST SO TIRED OF BLAMING MYSELF FOR NOT BEING ABLE TO FIX EVERYTHING.
AHHH—PERFECT, THANK YOU, AJANI.
BETTER TO HONOR THEIR MEMORIES BY HELPING PEOPLE, THAN BY PUNISHING OURSELVES, RIGHT?
AND YOU CALL ME WISE?
MAYBE I LISTEN MORE OFTEN THAN YOU THOUGHT, HUH?
I WENT TO AMONKHET BECAUSE I WANTED TO SHOW MYSELF THAT I COULD MOVE PAST IT.
WHOA, THANKS.
YOU'RE WELCOME.
THE LIFE-SIZE BOLAS THREW ME FOR A SECOND, BUT AFTER THE SHOCK WORE OFF, I KNEW.
I WAS READY TO LET GO.

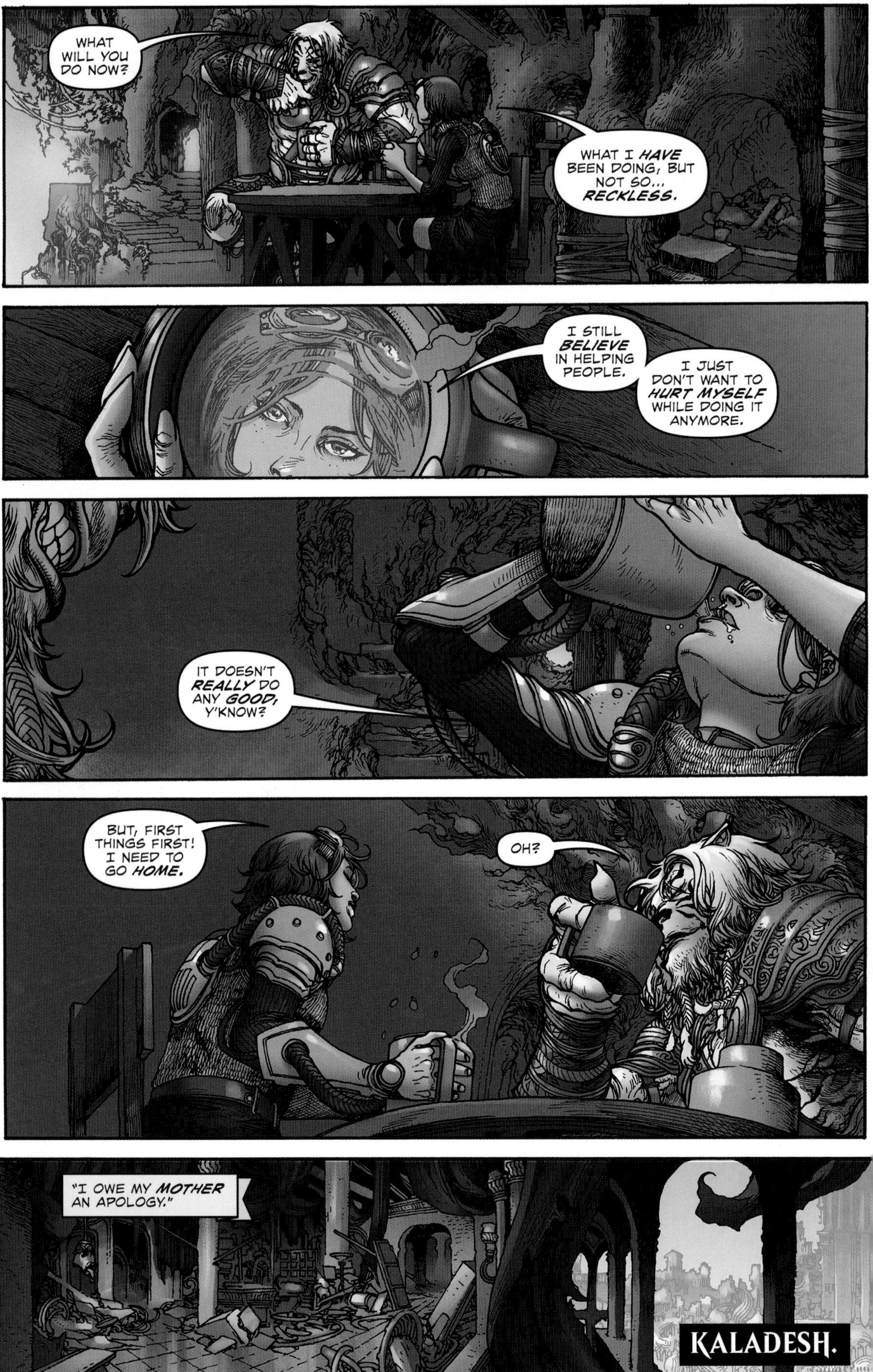
WHAT WILL YOU DO NOW?
WHAT I HAVE BEEN DOING, BUT NOT SO... RECKLESS.
I STILL BELIEVE IN HELPING PEOPLE.
I JUST DON'T WANT TO HURT MYSELF WHILE DOING IT ANYMORE.
IT DOESN'T REALLY DO ANY GOOD, Y'KNOW?
BUT, FIRST THINGS FIRST! I NEED TO GO HOME.
OH?
"I OWE MY MOTHER AN APOLOGY."
KALADESH.

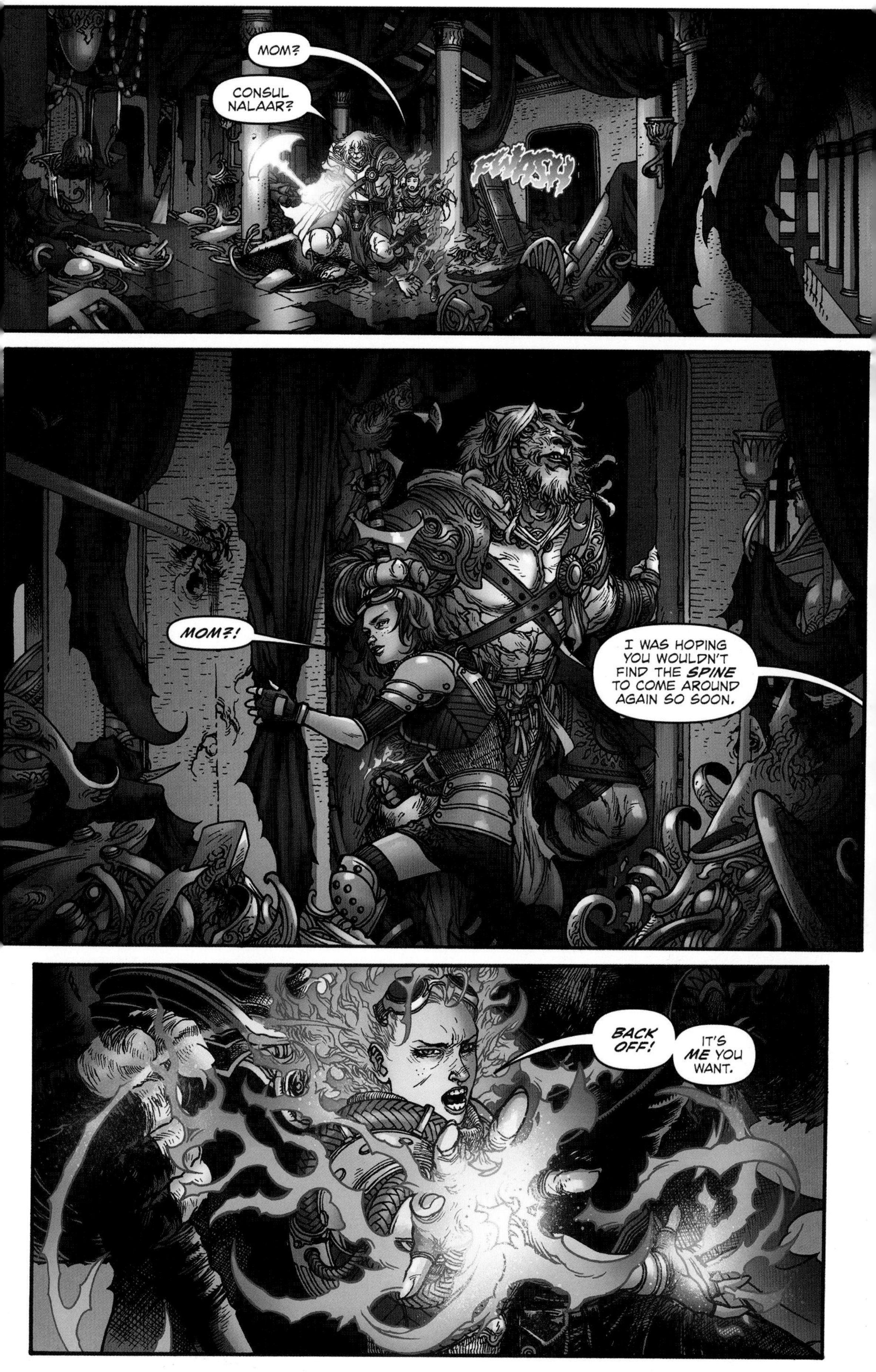
MOM?
CONSUL NALAAR?
FWASH
MOM?!
I WAS HOPING YOU WOULDN'T FIND THE *SPINE* TO COME AROUND AGAIN SO SOON.
*BACK OFF!*
IT'S *ME* YOU WANT.

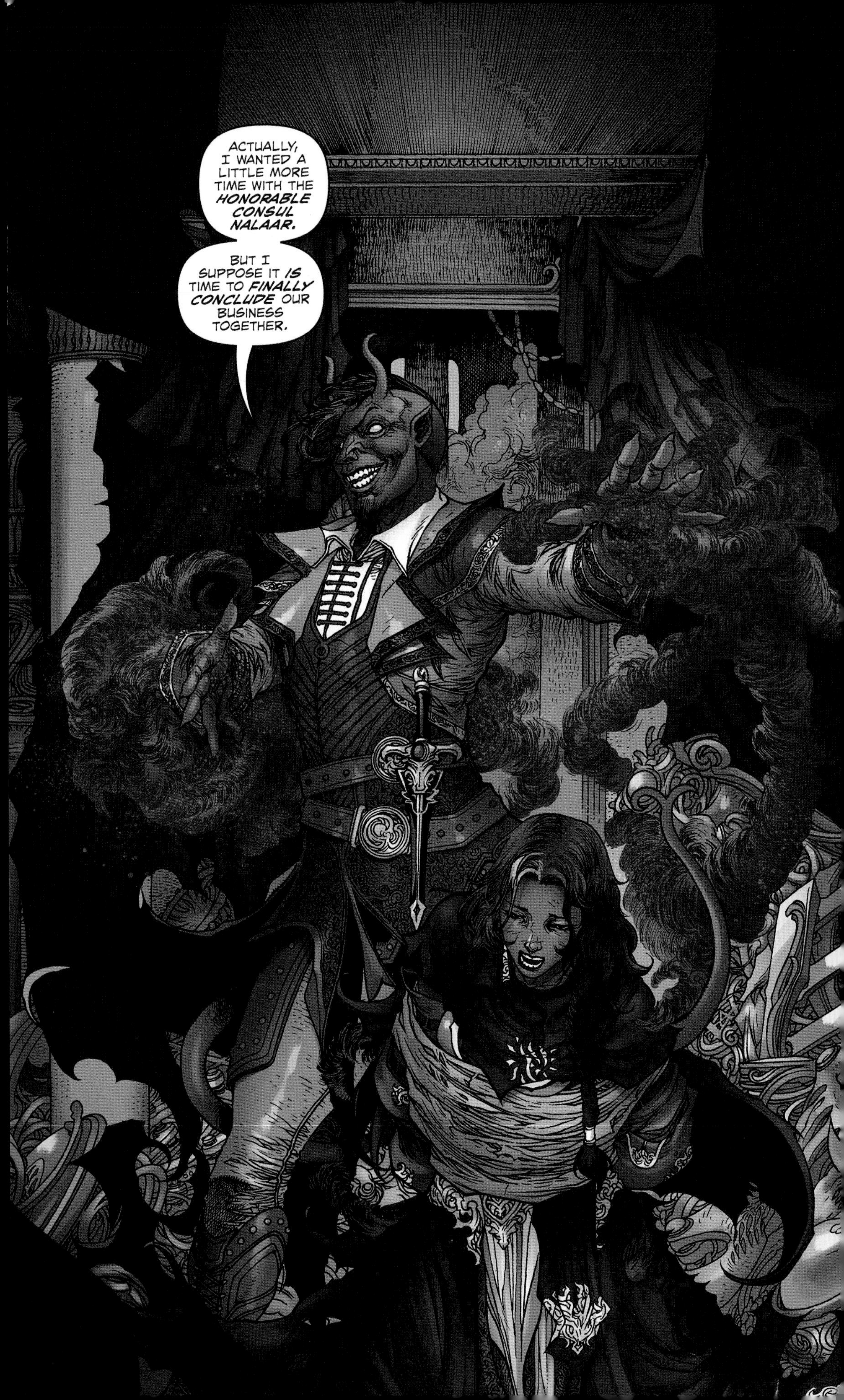
ACTUALLY, I WANTED A LITTLE MORE TIME WITH THE HONORABLE CONSUL NALAAR.
BUT I SUPPOSE IT IS TIME TO FINALLY CONCLUDE OUR BUSINESS TOGETHER.

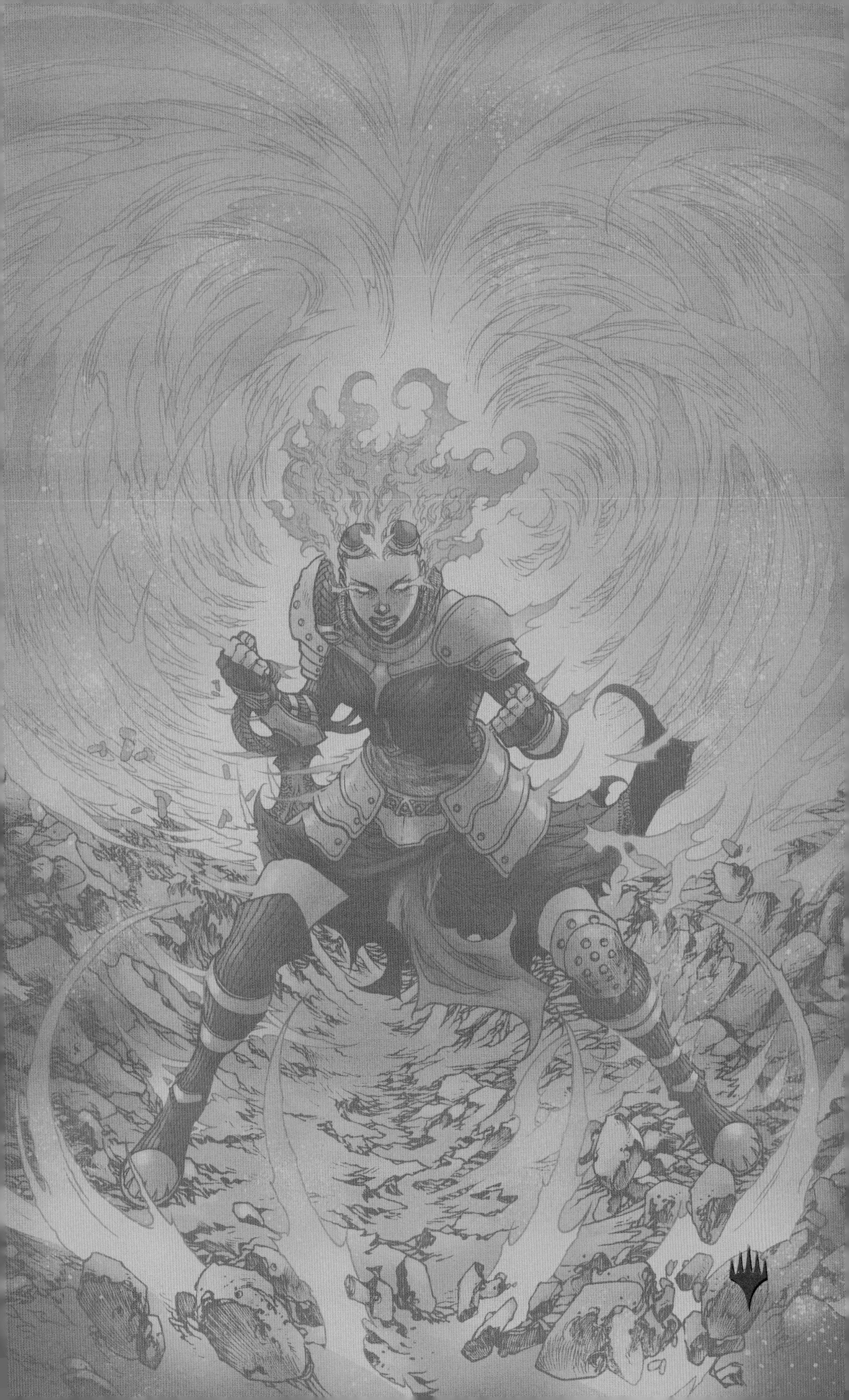

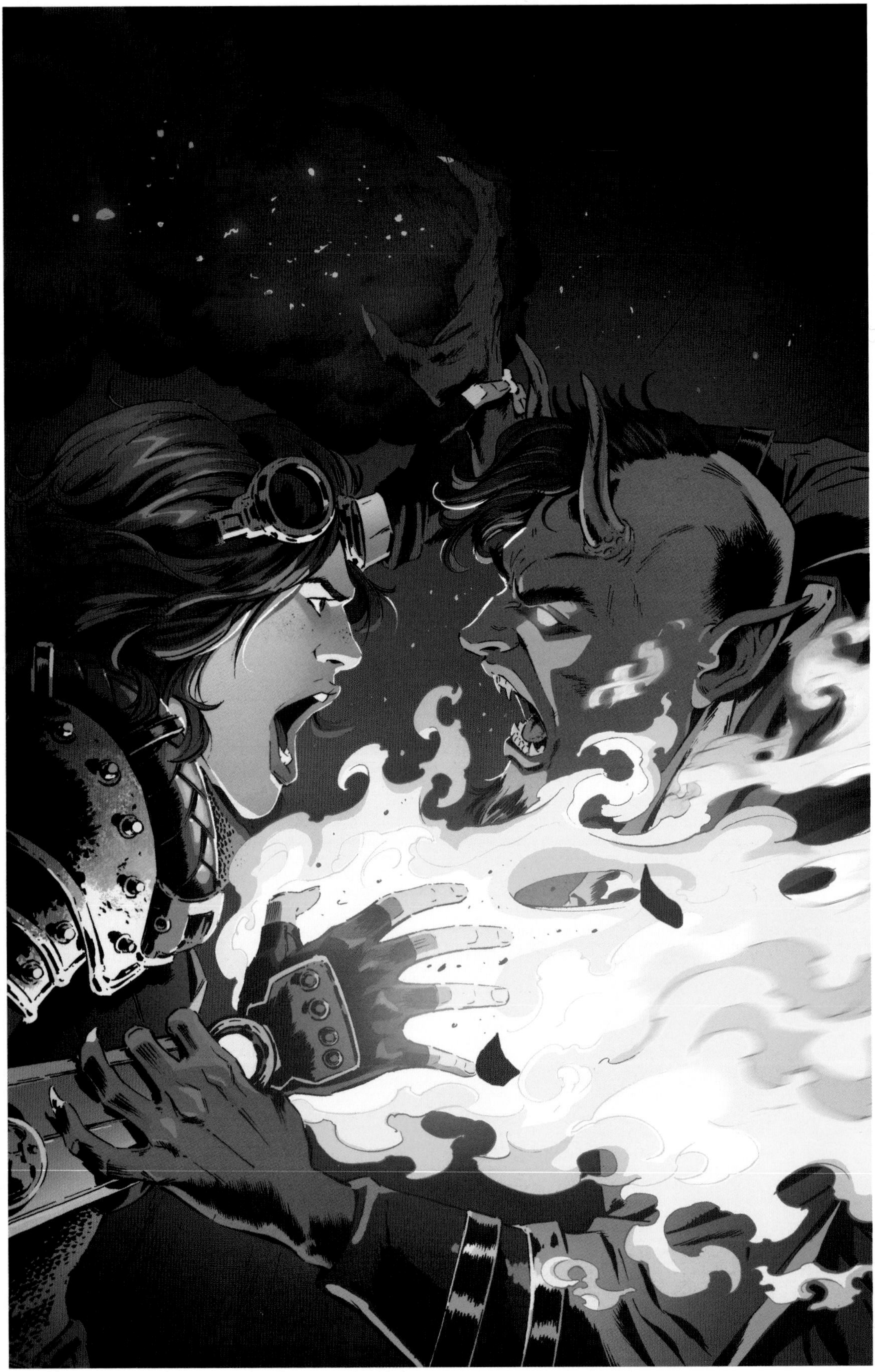

Art by SL Gallant • Colors by Matt Herms

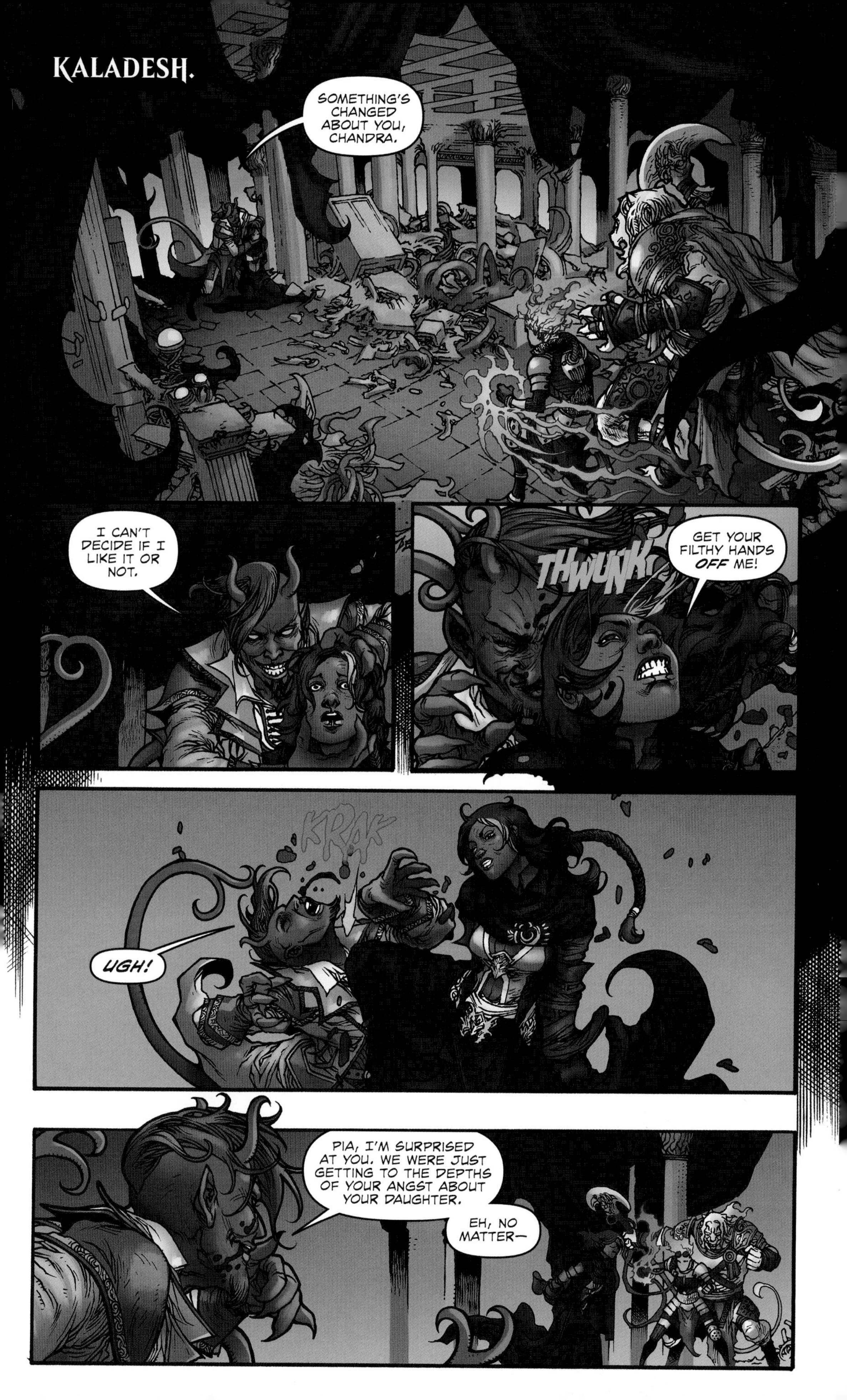
KALADESH.
SOMETHING'S CHANGED ABOUT YOU, CHANDRA.
I CAN'T DECIDE IF I LIKE IT OR NOT.
THWUNK!
GET YOUR FILTHY HANDS OFF ME!
KRAK
UGH!
PIA, I'M SURPRISED AT YOU. WE WERE JUST GETTING TO THE DEPTHS OF YOUR ANGST ABOUT YOUR DAUGHTER.
EH, NO MATTER—

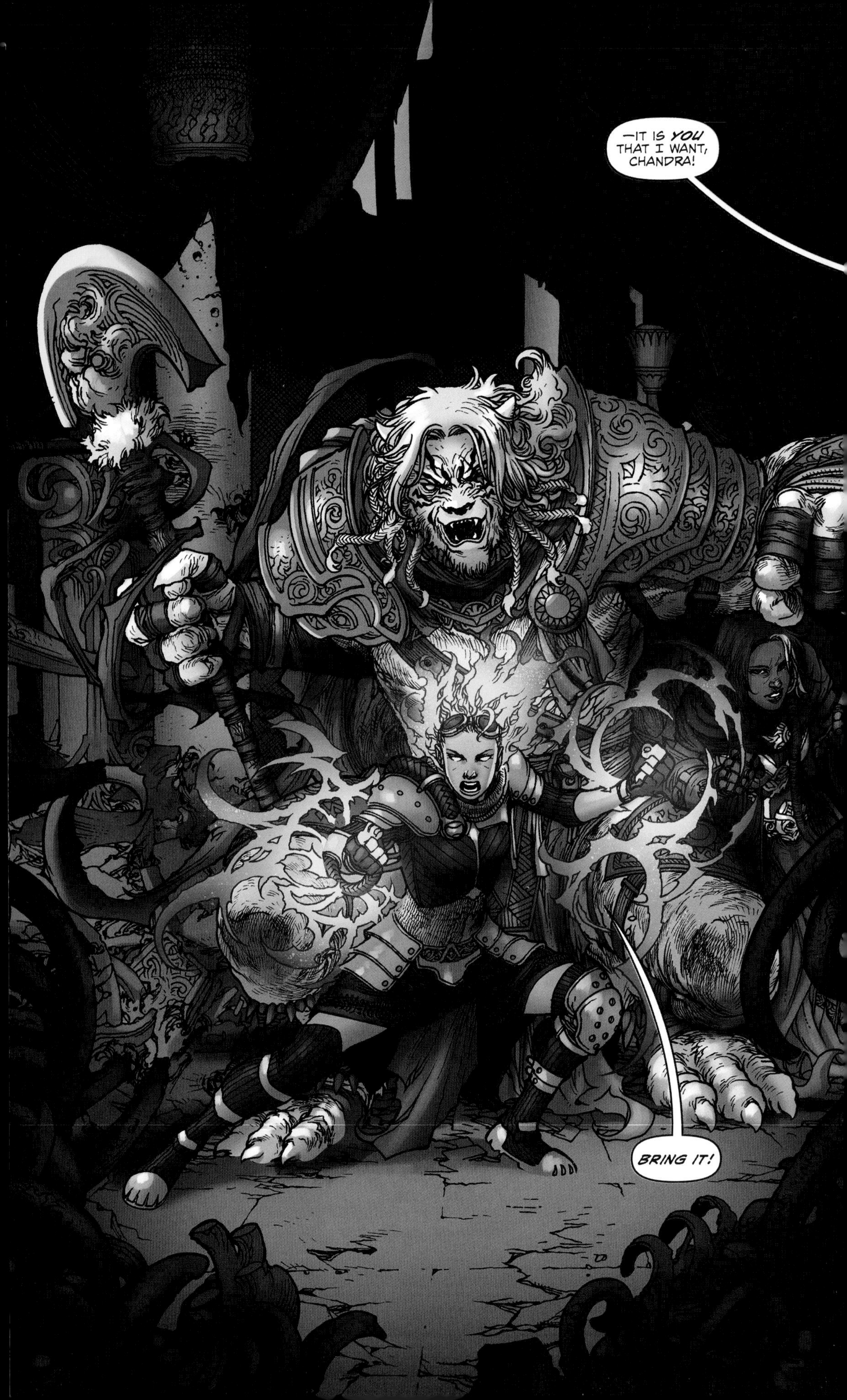
—IT IS YOU THAT I WANT, CHANDRA!
BRING IT!

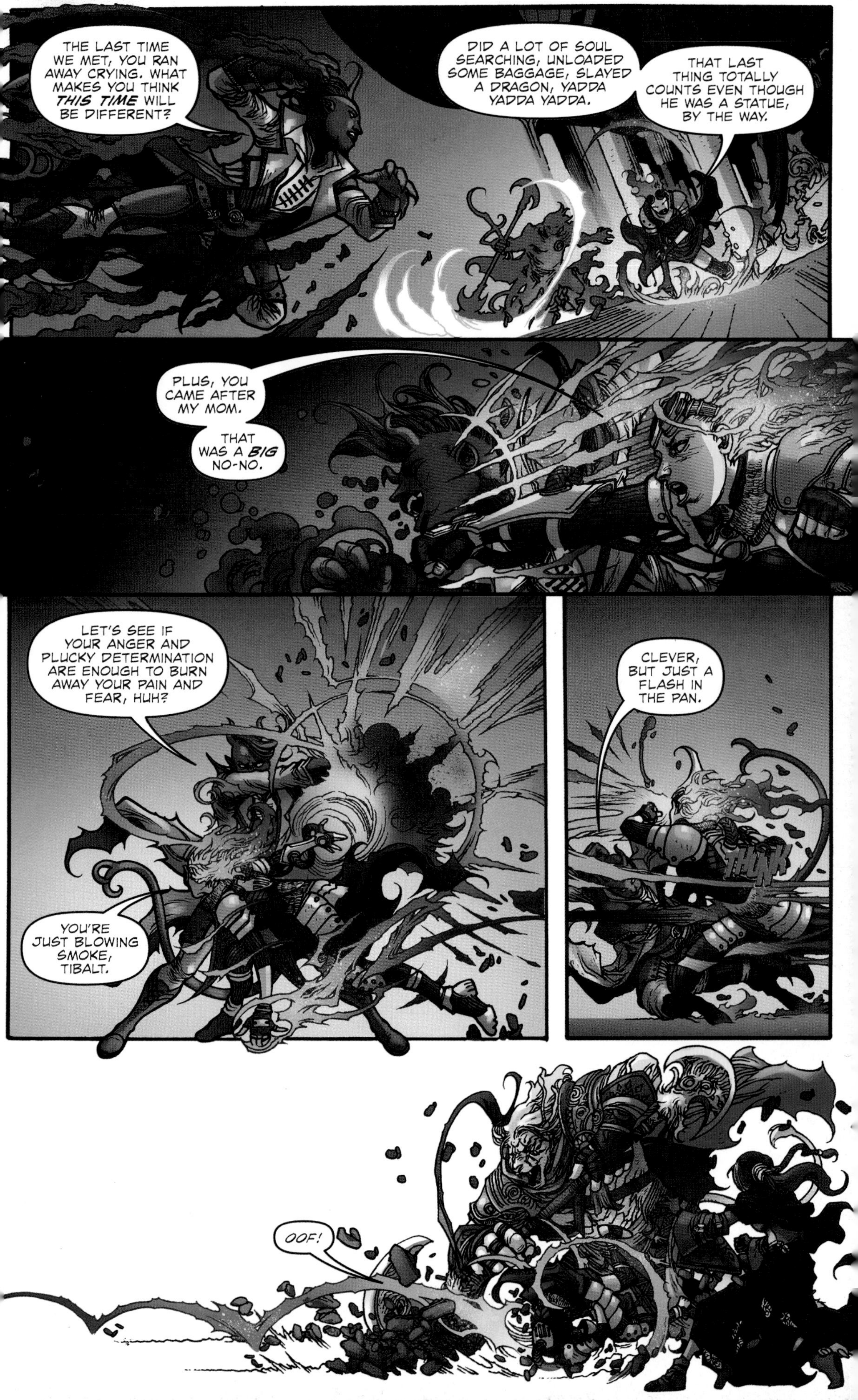
THE LAST TIME WE MET, YOU RAN AWAY CRYING. WHAT MAKES YOU THINK THIS TIME WILL BE DIFFERENT?
DID A LOT OF SOUL SEARCHING, UNLOADED SOME BAGGAGE, SLAYED A DRAGON, YADDA YADDA YADDA.
THAT LAST THING TOTALLY COUNTS EVEN THOUGH HE WAS A STATUE, BY THE WAY.
PLUS, YOU CAME AFTER MY MOM.
THAT WAS A BIG NO-NO.
LET'S SEE IF YOUR ANGER AND PLUCKY DETERMINATION ARE ENOUGH TO BURN AWAY YOUR PAIN AND FEAR, HUH?
YOU'RE JUST BLOWING SMOKE, TIBALT.
CLEVER, BUT JUST A FLASH IN THE PAN.
THUNK
OOF!

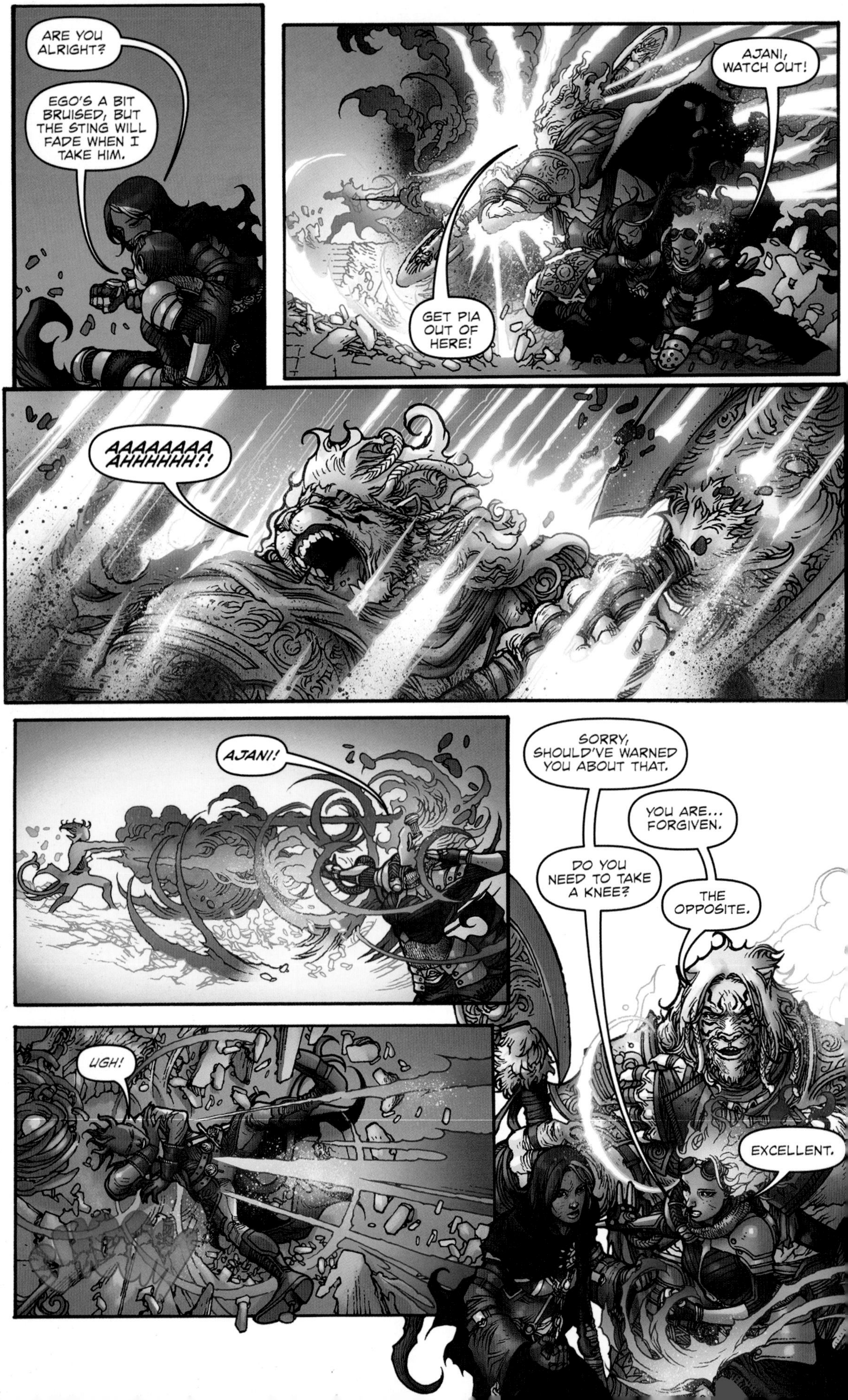
ARE YOU ALRIGHT?
EGO'S A BIT BRUISED, BUT THE STING WILL FADE WHEN I TAKE HIM.
AJANI, WATCH OUT!
GET PIA OUT OF HERE!
AAAAAAAA AHHHHHH!!
AJANI!
UGH!
SORRY, SHOULD'VE WARNED YOU ABOUT THAT.
YOU ARE... FORGIVEN.
DO YOU NEED TO TAKE A KNEE?
THE OPPOSITE.
EXCELLENT.

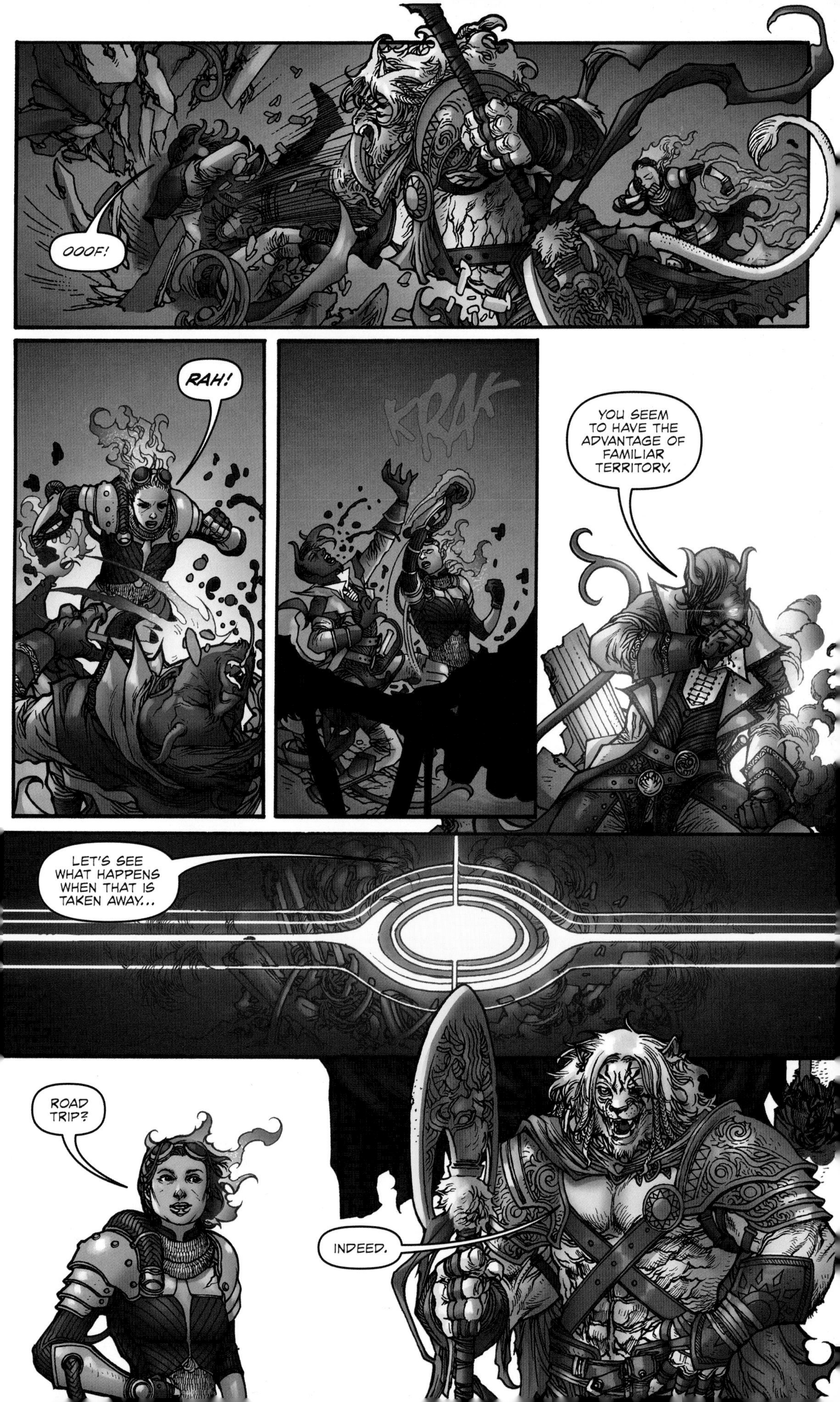
OOOF!
RAH!
KRAK
YOU SEEM TO HAVE THE ADVANTAGE OF FAMILIAR TERRITORY.
LET'S SEE WHAT HAPPENS WHEN THAT IS TAKEN AWAY...
ROAD TRIP?
INDEED.

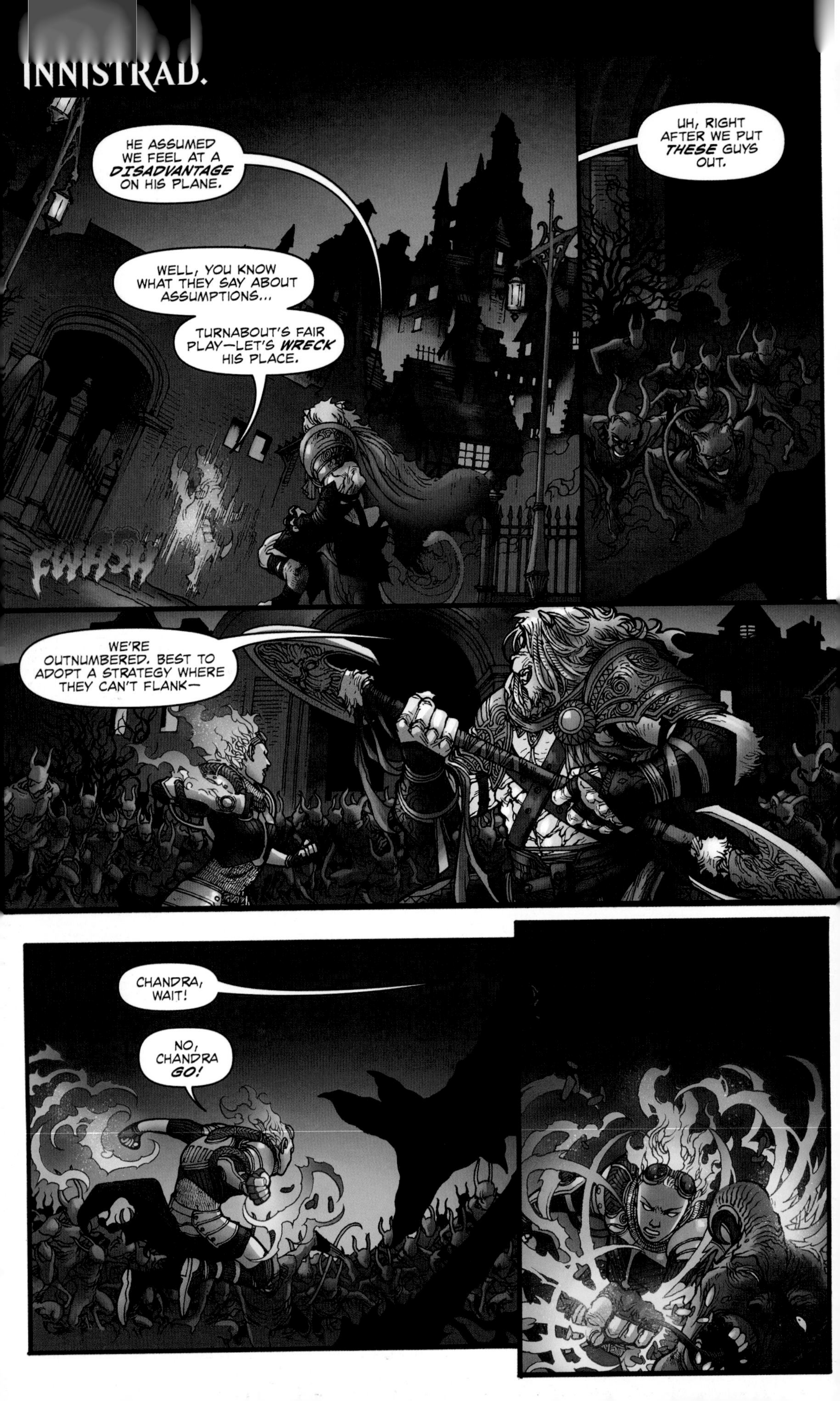

INNISTRAD.
HE ASSUMED WE FEEL AT A DISADVANTAGE ON HIS PLANE.
UH, RIGHT AFTER WE PUT THESE GUYS OUT.
WELL, YOU KNOW WHAT THEY SAY ABOUT ASSUMPTIONS...
TURNABOUT'S FAIR PLAY—LET'S WRECK HIS PLACE.
FWASH
WE'RE OUTNUMBERED. BEST TO ADOPT A STRATEGY WHERE THEY CAN'T FLANK—
CHANDRA, WAIT!
NO, CHANDRA GO!

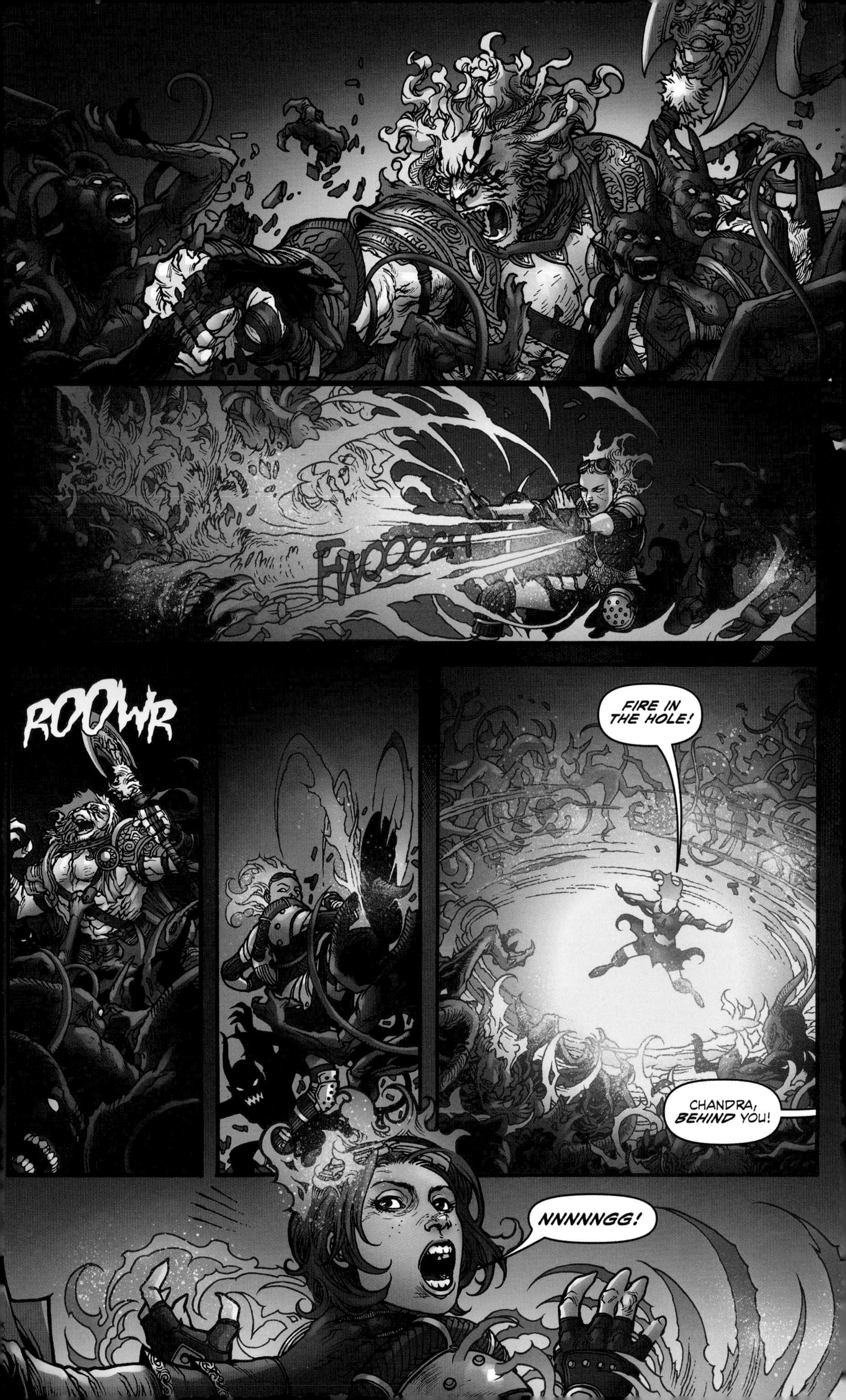
FWOOOSH
ROOWR
FIRE IN THE HOLE!
CHANDRA, BEHIND YOU!
NNNNNGG!

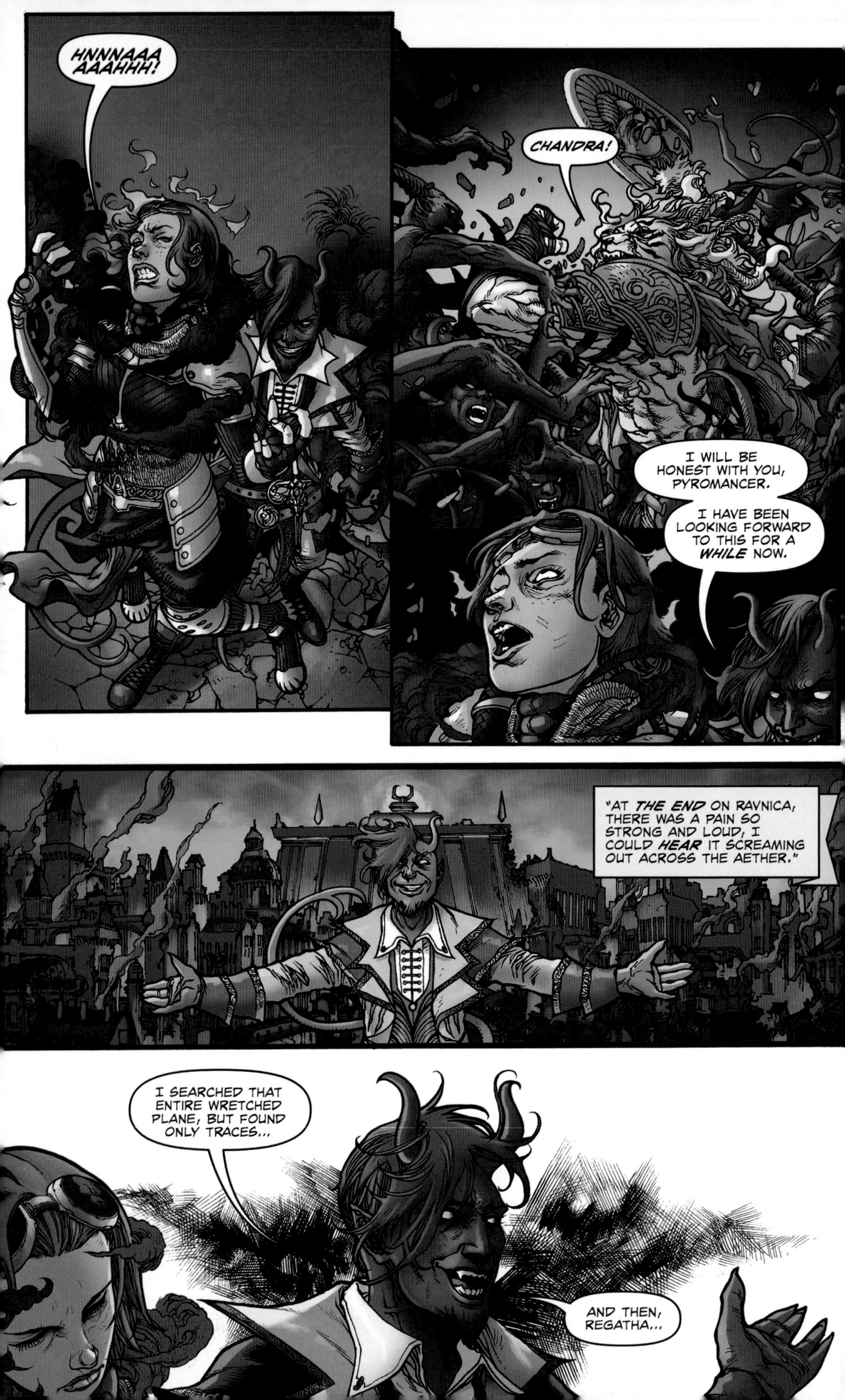
HNNNAAA AAAHHH!
CHANDRA!
I WILL BE HONEST WITH YOU, PYROMANCER.
I HAVE BEEN LOOKING FORWARD TO THIS FOR A WHILE NOW.
"AT THE END ON RAVNICA, THERE WAS A PAIN SO STRONG AND LOUD, I COULD HEAR IT SCREAMING OUT ACROSS THE AETHER."
I SEARCHED THAT ENTIRE WRETCHED PLANE, BUT FOUND ONLY TRACES...
AND THEN, REGATHA...

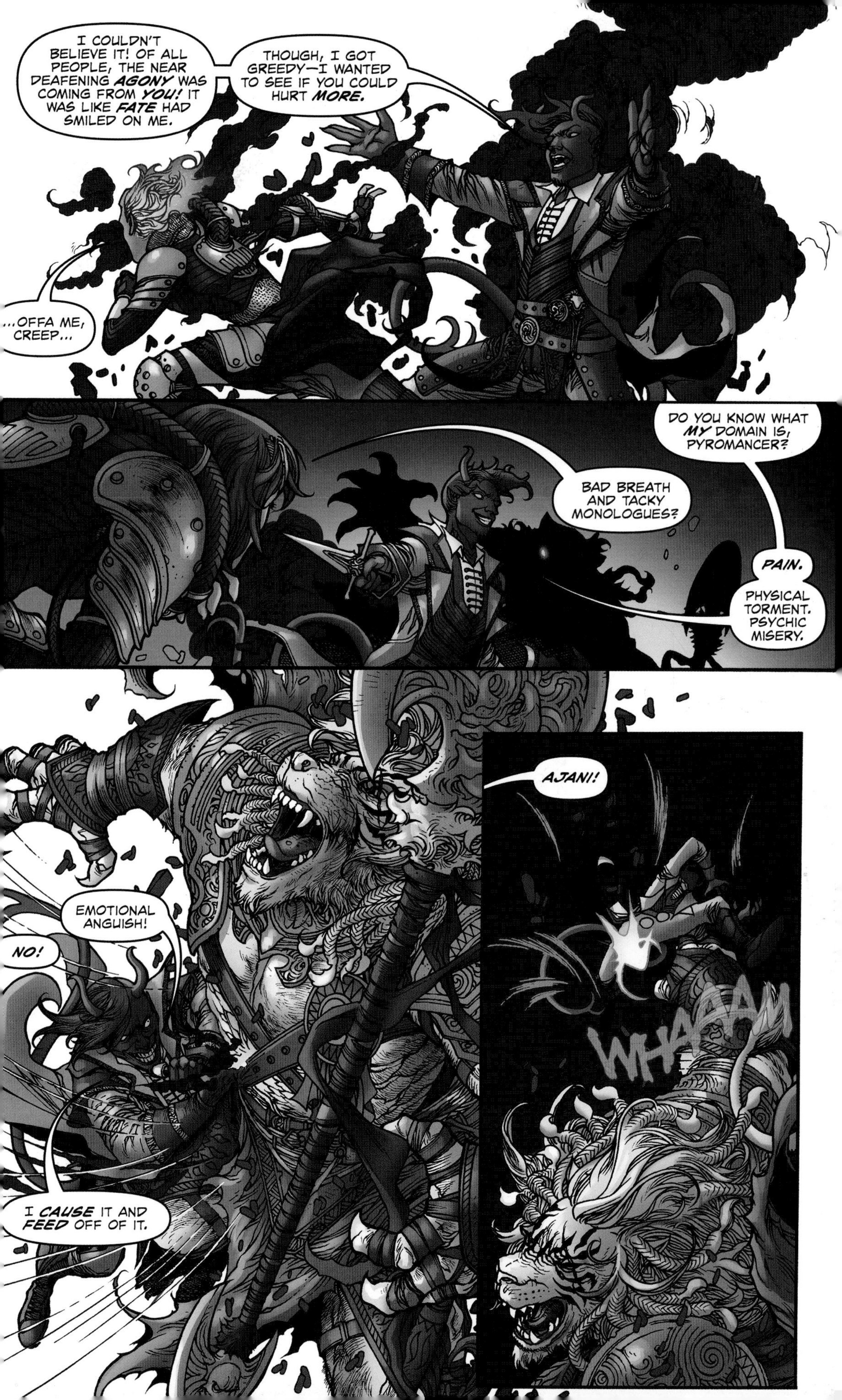
I COULDN'T BELIEVE IT! OF ALL PEOPLE, THE NEAR DEAFENING AGONY WAS COMING FROM YOU! IT WAS LIKE FATE HAD SMILED ON ME.
THOUGH, I GOT GREEDY—I WANTED TO SEE IF YOU COULD HURT MORE.
...OFFA ME, CREEP...
DO YOU KNOW WHAT MY DOMAIN IS, PYROMANCER?
BAD BREATH AND TACKY MONOLOGUES?
PAIN.
PHYSICAL TORMENT. PSYCHIC MISERY.
EMOTIONAL ANGUISH!
NO!
I CAUSE IT AND FEED OFF OF IT.
AJANI!
WHAAAM

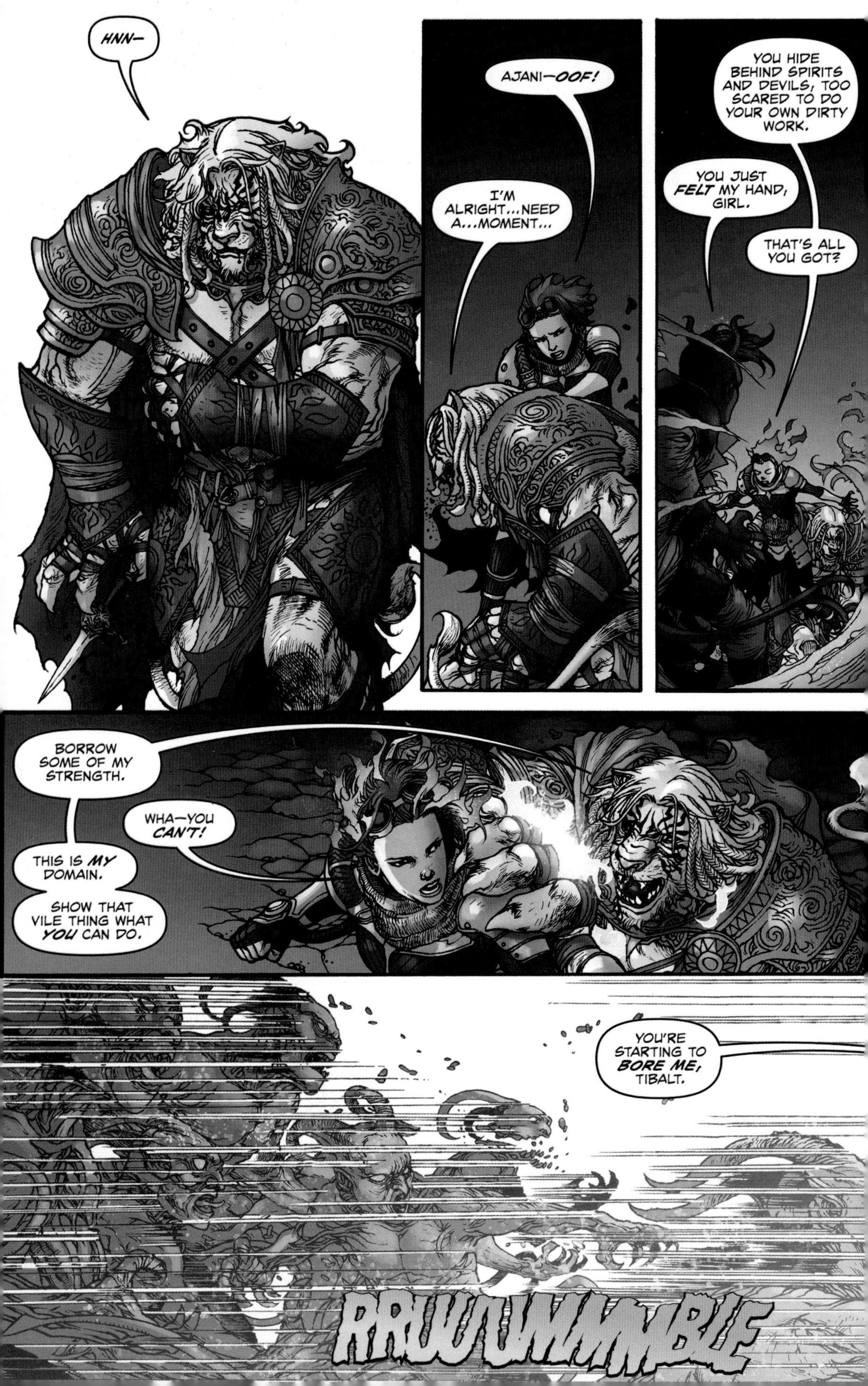
HNN—
AJANI—OOF!
I'M ALRIGHT...NEED A...MOMENT...
YOU HIDE BEHIND SPIRITS AND DEVILS, TOO SCARED TO DO YOUR OWN DIRTY WORK.
YOU JUST FELT MY HAND, GIRL.
THAT'S ALL YOU GOT?
BORROW SOME OF MY STRENGTH.
WHA—YOU CAN'T!
THIS IS MY DOMAIN.
SHOW THAT VILE THING WHAT YOU CAN DO.
YOU'RE STARTING TO BORE ME, TIBALT.
RRUUUMMMMBLE

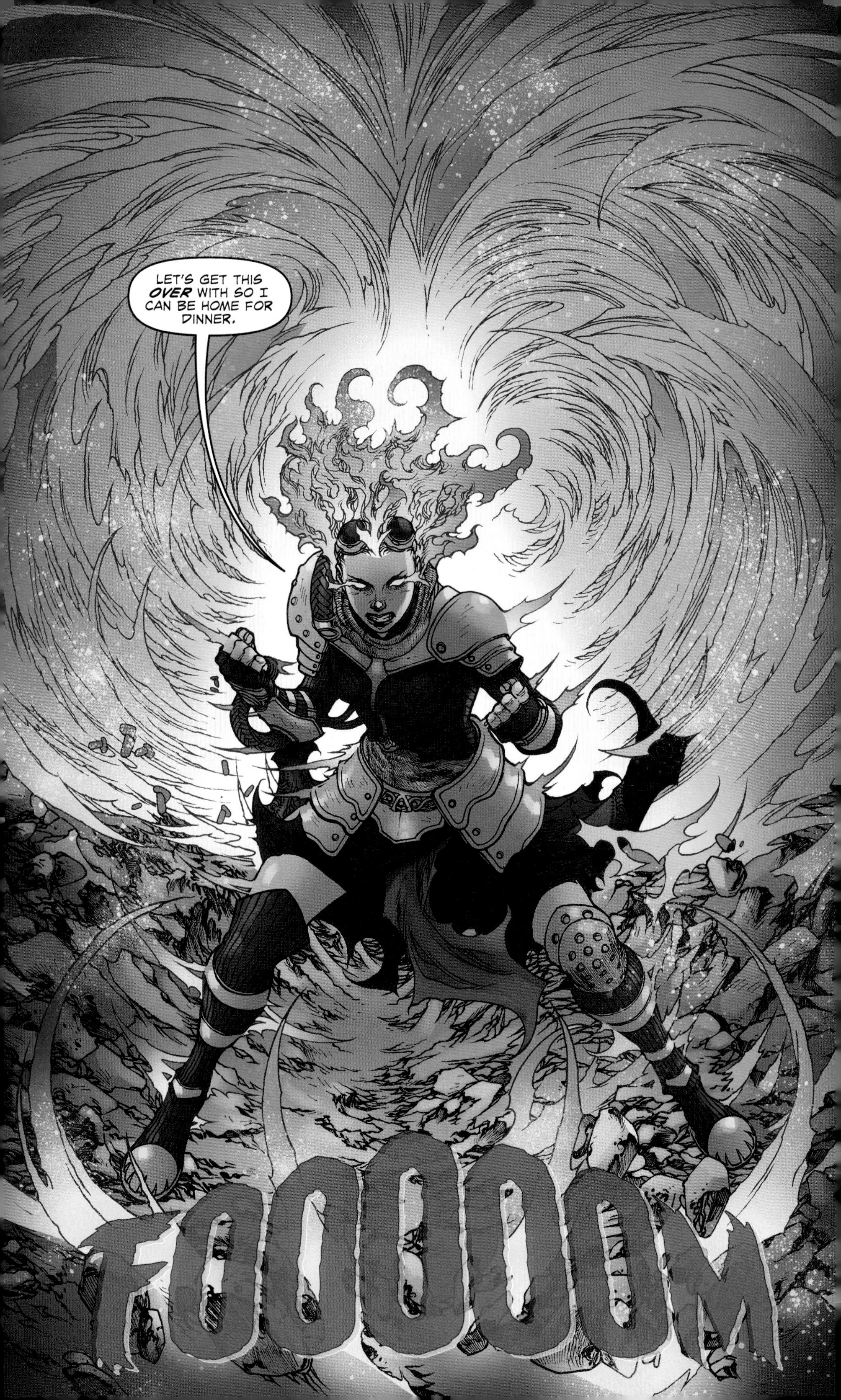

LET'S GET THIS OVER WITH SO I CAN BE HOME FOR DINNER.
TOOOOOM

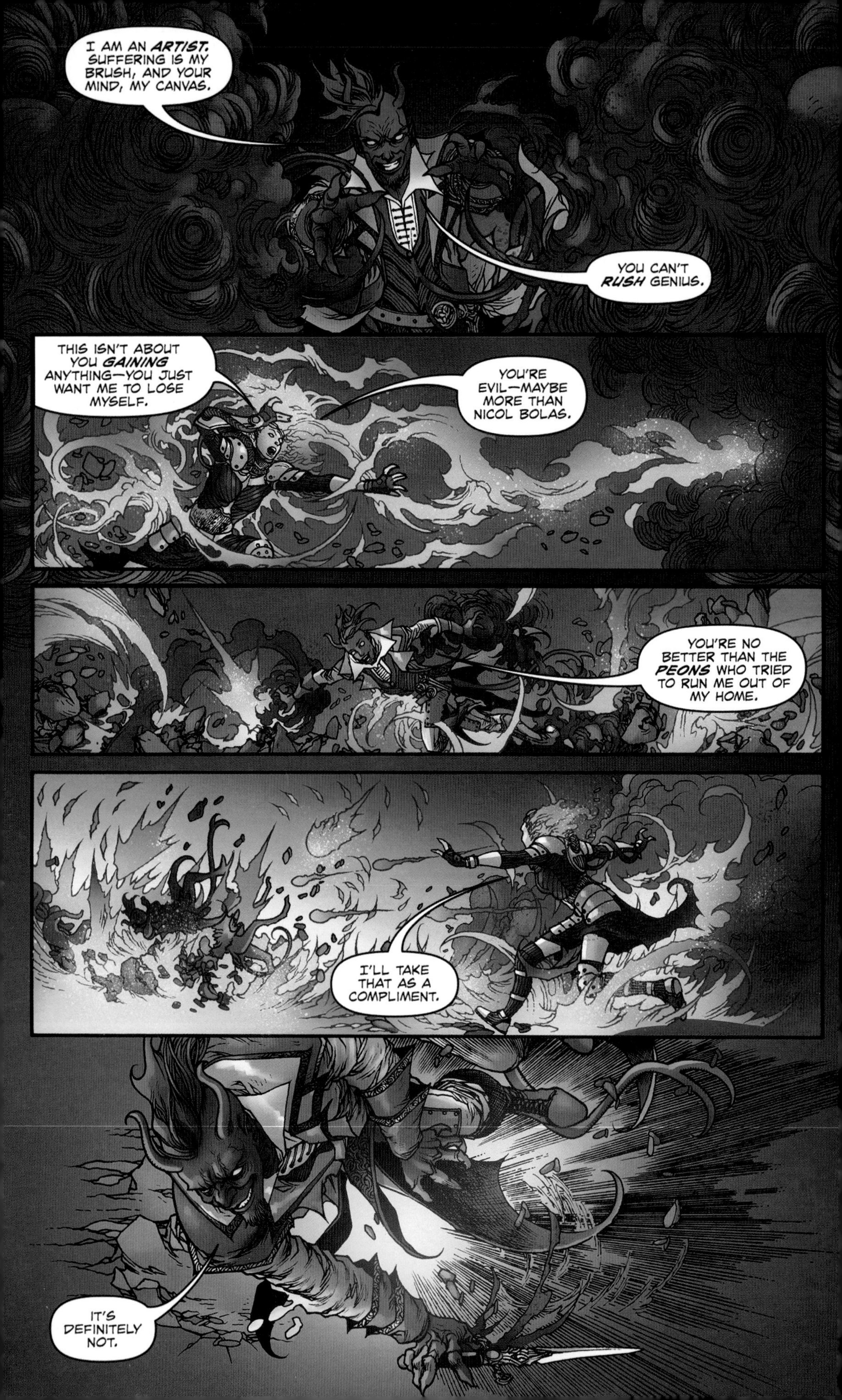
I AM AN ARTIST. SUFFERING IS MY BRUSH, AND YOUR MIND, MY CANVAS.
YOU CAN'T RUSH GENIUS.
THIS ISN'T ABOUT YOU GAINING ANYTHING—YOU JUST WANT ME TO LOSE MYSELF.
YOU'RE EVIL—MAYBE MORE THAN NICOL BOLAS.
YOU'RE NO BETTER THAN THE PEONS WHO TRIED TO RUN ME OUT OF MY HOME.
I'LL TAKE THAT AS A COMPLIMENT.
IT'S DEFINITELY NOT.

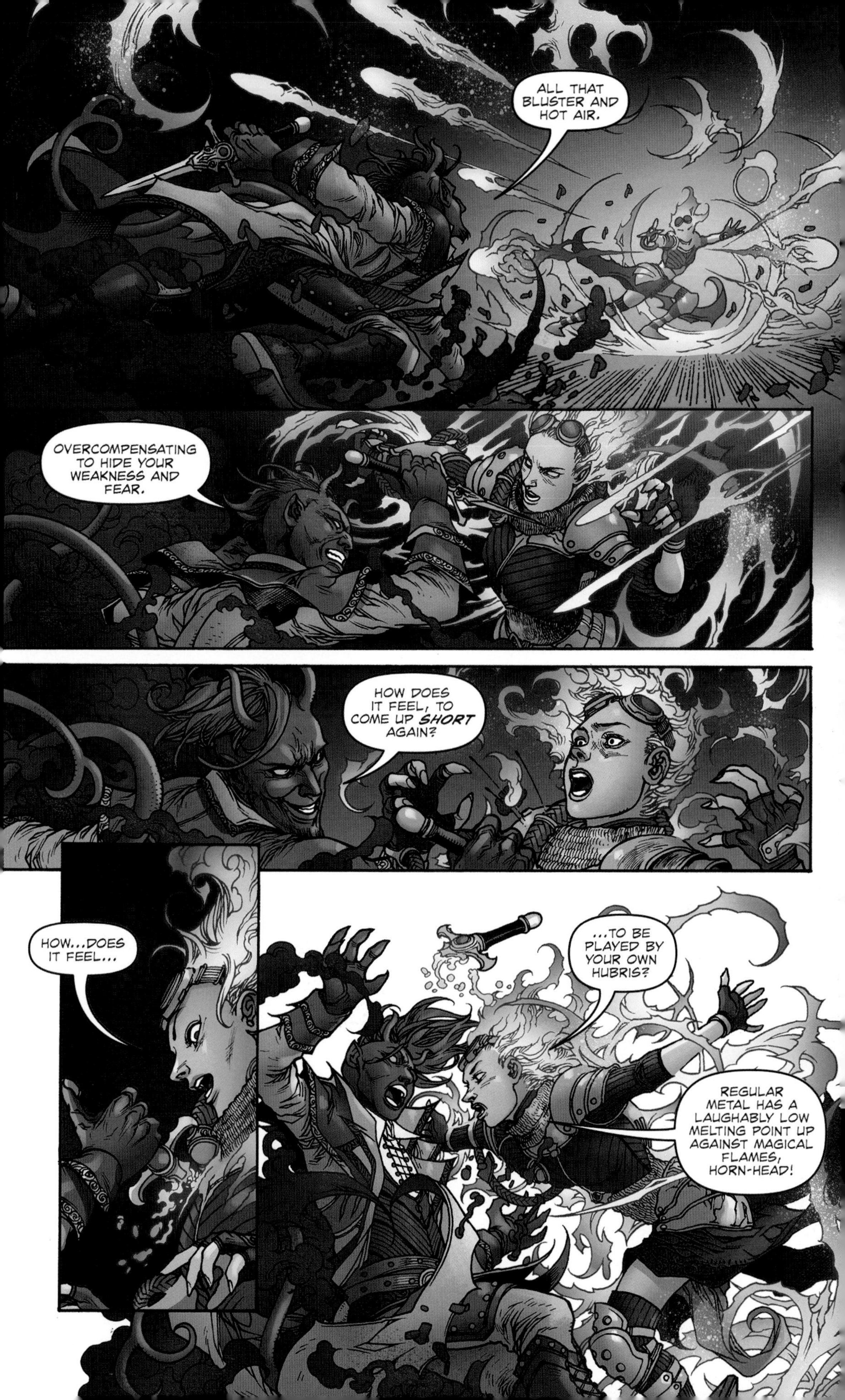

ALL THAT BLUSTER AND HOT AIR.
OVERCOMPENSATING TO HIDE YOUR WEAKNESS AND FEAR.
HOW DOES IT FEEL, TO COME UP *SHORT* AGAIN?
HOW...DOES IT FEEL...
...TO BE PLAYED BY YOUR OWN HUBRIS?
REGULAR METAL HAS A LAUGHABLY LOW MELTING POINT UP AGAINST MAGICAL FLAMES, HORN-HEAD!

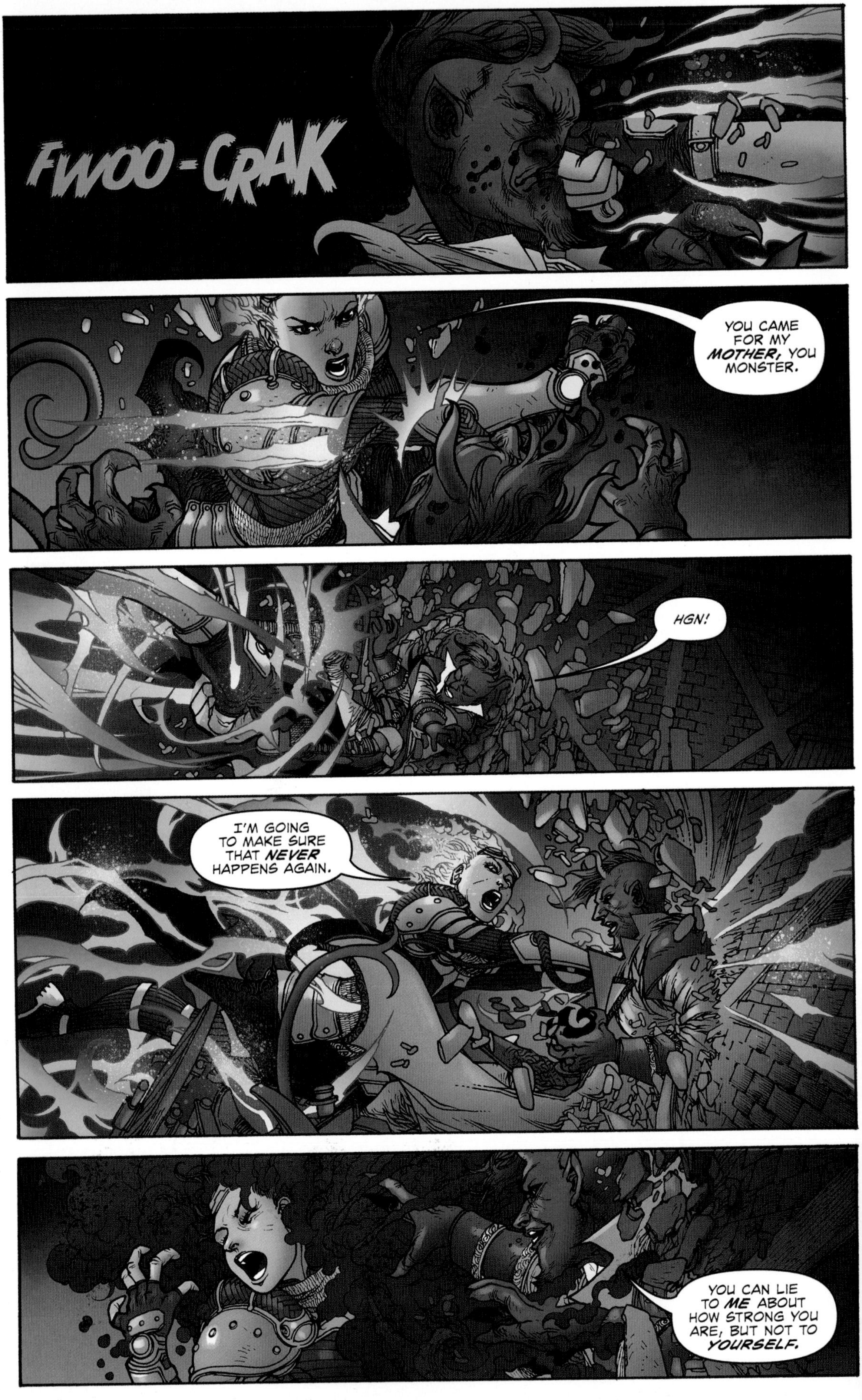
FWOO-CRAK
YOU CAME FOR MY MOTHER, YOU MONSTER.
HGN!
I'M GOING TO MAKE SURE THAT NEVER HAPPENS AGAIN.
YOU CAN LIE TO ME ABOUT HOW STRONG YOU ARE, BUT NOT TO YOURSELF.

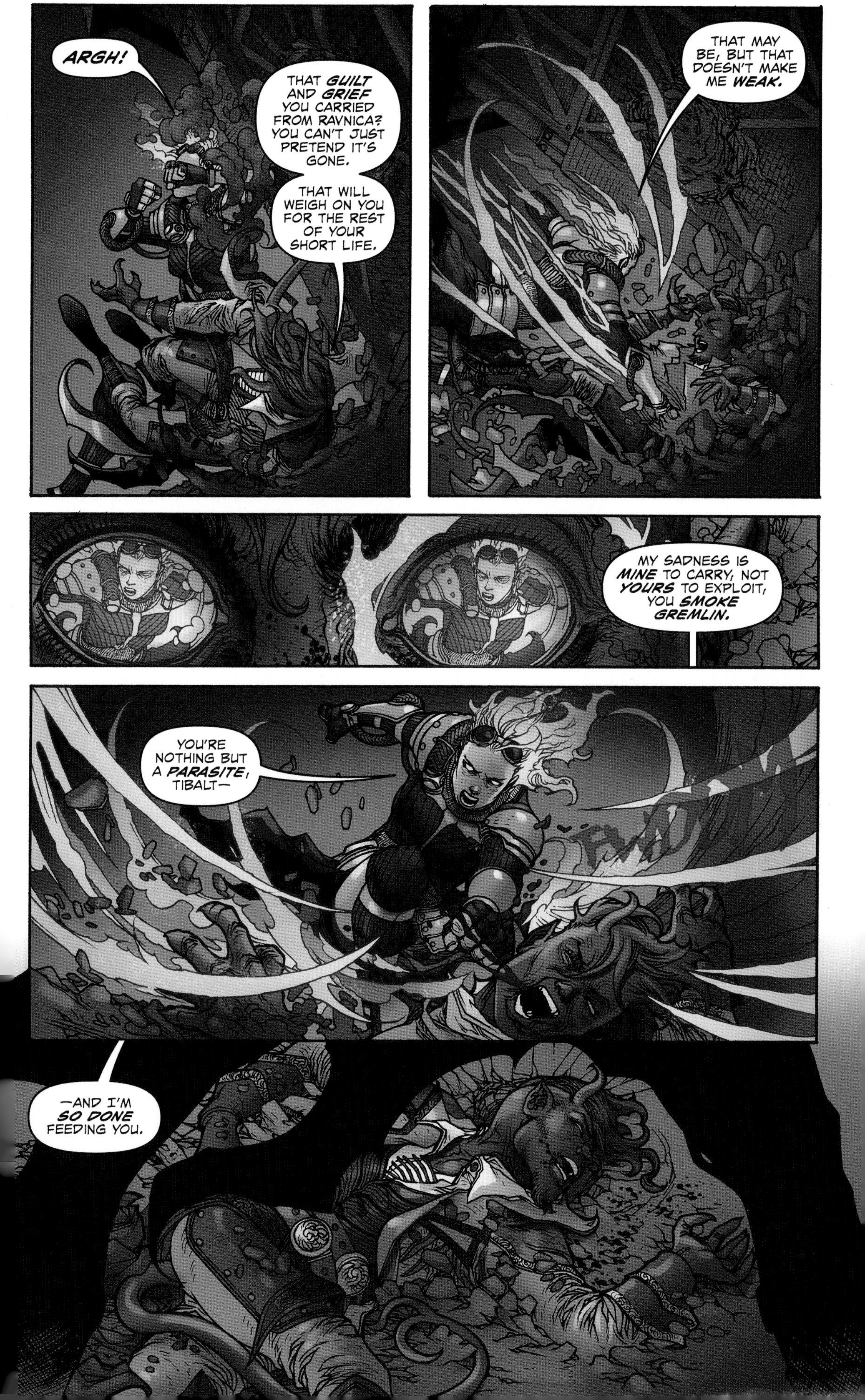
ARGH!
THAT GUILT AND GRIEF YOU CARRIED FROM RAVNICA? YOU CAN'T JUST PRETEND IT'S GONE.
THAT WILL WEIGH ON YOU FOR THE REST OF YOUR SHORT LIFE.
THAT MAY BE, BUT THAT DOESN'T MAKE ME WEAK.
MY SADNESS IS MINE TO CARRY, NOT YOURS TO EXPLOIT, YOU SMOKE GREMLIN.
YOU'RE NOTHING BUT A PARASITE, TIBALT—
—AND I'M SO DONE FEEDING YOU.

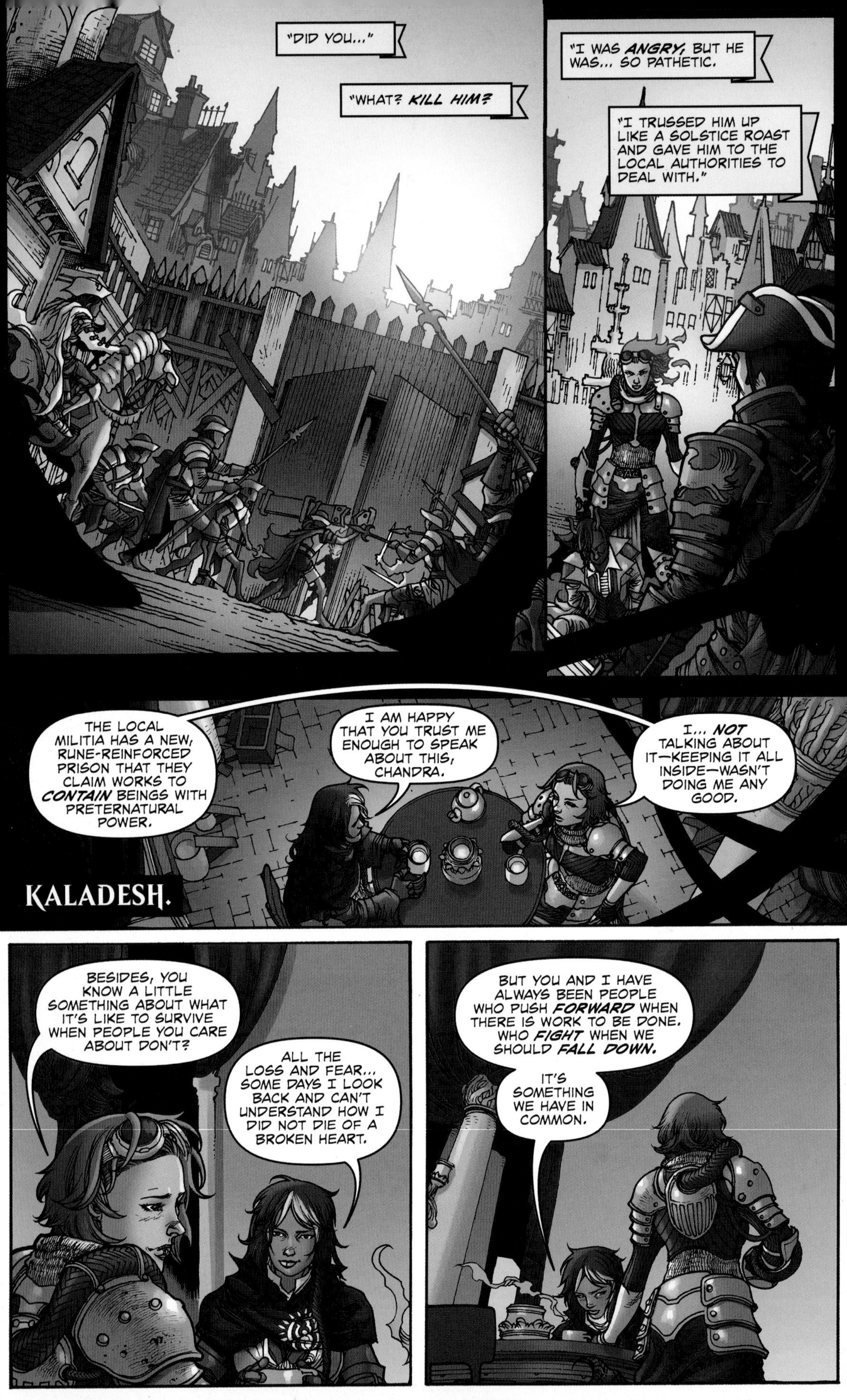
"DID YOU..."
"WHAT? KILL HIM?
"I WAS ANGRY, BUT HE WAS... SO PATHETIC.
"I TRUSSED HIM UP LIKE A SOLSTICE ROAST AND GAVE HIM TO THE LOCAL AUTHORITIES TO DEAL WITH."
THE LOCAL MILITIA HAS A NEW, RUNE-REINFORCED PRISON THAT THEY CLAIM WORKS TO CONTAIN BEINGS WITH PRETERNATURAL POWER.
I AM HAPPY THAT YOU TRUST ME ENOUGH TO SPEAK ABOUT THIS, CHANDRA.
I... NOT TALKING ABOUT IT—KEEPING IT ALL INSIDE—WASN'T DOING ME ANY GOOD.
KALADESH.
BESIDES, YOU KNOW A LITTLE SOMETHING ABOUT WHAT IT'S LIKE TO SURVIVE WHEN PEOPLE YOU CARE ABOUT DON'T?
ALL THE LOSS AND FEAR... SOME DAYS I LOOK BACK AND CAN'T UNDERSTAND HOW I DID NOT DIE OF A BROKEN HEART.
BUT YOU AND I HAVE ALWAYS BEEN PEOPLE WHO PUSH FORWARD WHEN THERE IS WORK TO BE DONE. WHO FIGHT WHEN WE SHOULD FALL DOWN.
IT'S SOMETHING WE HAVE IN COMMON.

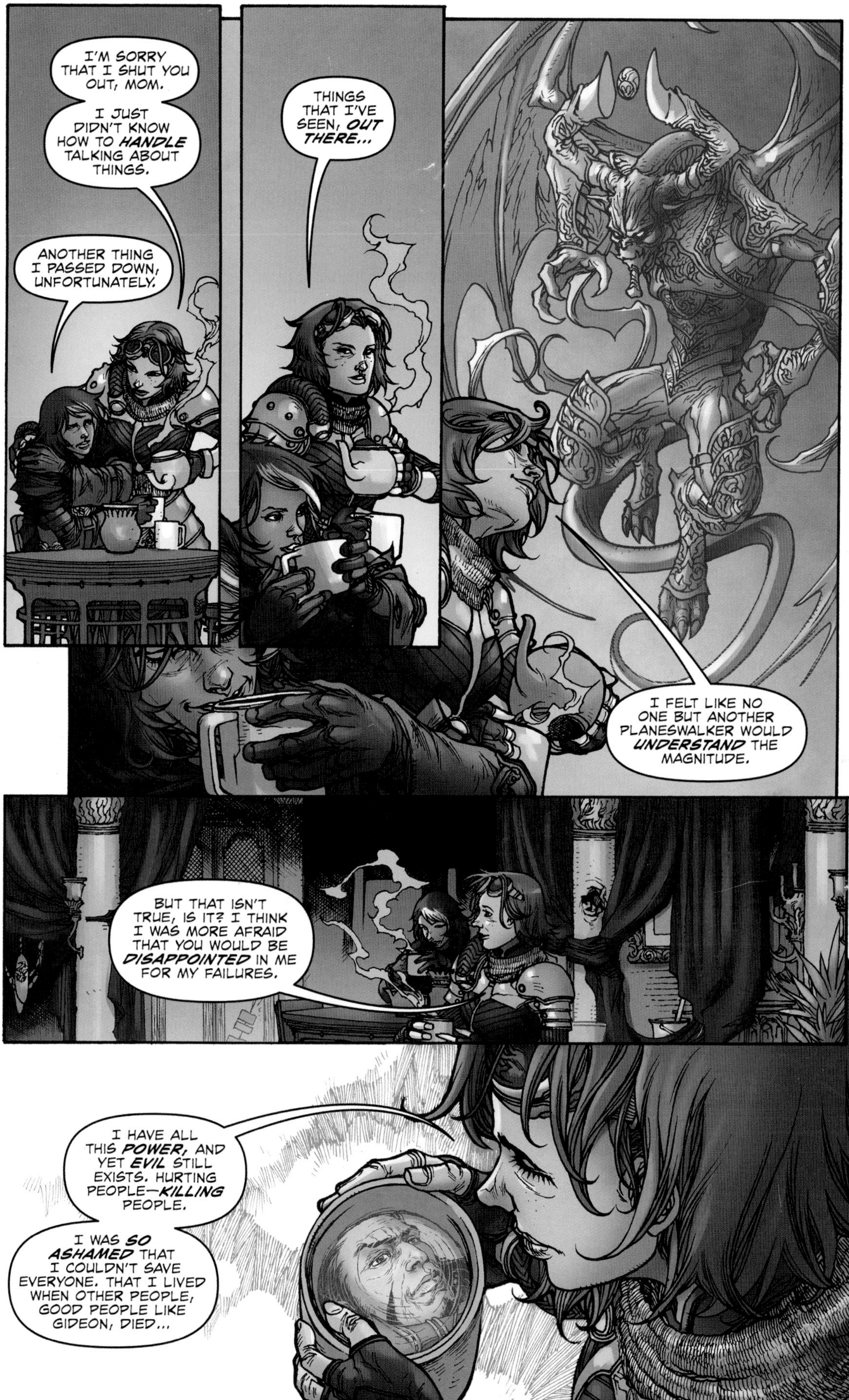
I'M SORRY THAT I SHUT YOU OUT, MOM.
I JUST DIDN'T KNOW HOW TO *HANDLE* TALKING ABOUT THINGS.
ANOTHER THING I PASSED DOWN, UNFORTUNATELY.
THINGS THAT I'VE SEEN, *OUT THERE...*
I FELT LIKE NO ONE BUT ANOTHER PLANESWALKER WOULD *UNDERSTAND* THE MAGNITUDE.
BUT THAT ISN'T TRUE, IS IT? I THINK I WAS MORE AFRAID THAT YOU WOULD BE *DISAPPOINTED* IN ME FOR MY FAILURES.
I HAVE ALL THIS *POWER,* AND YET *EVIL* STILL EXISTS. HURTING PEOPLE—*KILLING* PEOPLE.
I WAS *SO ASHAMED* THAT I COULDN'T SAVE EVERYONE. THAT I LIVED WHEN OTHER PEOPLE, GOOD PEOPLE LIKE GIDEON, DIED...

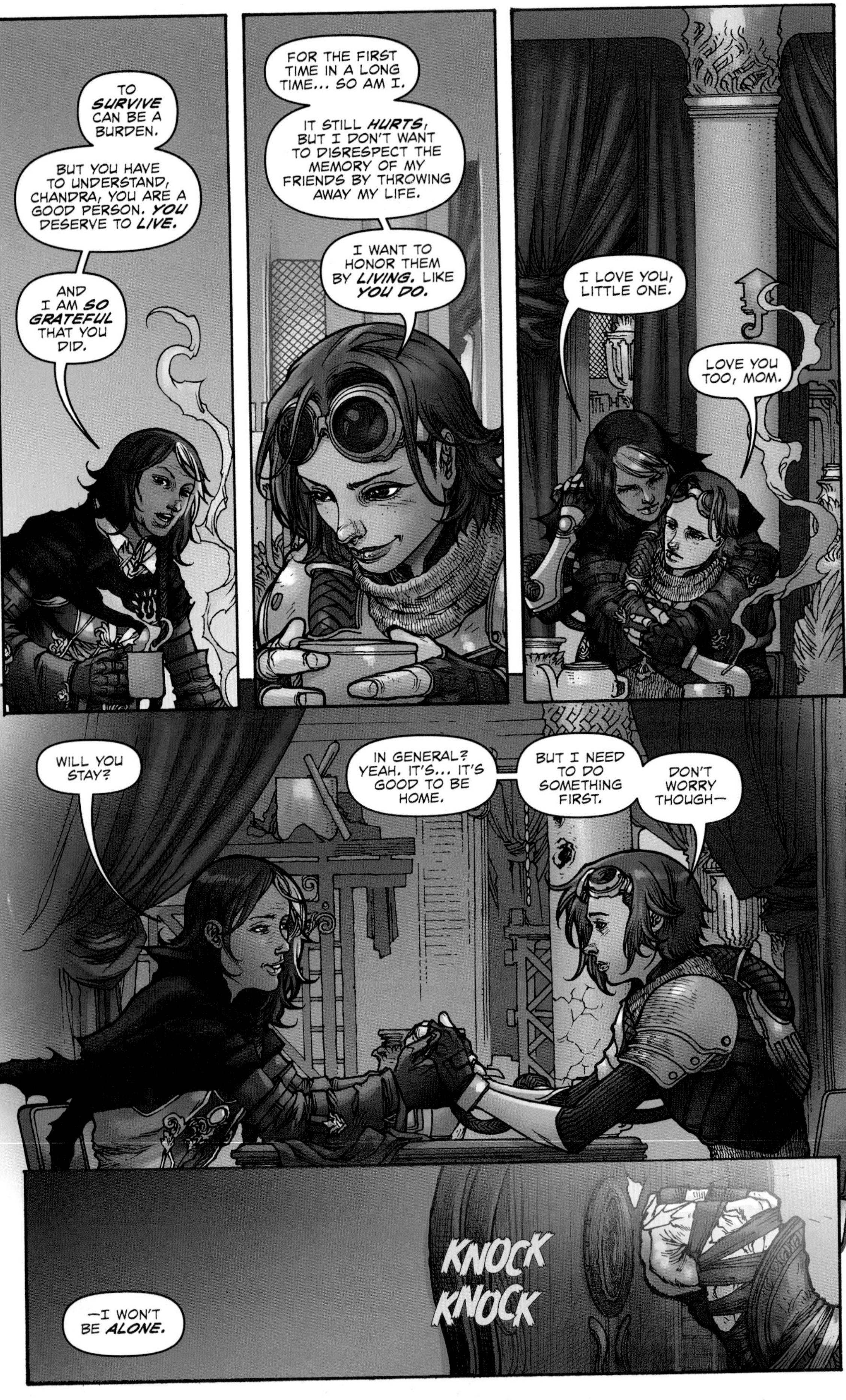
TO SURVIVE CAN BE A BURDEN.
BUT YOU HAVE TO UNDERSTAND, CHANDRA, YOU ARE A GOOD PERSON. YOU DESERVE TO LIVE.
AND I AM SO GRATEFUL THAT YOU DID.
FOR THE FIRST TIME IN A LONG TIME... SO AM I.
IT STILL HURTS, BUT I DON'T WANT TO DISRESPECT THE MEMORY OF MY FRIENDS BY THROWING AWAY MY LIFE.
I WANT TO HONOR THEM BY LIVING. LIKE YOU DO.
I LOVE YOU, LITTLE ONE.
LOVE YOU TOO, MOM.
WILL YOU STAY?
IN GENERAL? YEAH. IT'S... IT'S GOOD TO BE HOME.
BUT I NEED TO DO SOMETHING FIRST.
DON'T WORRY THOUGH—
—I WON'T BE ALONE.
KNOCK KNOCK

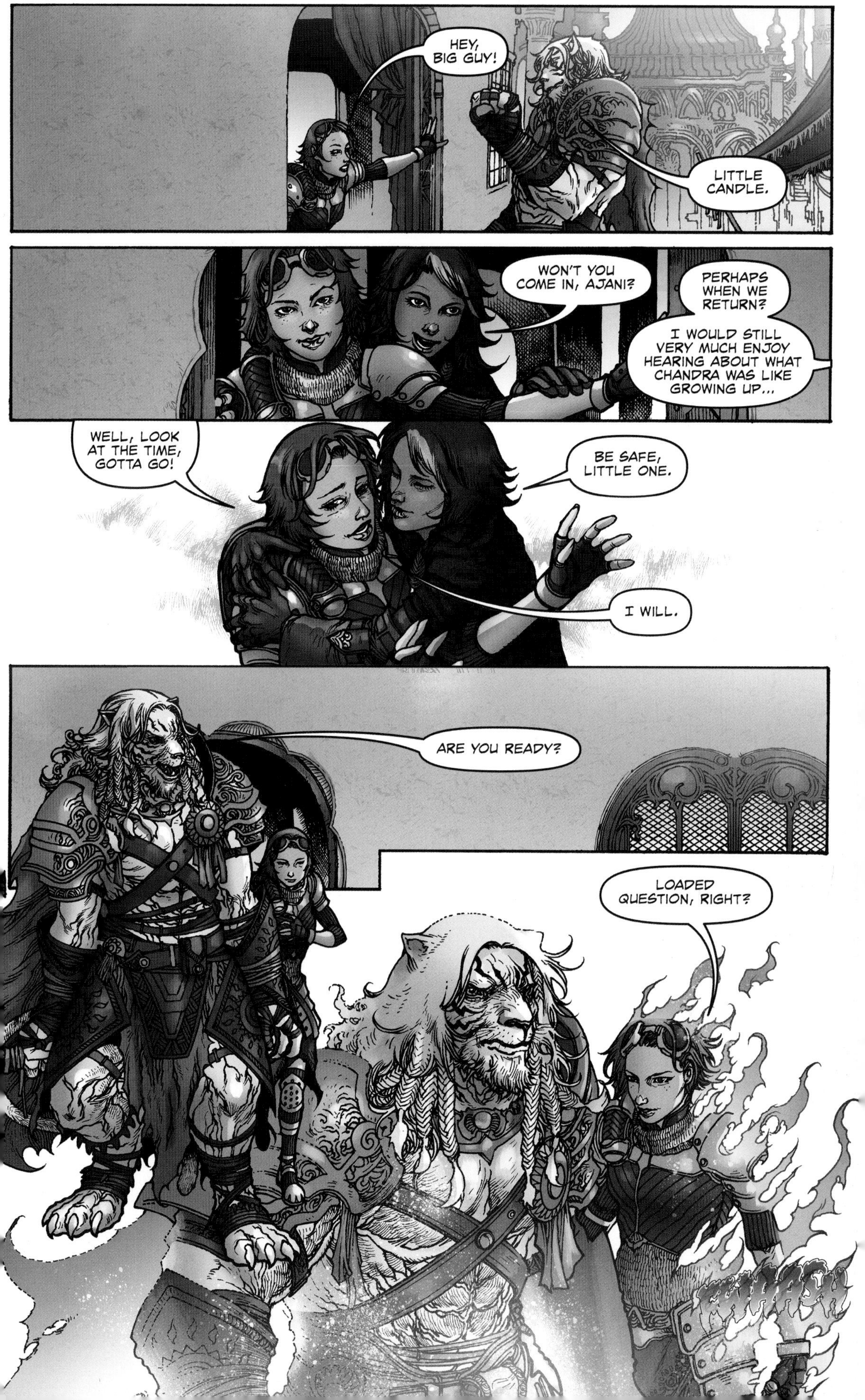
HEY, BIG GUY!
LITTLE CANDLE.
WON'T YOU COME IN, AJANI?
PERHAPS WHEN WE RETURN?
I WOULD STILL VERY MUCH ENJOY HEARING ABOUT WHAT CHANDRA WAS LIKE GROWING UP...
WELL, LOOK AT THE TIME, GOTTA GO!
BE SAFE, LITTLE ONE.
I WILL.
ARE YOU READY?
LOADED QUESTION, RIGHT?

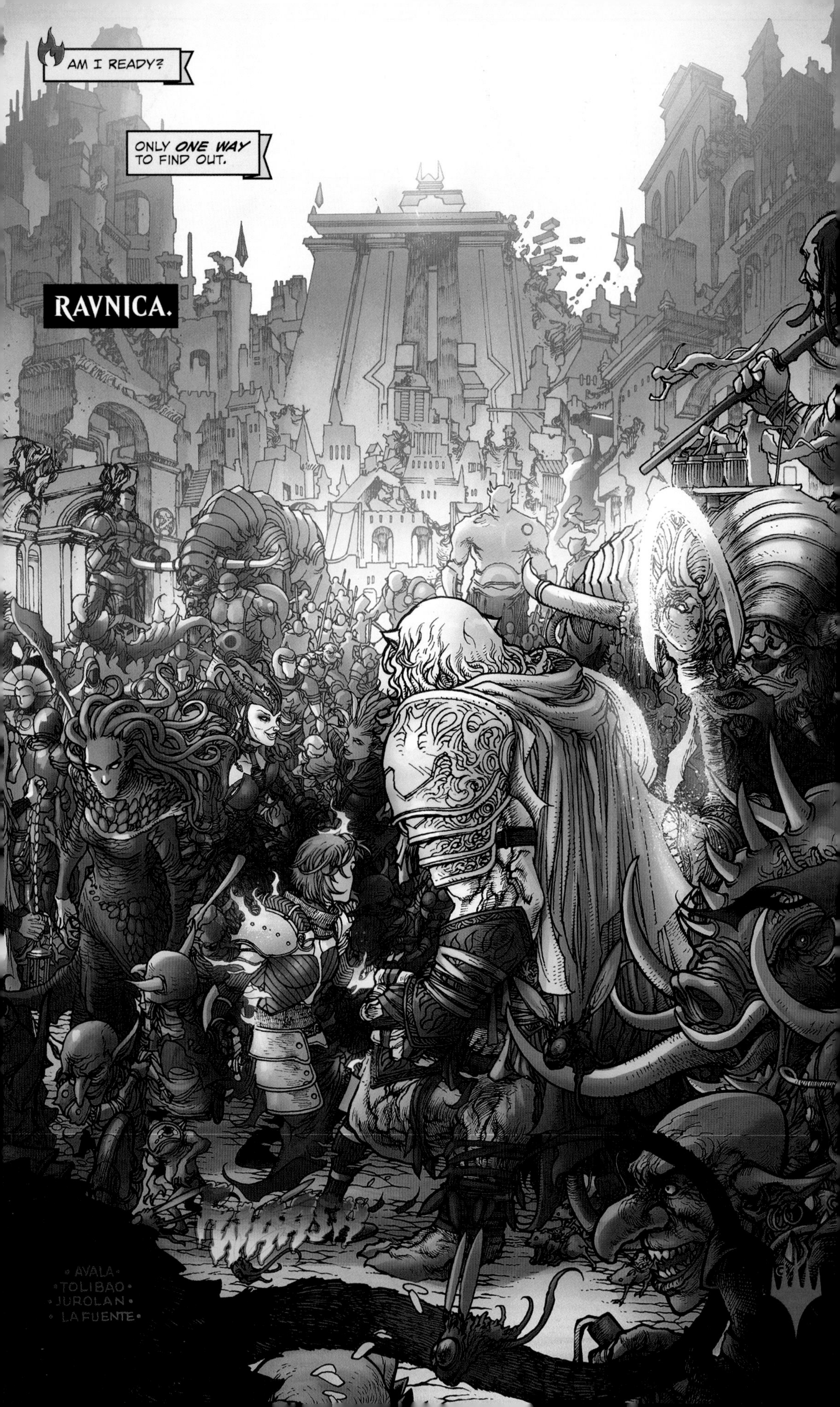
AM I READY?
ONLY *ONE WAY* TO FIND OUT.
RAVNICA.
AYALA
TOLIBAO
JUROLAN
LAFUENTE

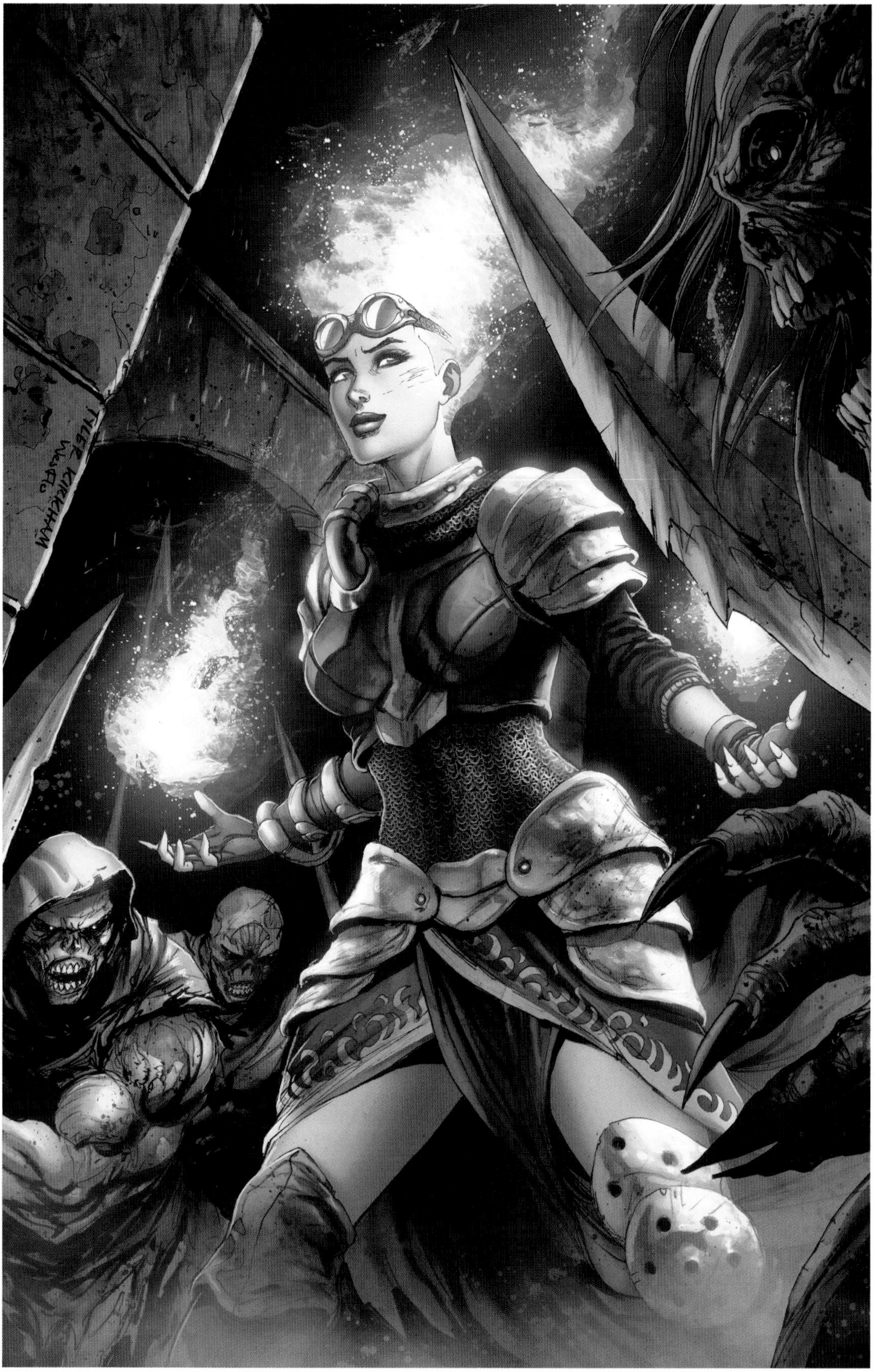

Art by Tyler Kirkham • Colors by Wes Hartman

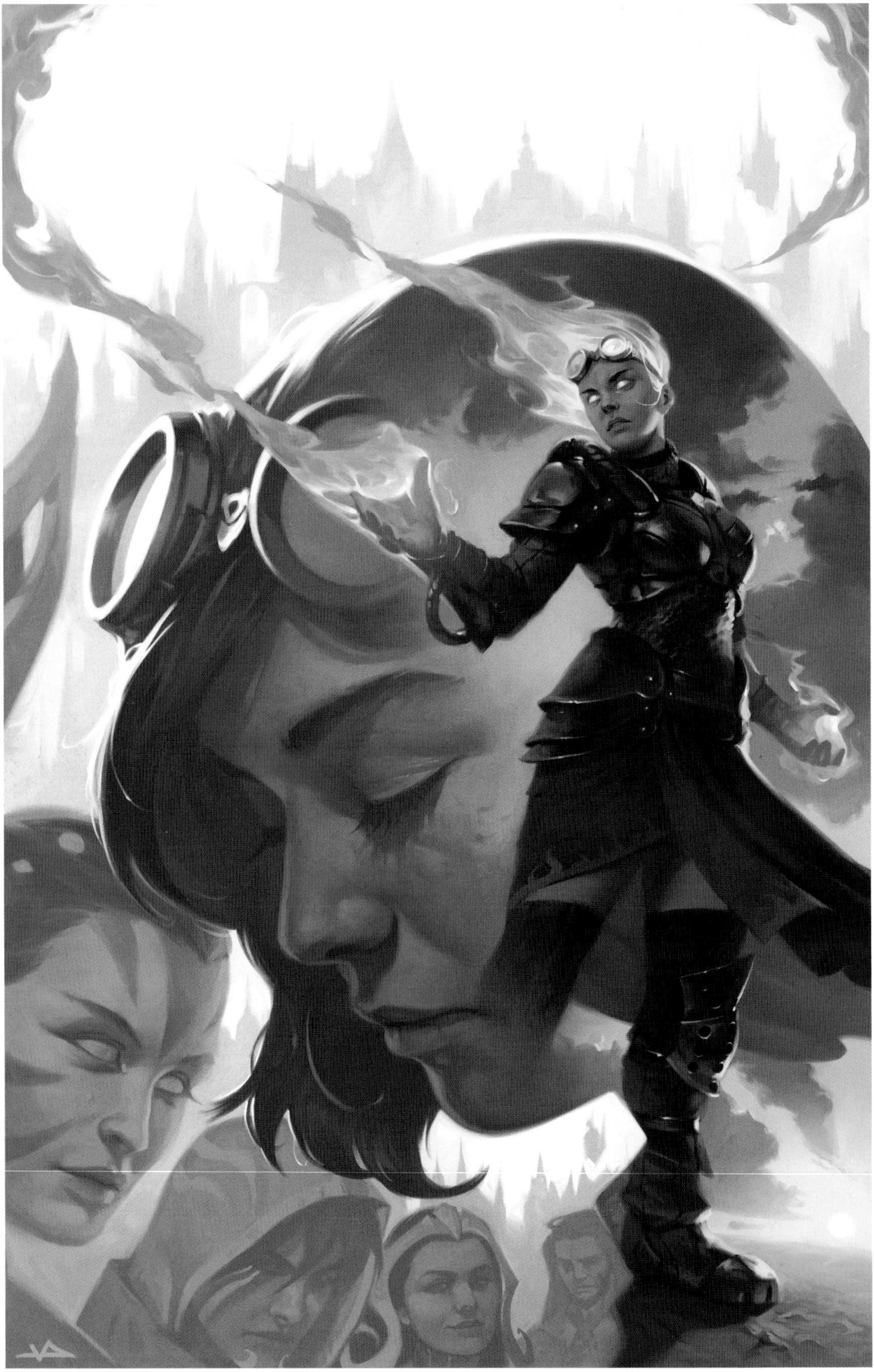

Art by Victor Adame Minguez

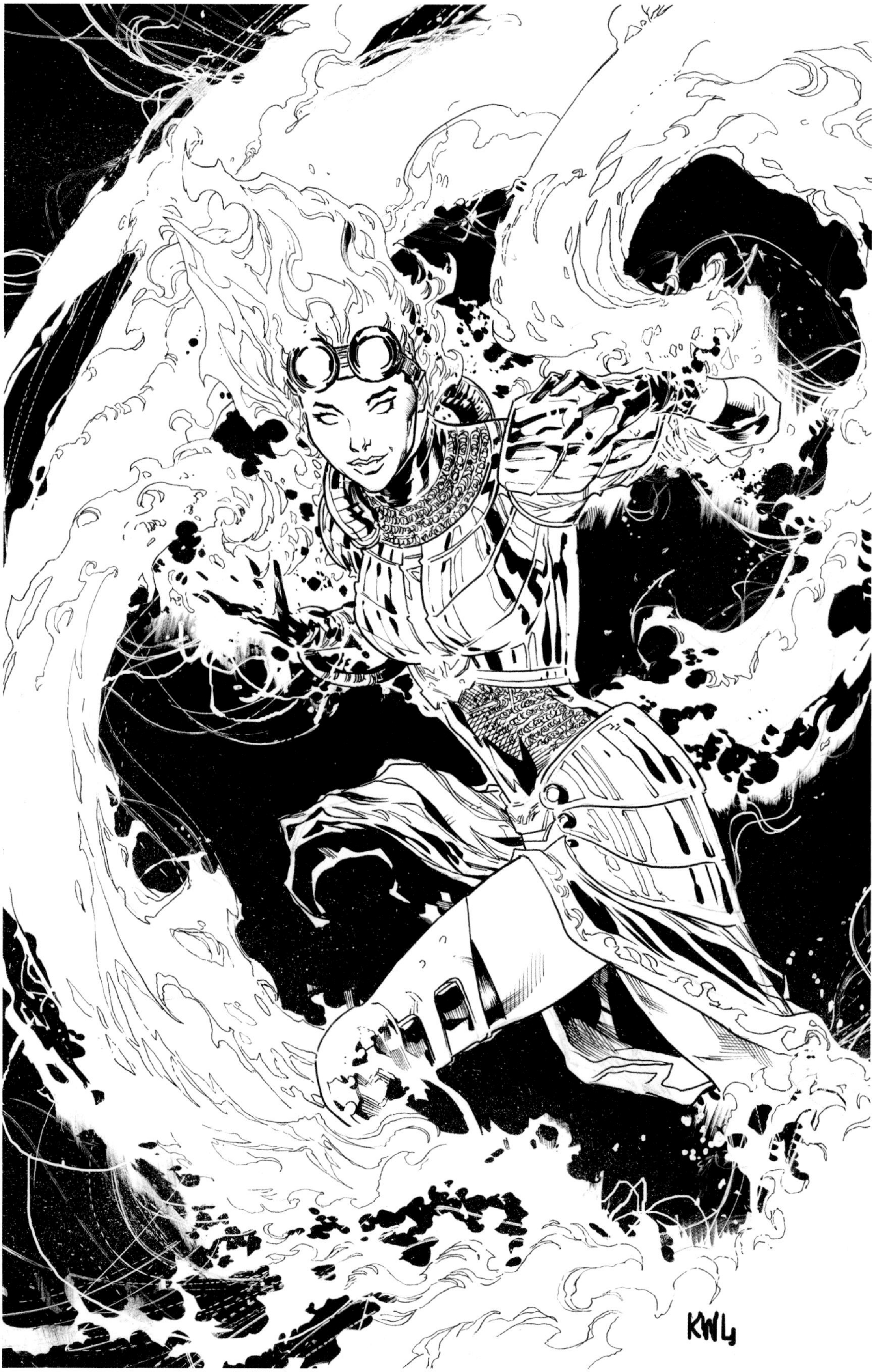
KWL

Art by Ken Lashley

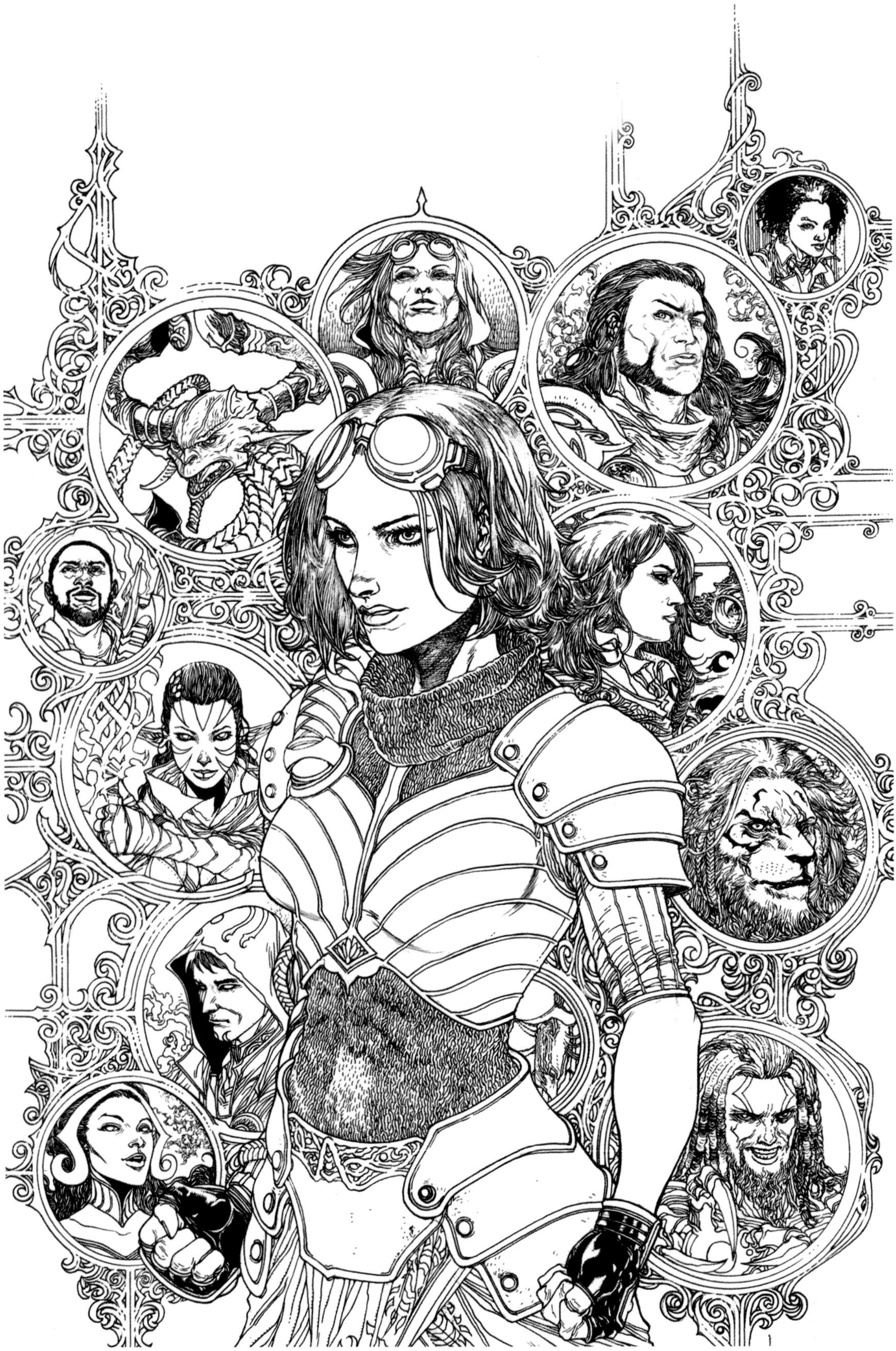

ART BY HARVEY TOLIBAO

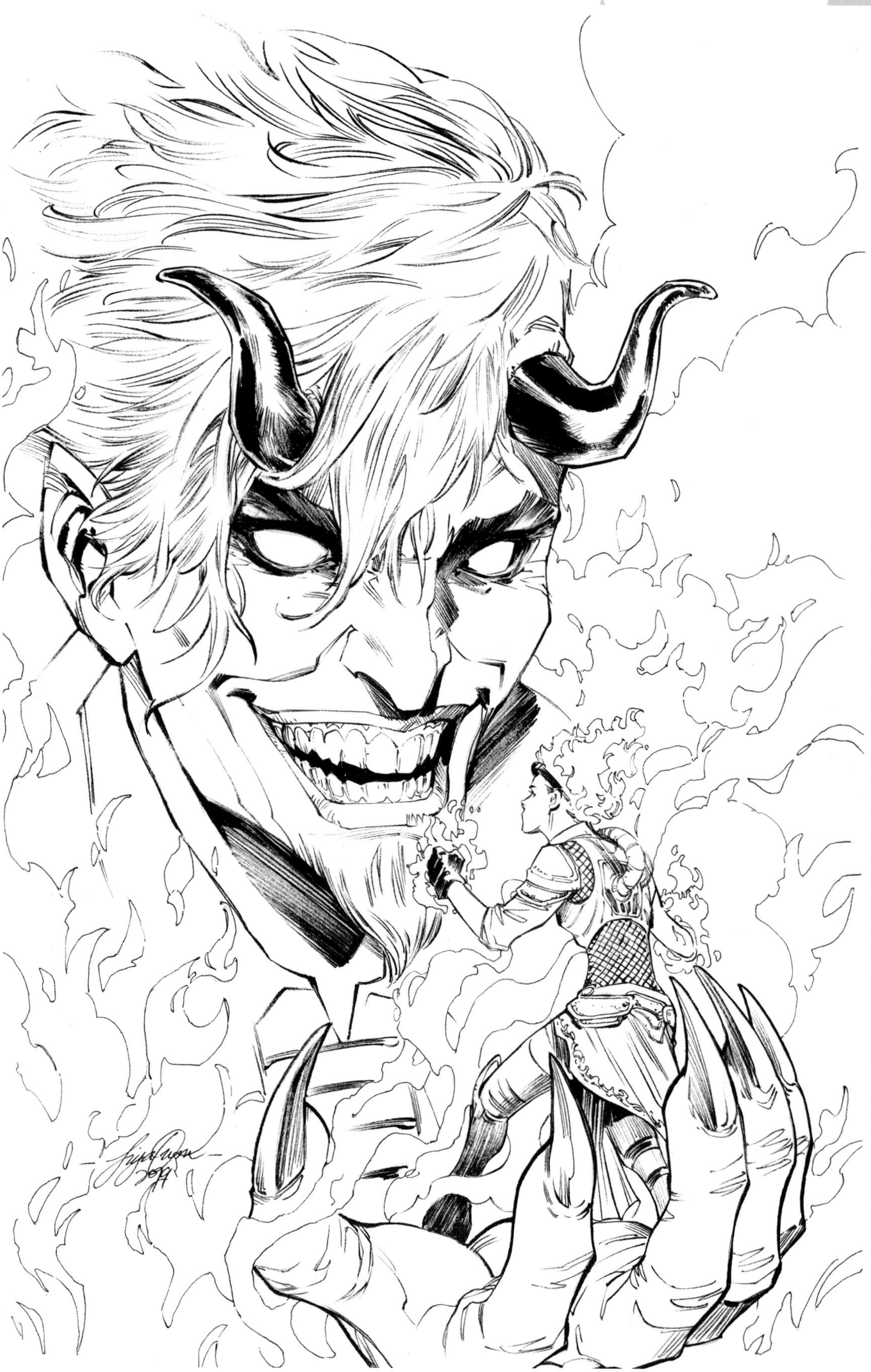

**Art by Siya Oum**

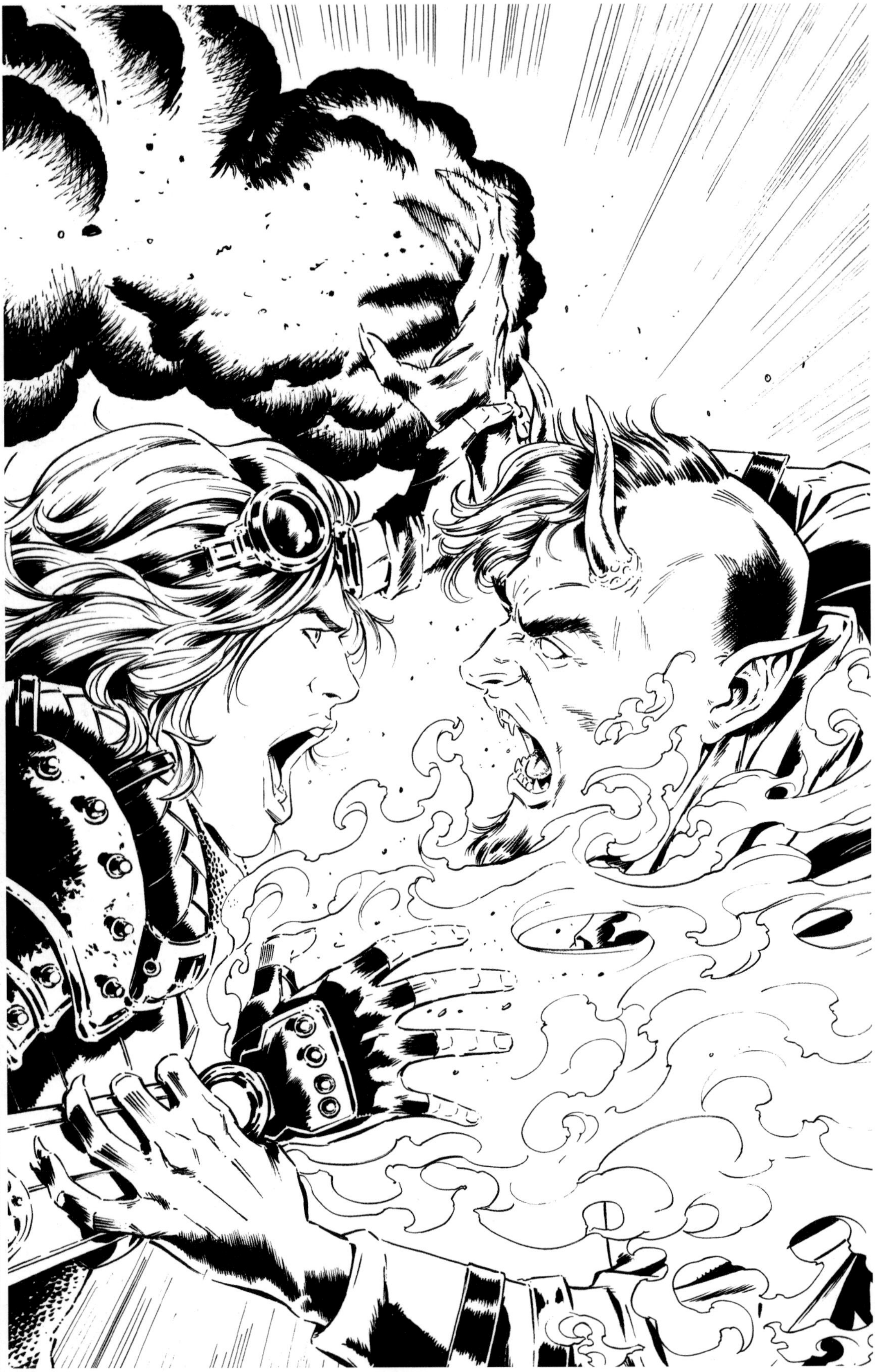

Art by SL Gallant